MURDER AT HOME

The smell was what I noticed first, even before I reached the den. An indistinct, slightly rank odor, like rotting leaves or a garbage disposal that hasn't been run through. Inside the room it was stronger and more fetid. I gagged slightly, thought about opening a window, then decided against it. Mona was not the fresh air freak I was.

I was halfway to the sofa before I noticed a shape mounded at one end, and even closer before it hit me.

The shape was Mona.

She was slouched against the back cushion, sweat pants twisted around her outstretched legs, one arm flung out to the side, the other draped across her chest. Her T-shirt had ridden up slightly, exposing a band of bare skin across her middle— skin that seemed oddly tight and waxy. Her head had rolled back so that she was facing the ceiling, her expression frozen and masklike.

I closed the distance between us in a flash, grabbed her arm, and felt for a pulse. The flesh my fingers touched was cold. Clammy and lifeless, as I'd known it would be. . . .

Books by Jonnie Jacobs

Kali O'Brien Novels of Legal Suspense

SHADOW OF DOUBT

EVIDENCE OF GUILT

MOTION TO DISMISS

WITNESS FOR THE DEFENSE

The Kate Austen Mysteries

MURDER AMONG NEIGHBORS

MURDER AMONG FRIENDS

MURDER AMONG US

MURDER AMONG STRANGERS

Published by Kensington Publishing Corporation

JONNIE JACOBS

MURDER AMONG
FRIENDS

Kensington Books
Kensington Publishing Corp.

http://www.kensingtonbooks.com

For David, Matthew, and Rod

ACKNOWLEDGMENTS

I wish to thank the following people for generously sharing their ideas and expertise: Detective Steve DeWarns, Piedmont Police Department, and Dr. Charles Linker, U.C. Medical Center, for their help with technical matters; Charlotte Cook, Margaret Lucke, Lynn MacDonald, Sally Richards, and Penny Warner, for their suggestions on the manuscript. A special thanks to my editor, John Scognamiglio, for making it happen, and to my husband and sons, for their unfailing encouragement and support.

1

Mixing business and friendship is always something of an iffy proposition, even when you expect things to go smoothly. I had no such expectation where Mona Sterling was concerned. Not that Mona wasn't wonderfully sincere and warm-hearted, because she was, in spades. But she was also opinionated, self-centered, and sometimes downright insensitive.

Although Mona and I had been drawn together initially by the bond of divorce, we'd soon moved beyond discussion of marital termination agreements and child support guidelines to more cheery subjects such as dieting, age lines, and PMS. Whatever the subject, Mona would invariably carry on at length and with mind-numbing conviction. As fond as I was of the woman, I sometimes found her a daunting companion.

When she'd called and insisted we simply had to meet that Monday, which happened also to be a holiday at my daughter's school, and then announced that she was available only between the hours of 11:00 A.M. and 1:00

P.M., I'd managed to shrug off my initial irritation. After all, I'd known that working for Mona was going to tax my patience. I was hoping it would also bring me a slew of flush new clients. Mona was, among other things, well connected with the monied elite of Walnut Hills—and as a fledgling entrepreneur, I needed all the help I could get.

I reminded myself of this as I stood at Mona's massive front door and rang the bell. A sharp, wet, February wind whipped strands of hair across my face and tunneled down the neck of my old raincoat. After seven years of drought, El Nino or the hole in the ozone or whatever other mysterious force was responsible had finally shifted, and we were having one of the coldest, wettest winters in California history. Like cod liver oil, it might be good for us but it wasn't pleasant.

Shivering, I tried the bell again, poking it several times in quick succession the way my five-year-old, Anna, does when I don't answer instantly. I waited for a minute, which is something Anna never does, then sighed, brushed the hair out of my eyes and reached into my purse for the keys Mona had given me.

"I might be a few minutes late," she'd told me. "Just go on in and get started. I shouldn't be too long." Mona was invariably late so I'd planned for the fact and arrived almost twenty minutes after the hour myself. Apparently I'd still beat her there.

I fumbled around in my bag, stabbing my finger on one of Anna's stray jacks before finding the keys under the phone bill I'd forgotten to mail. There were two keys. The rounded one for the top lock, the narrow one for the bottom. Or was it the other way around? I'd been dashing off to drive the afternoon carpool when Mona had gone over it, so I'd only listened with half an ear.

I tried the narrow key in the bottom lock. Wonder of wonders, it worked. I stuck the other in the top lock, preparing to turn it with my left hand while using my right to depress the latch, the way Mona had showed me. But the door opened immediately. All those instructions and she hadn't even bothered with the dead-bolt after all!

I pushed open the door and called out in case she simply hadn't heard the bell. No answer. No sound of running water or footsteps either. Propping the door open with my purse (Mona had warned me that it locked automatically when shut), I went back to the car to retrieve the lithographs, which were the primary reason for my being there that morning. I'm an art consultant, a business I'd sort of back-stepped into when Andy and I separated and a friend offered me a job in her gallery. I'm an artist too, but that's an endeavor which provides more pleasure than profit. Not that I make such a killing from my consulting business. I'm counting on the fact that things will pick up over time.

I had two pieces with me that morning. One was a monochromatic abstract which Mona had purchased, with my help, several weeks earlier. It was back now from the framers and ready to be hung. The other was something I'd stumbled across at a new gallery in Berkeley. I was pretty sure Mona would like it, but I didn't know if the colors were right for the room.

The pictures were large (which is what Mona wanted) and heavy (which sort of comes with the territory when you're talking large). With the ground so damp and the wind gusting about the way it was, I decided it would be best if I carried them to the house one at a time. You drop a fifteen-hundred dollar painting and you're liable to spend the rest of your life cursing your stupidity.

By the time I got them both into the house and unwrapped, it was 11:40 A.M. and Mona still hadn't shown. Grumbling, I carted the pictures into the spacious living room and propped them against the wall.

Mona's house is large and sprawling, unlike my own which is so cramped that people and furniture have trouble co-existing. Andy and I had planned to add on, but we'd never managed to save enough money to do more than dream. Now, with the impending divorce, money was even tighter. It wasn't that Andy was being nasty about it. Bottom line is, he's a pretty decent guy. Unfortunately, he's also unreliable as all get out and practically penniless.

The financial fallout from Mona's divorce was different. Her husband was a first-class sleaze, but a rich one. Though he'd fought her tooth and nail over everything from the country club membership to the leftover Christmas wrap, Mona had wound up with a more than satisfactory settlement. She got the house and a sizable portion of their assets, while Gary got the furniture, Persian carpets, and china, all of which he was eager to install in the even bigger house he and his wife-to-be were building on the edge of town.

I'd only seen Mona's house once in its former, sumptuous state. It had been decorated to the nines with massive and, to my taste, overly ornate antiques. Impressive certainly, in a formal, heavy-handed way, but not the sort of place where you'd want to kick off your shoes and stretch out. At that time the walls had been adorned with gold-framed hunting scenes and pseudo Rembrandts. In forging her life anew, Mona had gone from one extreme to another. She was now into serious minimalism. The walls were white, the floors and windows bare, the furnishings sparse. Libby's was the only room that actually looked inhabited. And it was a mess. Exactly what you'd expect from the teen-aged daughter of a woman who'd elevated empty space to new heights.

I checked my watch again, then stood back against the fireplace to get a feeling for the two pictures together. I liked the effect, though of course Mona would have the final say. If she ever got there. I couldn't imagine what was keeping her. Or why she didn't at least call.

Damn her anyway, I thought. I'd arranged my whole morning around her schedule. Mentally giving her the what-for, I stomped off into the kitchen, newly refurbished in white and chrome, and put on a kettle of water for coffee. Mona had told me she had something to discuss, and with Mona this meant coffee. It would speed up the process considerably if the coffee was ready when she was.

And that would have to be soon or we'd never get to the conversation part of the visit, which seemed, from Mona's tone, rather pressing. She wasn't the only one with an afternoon commitment. I had a one o'clock meeting, a final planning session for the upcoming school auction, and I'd promised Sharon I'd stop by the bakery on my way over. God forbid we should have to do all that planning without the benefit of oatmeal bars and brownies.

The water began to boil. I measured the coffee and then pulled down the cups, taking care not to knock against the two crystal tumblers sitting next to the sink. They hadn't been emptied completely, and had that heavy, boozy odor you never notice until the next morn-

ing. I dumped the contents, then rinsed them carefully.
While I was at it, I dumped the ashtray as well. Company
and a late night, I thought, maybe that explained it.
Mona had probably slept through her alarm this morning and had been running late ever since.

If that was the case, though, she probably hadn't had
time to pull together the samples I'd asked for. We were
looking for a large, horizontal piece to hang above the
couch in the den. I wanted to measure the space and
maybe take one of the throw pillows to use in matching
colors. I poured the water through the coffee, and then
while it dripped, went to complete the work myself.

The smell was what I noticed first, even before I
reached the den. An indistinct, slightly rank odor, like
rotting leaves or a garbage disposal that hasn't been run
through. Inside the room it was stronger and more fetid.
I gagged slightly, thought about opening a window, then
decided against it. Mona was not the fresh air freak I was.

I was halfway to the sofa before I noticed a shape
mounded at one end, and even closer before it hit me.

The shape was Mona.

She was slouched against the back cushion, sweat pants
twisted around her outstretched legs, one arm flung out
to the side, the other draped across her chest. Her tee
shirt had ridden up slightly, exposing a band of bare skin
across her middle, skin that seemed oddly tight and waxy.
Her head had rolled back so that she was facing the ceiling, her expression frozen and masklike.

I closed the distance between us in a flash, grabbed her
arm and felt for a pulse. The flesh my fingers touched was
cold. Clammy and lifeless, as I'd known it would be. The
prescription bottle and half-empty fifth of scotch on the
table left little room for doubt.

"Mona. My God, Mona, why?" My mouth was too dry to actually form the words, but inside my head someone was shrieking, and sobbing her name over and over again.

I stumbled back to the kitchen where I called the paramedics, although I knew there was nothing they could do. Then I hung up and placed a second call to Lieutenant Michael Stone.

2

The paramedics arrived first. A dark-haired man with a sizable beer gut and a lanky, freckle-faced woman. Neither of them looked a day over twenty. They moved briskly and efficiently, communicating with each other in a sort of verbal shorthand. I huddled in the kitchen, trying hard to distance myself from the unfamiliar thumping and rustling of their movements, and the sharp, staccato rhythm of their dialogue. After an initial flurry of activity, everything was quiet. Several moments later, the woman joined me in the kitchen.

"I'm sorry," she said. "I'm afraid there's nothing we can do at this point."

I nodded numbly. I hadn't expected it to be otherwise.

"She a relative?"

"A friend."

"The police should be here any minute. And someone from the coroner's office."

I nodded again. The words floated past, like skywriting blurred by the winds. I understood but I didn't. How could Mona be dead?

Two uniformed cops arrived a few minutes later, followed soon after by Michael.

Lieutenant Michael Stone, whose taut, lean body had left my bed not more than seven hours earlier, sliding into the frigid morning darkness before Anna awoke. He and I are, as they say, "involved," although we're having a little trouble figuring out what, exactly, we're involved in.

I met him in the hallway. "What took you so long?" The words, which were not at all the ones I'd intended, squeaked out, jerky and uneven.

Michael ignored my question and put an arm around me instead. "You okay, Kate?"

"Yes, I think so." My throat constricted and my stomach did a funny little two-step. "No, maybe not." I rested my forehead against his chest and took a deep breath. "All of the above, I guess."

"Can you tell me what happened?"

"I was supposed to meet her here at eleven. I brought pictures for the living room. We were going to start on the other rooms too. She'd given me a key because she knew she might be a few minutes late." I paused for another breath. "I went into the den to get a couple of pillows to take with me—fabric samples for matching colors—and that's when I . . . when I found her."

"She was already dead?"

I nodded, feeling again the unyielding stiffness of her flesh under my fingertips. I shivered.

"How well did you know her?"

"She was a friend as well as a client, but I didn't know her all that well. She was more Sharon Covington's friend really. That's how I met her in the first place. The two of them go way back." Poor Sharon. I hadn't thought about that part of it. Mona's death was going to hit her hard.

Just then a uniformed officer appeared in the doorway. "Hey, lieutenant, what are you doing here?"

"You can relax Jerry, it's unofficial."

Jerry Watkins, fair-haired and baby-faced, was the sort of young man who'd look more at home in a football jersey than a police uniform. But since he was the captain's favorite nephew, he'd probably never been given the choice. He frowned for just a moment, then shrugged.

"Since you're already here," Jerry said, "you might as well have a look. I'd have probably called you anyway. Better make it fast though. The guy from the coroner's office is anxious to get the body moved."

The body. Mona Sterling, the body.

"I'll be back in a minute," Michael said to me, then paused at the doorway to catch my eye. "You'll be okay?"

"I'll be fine," I replied, as much to reassure myself as him.

He headed off to the back of the house. I opened the outside kitchen door for a breath of air. A fine, gray drizzle had begun falling. I wondered if *the body* would get wet on the way to the coroner's van. I wondered if it mattered.

Suddenly, I was gripped by a numbing cold that had nothing to do with temperature. To take your own life like that, to make that final irreversible decision. What terrible sadness, what unbearable dread would lead a person to do such a thing? And why hadn't any of us seen it coming?

I went back inside and found the female paramedic. "You think it would be okay if I used the phone?" I asked.

"Sure, I don't see why not."

It was clear I wasn't going to be stopping by the bakery on my way to the auction meeting. Assuming I made it at all. Telling Sharon that would be the easy part. Telling her about Mona was going to be much harder.

Had it not been for Anna, I might well have put off making the call altogether. When it comes to things that make me uncomfortable, I'm a skilled procrastinator. But I'd farmed Anna out with Sharon that morning, and I had a sudden, irrational urge to make sure she was okay. News of even distant misfortune sends my maternal worry meter into high gear. Finding a corpse had sent it clear into overdrive.

I'd intended to break the news to Sharon gently (however one does that), but instead, I blurted it out the moment she picked up the phone.

"Dead?" Sharon said. Even though it was a one syllable word, her voice broke in the middle. "How could Mona be dead?"

I told her what I knew, which answered neither her question or the more troubling "Why?" We went back and forth for five minutes of "I can't believe it," and then there was a long silence.

"I guess I'd better call everyone and cancel the meeting," Sharon said finally.

I mumbled agreement. "I'll come get Anna as soon as I can. She's doing okay?"

"She's fine."

We went through a second round of "I can't believe Mona's really dead," then I let Sharon go so she could call the others. I tried to stand, but my legs refused to cooperate, so I sat by the phone and stared blankly at the remnants of Mona's life spread out across her kitchen desk. A stack of bills, a grocery list scratched on stationery from The Timbercreek Lodge in Mendocino, a flyer from a window-cleaning service, a student essay entitled, rather unimaginatively, *Assignment #11*, by *Eve Fisher*. Mona taught English at the local community college, although she was quick to point out that "teach" was a somewhat misleading term for what actually took place.

In an effort to shut out the demons, I picked up the paper, which was typed with so many strike-overs it looked at first glance like something written in Sanskrit, and started to read.

When the winter winds blow harsh and cold, she thinks of snuggling by the fire with Madelaine. And dies a little more inside. When the summer sun is bright and warm, she thinks of wading in the creek with Madelaine. And dies a little more inside. Washing her face at dawn and the dishes at night, in the dentist's chair and the grocery line, the memories spring forth with a life of their own. The void is so great . . .

At that point I stopped really reading and skimmed the rest of the page. It seemed to be about the memory of a child, though whether the child was dead, grown, a figment of the author's imagination, or simply indifferent to her mother, was hard to say. Even I could tell that it was poorly written. Awkward and mawkish, the kind of thing that Mona would have hated. Given my present state though, the sentiment struck a chord. I felt a lump forming in my throat.

Michael re-appeared just then, saving me from my own dark thoughts. "You doing okay?" he asked.

I nodded and shrugged at the same time. Then swallowed.

"I told Jerry I'd take your report. Do you think you're up to talking about it?"

I nodded again, swallowed again.

"Good." He glanced over at the stove. "That coffee fresh?"

"I made it when I was waiting for, uh, when I thought I was waiting for Mona. It's probably cold by now though."

Michael wandered over to the stove, turned on the burner, and found a cup. "You want some?"

My stomach turned just thinking about it.

He poured himself a cup, then nodded in the direction of the front room. "Let's talk in there. It looks a bit more comfortable." He gave me a twisted smile and added, "Though not by much."

Michael settled into Mona's simple, square-lined sectional, and leaned forward, arms resting on his knees. I sat next to him and let my mind drift for a moment from the business at hand. Michael has that effect on me, has since the day I first met him. A day in some ways not unlike this. I hadn't found the body that time, but I had known the woman.

Michael doesn't look like a cop. Not unless you're talking about some big-screen, Hollywood version. His voice is too gentle for one thing. As are his eyes. They're a liquid gray-blue, and they look right at you instead of over or through you. For another thing, his hair is all wrong. It's dark and thick, and considerably longer than the captain would like, though they seem to have reached an unspoken truce about this as well as other things.

Michael sipped his coffee and let his eyes drift around the room. "So, let's start at the beginning," he said finally. "Name's Mona Sterling, right?"

I nodded.

"Married?"

"Divorced. It was final just last month. Her ex-husband is a developer. Owns a number of commercial properties too. It was a nasty divorce, but it worked out okay in the end. Mona got a good settlement. Awfully good in fact.''

"She must have had Keeler for a judge," Michael humphed. He's had experience with Keeler himself, first hand.

"Actually, they never went to court. In spite of all the animosity, the lawyers somehow managed to work out a settlement both Mona and Gary agreed to. Though to hear Gary complain about it, you'd think he'd had it shoved down his throat.''

"What about Mona? She work?"

"She taught at Valley Community College, in the English department. She was faculty coordinator of the Women's Re-entry Program as well.''

Michael looked puzzled. "That some kind of astronaut training?''

"Re-entry into the work force," I explained. "For women who've been wives and mothers for so long they've forgotten how to handle anything that doesn't involve peanut butter or carpooling.''

Michael ran a hand through his hair. The puzzled look faded but did not entirely disappear. He scratched something in his notebook. "Any kids?"

"One. A daughter, almost sixteen. She's on a school ski trip at the moment." I didn't know Libby well, but the very thought of a child left motherless brought on a momentary swell of panic. This was true despite the fact that the child insisted she was, for all practical purposes, an adult herself, and seemed to spend the better part of every day bitching at her mother.

"Any idea who we notify as next of kin?"

"There's a sister in Seattle. Alice something. Sharon will know how to reach her. Because of Libby I guess you'll have to notify Gary too, but I know for a fact Mona wouldn't want him to set foot in her house.''

"They were still going at it then?"

"With a vengeance."

"How about the daughter? She close to her dad?"

From the little I'd seen, Libby wasn't close to either parent. But my perspective was skewed by the fact that Anna adores her father and is young enough to still consider me, on most occasions, a confidant and kindred spirit. Mona had warned me it wouldn't last.

"She didn't see her father very often," I told Michael. "But I don't know whether that's the way she wanted it, or just the way it worked out."

He chewed on his lower lip. "How about Mona's health?"

"I don't know, she seemed fine." Except for recurring yeast infections and hot flashes that is, but you don't take your life over something like that. "I'm sure I'd have heard if there was something seriously wrong."

"She seem depressed lately?"

I shook my head.

"Upset? Worried?"

"Nothing out of the ordinary. Mona was always grousing about something, but I never took it very seriously."

Michael sighed, took a moment to stare out the window, then leaned forward and set his cup on the coffee table. "Lord, it's hard having to break news like this to the family."

I nodded in sympathy. There are lots of things about Michael's job that would bother me. It isn't all protecting the good and punishing the wicked.

"Mona always struck me as being so together," I said. "So resilient."

He shrugged. "People are full of surprises."

"I can't help thinking there had to have been something I could have done. Something I *should* have done."

I found myself searching my memory for the signs I'd missed, the desperate cry for help I'd blindly ignored. It was true Mona had wanted to talk to me. "Heavy duty stuff," she'd said, but she hadn't sounded desperate. Then, with a wave of guilt, I remembered that she'd initially wanted to get together over the weekend. But Michael had the time off and Anna was with her dad. Talking to Mona had been a pretty low priority in my life and I'd put her off until today. Would it have made a difference if I hadn't?

Michael gave my hand a gentle squeeze. "You can't start blaming yourself, Kate. Anyway, it might not have been suicide. There's the possibility of accidental overdose too. A person feels a little low, tries to forget her sorrows with booze and drugs, and pretty soon she's lost touch with a whole lot more than her troubles."

"You think that's what it was?"

"Hard to tell. The coroner may be in a better position to say, but truth is, we'll probably never know for sure. Not unless she left a note, and nothing along those lines has turned up so far."

Either way, I couldn't help feeling I ought to have picked up on the fact she was troubled. "How long do you think she's been dead?"

"I can't say for sure. More than twenty-four hours though."

Just then a uniformed officer I didn't recognize came into the room and handed Michael a folded section of newspaper. "Jerry said to let you know we found this under the sofa. Just an old out-of-town newspaper, but he

said he wouldn't want you to think he was holding out."
The officer looked embarrassed. He was obviously no
stranger to Jerry's defensive posturing and rather vocal
resentment of the detective division.

Michael flipped the paper open. "*St. Louis Post-Dispatch.* Is that where she's from?" he asked me.

"No. She's from somewhere around Boston. Went to
school in the east as well."

He shrugged and handed the paper back. "Tell Jerry
thanks."

There were footsteps in the hallway just then, and a
muffled shuffling sound. I turned in time to see a
stretcher being wheeled down the hallway. A stretcher
bearing a shapeless form covered from head to toe with
black plastic. My stomach lurched suddenly, as though
the floor beneath me had taken a sudden drop. I stood
unsteadily and made a beeline for the bathroom. Some
nice person had already lifted both the lid and seat. Good
thing, I wouldn't have made it otherwise.

When my stomach finished acting up, my eyes started
in. Huge wet tears appeared from nowhere and began
snaking down my cheeks.

Mona. *The body.*

How could this have happened? What had pushed her
to the limit?

My head filled with images of Mona as I had known her
in life. Always talking, always moving, often laughing.
She'd been an attractive woman. Tall and shapely, the
kind of sleek, dark-haired figure that caused heads to
turn. It was hard to reconcile those memories with the
puffed, waxy face and the lifeless expression I'd encountered in the den.

Michael appeared at the door a moment later with a

glass of water and a sympathetic half-smile. "It's never easy," he said.

I took the water, wiping my eyes with my fist.

"You want me to give you a ride home? We can come back for your car whenever you feel up to it."

"I'll be okay. I've got to go by Sharon's and get Anna anyway."

"How about I stop by this evening with an order of Chinese food?"

My stomach took another sweeping roll. It must have registered on my face.

"Sorry," Michael said, "I guess I shouldn't have mentioned food."

"Definitely not." I took a couple of deep breaths. The queasy feeling passed. "It wouldn't work anyway. Andy's coming for dinner tonight."

Michael raised a brow, then cemented his lips into a thin line. I knew he was fighting the urge to make some biting remark. Finally, discretion won out. He shrugged and said, "Another night then."

3

From the outside, Sharon's house is as grand and imposing as Mona's. Inside, they are worlds apart. Sharon's decor, like her personality, tends toward the casual and comfortable. She pulls it off with flair though, so the ambiance is one of inviting warmth rather than clutter.

We sat in her kitchen sipping coffee and trying to make sense of Mona's baffling death. We weren't having much luck.

"How could she have done this?" Sharon lamented, pressing her fingers hard against her temples.

I shook my head. I'd been asking myself the same question for several hours and I was no closer to an answer.

"How could she laugh and gossip with me over a routine cup of coffee, then a couple of days later go kill herself? Why didn't she say something?"

"Maybe she didn't want to worry you." It was lame, but I was kind of short on answers.

"It doesn't make sense, Kate. Besides, Mona wasn't the type to take her own life."

"There's a type?"

"There's definitely a non-type."

"You think it was accidental then?"

"It had to be." Sharon sighed, ran a hand through her dark curls, and scowled into her coffee. "Except that Mona was usually pretty careful about mixing drugs and booze."

"She had company earlier that evening." I explained about the full ashtray and the glasses which smelled of alcohol. "Maybe she'd had more to drink than she realized. You know how she was when she got to talking."

Sharon nodded lamely. "I guess it's possible."

We lapsed into glum silence while Sharon refilled our cups.

"Did you reach everyone about canceling today's meeting?" I asked, grasping at the chance to talk about something besides death.

"Everyone except Claire. She wasn't going to be able to make it anyway. Jodi has one of her ear infections so they were going to see the doctor. I left a message on her machine, although she'll probably see the police cars first. You know Claire, she'll have worked herself into a grade A state of agitation before she even gets my message."

Claire Jorgensen and her daughter lived at the back of Mona's property in what had once been the caretaker's cottage. Claire was a humorless, slouch-shouldered woman who found more things to worry and whine about than the Communist conspiracy folks. None of us knew her well since she'd moved to town only that fall, and then kept pretty much to herself. I'd thought that being involved with the auction might bring her out of her shell, but so far she'd managed to miss half the meetings and do nothing at those she did attend but chew on her bottom lip.

"We're going to have to reschedule," Sharon said, "but there's no way I can deal with that right now."

I nodded. The school auction, the major fundraiser of the year, was only a week away. The kindergarten parents had been assigned ticket sales, so we weren't (thank goodness) involved in any of the last minute preparations. Still, there were a few loose ends we needed to tie up.

The phone rang just then and Sharon reached for it. "It's probably George. I called earlier but he was out." George was Sharon's husband and longtime friend of Mona's ex. "I can't believe Gary's going to need much consoling," she said, "but George would be furious with me if I didn't let him know about Mona right away."

While Sharon broke the news to her husband, I went upstairs to find Anna. She and Kyle were in the second of Kyle's two bedrooms, the one given over to bins and boxes of toys. Tiny soldiers and plastic action figures were strewn about the room. Kyle sat near the door, sorting through his baseball cards and carrying on a nonstop monologue about stolen bases and RBIs. Anna sat at the other end of the room, her back to Kyle, arranging his collection of stuffed animals in what I recognized as party formation.

When she saw me, she jumped up and left the animals with a stern warning to stay put. She threw her arms around my middle and hugged me. "You're just in time," she said. "We're going to have tea and crumpets."

Crumpets were new. It was usually tea and scones though, to my knowledge, Anna has never actually had either.

"I can't stay for the party, honey. I just thought I'd come up and say hi. We'll be going home in a bit anyway."

Ignoring my protests, Anna handed me an invisible cup. "Here," she said sternly. "Just sit and catch your breath for a minute or you'll wear yourself out."

I hated to think how many times each day I must have uttered those exact words to her.

I swallowed my tea and ate a bit of crumpet, although I made the mistake of calling it a biscuit. Anna looked at me like I'd dropped plum jam on the Duchess's white carpet.

On my way down the stairs the doorbell rang. "Can you get it?" Sharon called, "I'm still on the phone."

I opened the door just as the bell chimed a second time. Mary Nell greeted me in hushed tones. "How is she doing?" she asked.

"Who?"

"Sharon. She and Mona were so close, it must be just awful for her." Mary Nell held up a large picnic basket stuffed with food. "I brought dinner so she wouldn't have to worry about cooking."

This was typical Mary Nell. She was always dropping by with home-baked bread or a jar of the jam she'd been putting up. She remembered birthdays too, and sent get-well cards for simple colds.

Until she and her husband moved to Walnut Hills two years ago, she'd lived her whole life in a small town somewhere in Kansas. And she'd give anything to move back. If she could, she'd probably set the clock back about thirty years as well. Mary Nell finds life in California bewildering and often unpleasant, but to her credit, she makes a valiant effort to fit in.

"Come on," I told her. "Sharon's in the kitchen."

"Oh, no, I wouldn't want to intrude."

"You're not intruding."

"I didn't know Mona all that well myself. Only through the club and our work on the Guild project for battered women. I wouldn't want Sharon to feel I was being presumptuous."

"Oh for heaven's sake. You don't have to stay, but at least come in and give her the basket."

Mary Nell cleared her throat. "Well, if you think I should."

I nodded, and she followed me into the kitchen.

We'd barely gotten ourselves seated when the doorbell rang again. I went to answer it while Sharon finished unloading the basket. She'd already oohed and aahed over a tuna noodle casserole topped with crumbled potato chips, lime jello salad, marshmallowed carrot strips, and an Oreo-crumb strawberry jam tart. Mary Nell may not know the meaning of nouvelle cuisine, but she's a whiz at assembling a meal on short notice.

Sharon was mumbling still another "Oh you shouldn't have" when I reached the door. It was Claire, looking paler and more overwrought than ever. Jodi stood behind her, clinging to her mother's leg.

"I got Sharon's message," Claire said, speaking in a low voice so Jodi wouldn't overhear. "I tried calling but the line was busy. She didn't give many details."

"There's not a lot to tell. Mona was dead when I got there."

Claire sucked in her breath. "*You* were the one who found her?"

I nodded, envisioning once again the lifeless form sprawled across the sofa.

"How awful."

I knew I was going to have to go through the whole, dreadful thing one more time. "Come on in. Mary Nell's here too."

We'd no sooner made it to the kitchen than the bell rang once again. Sharon went to answer it, returning with Laurelle Simms, who was pregnant with baby Simms number four.

"I thought you told me the meeting was canceled," she huffed. "Then I happen to drive by and see that everyone is here after all. Everyone but me, that is. I'd like some explanation."

"Kate found a body," Mary Nell said. "A woman she knew. A woman we all knew, although Sharon knew her best. We're here because of that, not because of the auction meeting."

"A body? You mean, as in a *dead* body?" Laurelle looked at me as though I'd gone out digging up graves.

"We think she probably committed suicide."

"How ghastly." Laurelle unwrapped the blue cashmere scarf from around her neck and tossed it over the chair back. "Who was it?"

"Mona Sterling. You know her?"

Laurelle blinked, shot a quick glance at the faces in the room, then dropped heavily into the chair next to Claire. "Never heard of her," she said.

"Her daughter's in high school," Sharon offered by way of explanation. The child-classmate connection was one of the main arteries of social contact.

"Your father handled her divorce," I added. He was handling mine too, although I was beginning to wonder if hiring him had been a mistake. He wanted to wage war, whereas all I wanted was the dotted line, ready for my signature.

"That means your husband probably knew her as well," Mary Nell added. Laurelle's husband and father were law partners.

Laurelle squared her shoulders and ran a hand across her protruding belly. "Well, *I* didn't know her."

Claire looked up, frowning. "You asked me about her just last week."

Laurelle swallowed a hiccup. "I did?"

"Remember, you knew I rented the cottage from her."

"Oh, that." The thin line of Laurelle's mouth relaxed. "I didn't make the connection at first. I guess I have *heard* of her."

"How about I put on another pot of coffee," Sharon suggested. She stood to fill the pot with water, then set it back on the stove, empty. "Hell's, bells," she said. "Let's skip the coffee and open a bottle of wine. I don't know about the rest of you, but I could certainly use a drink."

Because she was pregnant, Laurelle took only a small amount. Claire, who never drank alcohol, passed on coffee as well. But Mary Nell, Sharon, and I each had a full glass, and what's more, Mary Nell didn't bat an eye. I refrained from pointing out to her that she was becoming more thoroughly steeped in California tradition by the day.

While we drank our wine and munched on pretzels, we debated the suicide question. Mary Nell made sure we all understood that in the eyes of God, suicide is a sin. Nonetheless, she said she understood how a person might be so despondent as to seek relief in death. Sharon, who didn't give a hoot what God thought, argued that suicide made perfect sense in certain situations, but that it made no sense whatsoever where Mona was concerned.

"Well, she *was* just divorced," Mary Nell said. "Losing her husband, and to a younger woman at that. It makes sense she'd be depressed. And then with Gary getting married again right away and all . . . I'm not saying Mona was justified in doing what she did, but I think we can't judge her too harshly, after all she'd been through."

Sharon squinted one eye at Mary Nell in a look of utter disdain. "Hell, she was glad to be rid of the guy. It was like a new beginning for her. And she certainly wasn't jealous of Bambi. The woman's a high school dropout with the IQ of a flea. She used to work in some south of Market manicure salon, for God's sake."

"I don't see what that has to do with anything," Mary Nell replied.

"She could have been upset about something else," said Laurelle, who hadn't known Mona at all but wasn't one to let that stop her. "I read an article about suicide not too long ago. You wouldn't believe the things that can push people over the edge. I mean it can be the littlest, most inconsequential thing. It's all in how a person perceives it. People who feel guilty are particularly vulnerable."

"Why would Mona feel guilty?"

Laurelle shrugged. "It was just a thought. Everybody has something they feel guilty about."

Sharon rolled her eyes and sighed, but she was facing away from the others so I was the only one who caught it, which was probably just as well.

Claire was sitting quietly, tracing invisible squares on the tabletop with the end of a pretzel. She is one of those women to whom nature has not been kind. She has a pinched, mouselike face with a slight overbite and a receding chin. And she does nothing on her own to improve things. She turned suddenly, addressing me without actually raising her eyes. "What happened when you found her?" she asked.

Mary Nell swiveled to look at me with astonishment. *"You* were the one? Oh dear, poor Kate." She reached over to pat my hand. I could tell she was thinking she should have prepared a food basket for me as well.

Claire tried again, her voice squeaking a little at odd intervals. "Did you know right away that she was dead?"

A vision of Mona's face appeared before me. I pushed it aside. "I was pretty sure she was. I called the paramedics anyway. And then the police."

"The police? What did they do?"

"I don't know really. I stayed in the other room, and then left right after they took the . . . after they took Mona out."

"I believe I read somewhere," said Mary Nell, "that there are more suicides in California than in any other state. When you consider how cavalier most people out here are about traditional values, I guess it's no wonder."

Sharon sent me a pleading look and reached for the bottle of wine. "There are more *people* in California than any other state," she said. "So even if your statistics are right, it doesn't mean much. In any case, I can't believe that Mona was one of them."

"What do you think, Claire?" Mary Nell spoke as though trying to entice a child into conversation. "Living in her cottage, you probably saw a different side of her than the rest of us."

Claire looked up. "What do I think about what?"

"Accident or suicide."

She shrugged, but it was a deliberate and somewhat strained gesture. She returned her gaze to the table top. "It doesn't much matter at this point. Either way, she's dead."

There was something about the look on Claire's face. It made me wonder if her husband's death had been a suicide as well. She never spoke about it except to say that he'd died before Jodi was born, but it would certainly explain her dour outlook on life.

Before I could think of some appropriately empathetic comment, Laurelle stood and announced that since this wasn't *really* a meeting after all, she had other, more pressing matters to attend to. Mary Nell and Claire left not long after. Sharon and I sat awhile more, scrutinizing every conversation we'd had with Mona over the last few weeks. Even with the benefit of hindsight, we agreed there had been nothing to indicate she was upset.

Finally, we'd gnawed and chewed at the problem long enough that there was nothing left to say. I gathered Anna and the assortment of coloring books she'd insisted on bringing. They had somehow ended up strewn around the family room floor.

"Sorry about the mess," Sharon said, gesturing to the piles of manilla folders spread out at one end of the room. "Soccer registration. When I volunteered I never realized how much *paper* was involved. There's the application, the check, the birth certificate, the recent photo, the doctor's statement, the waiver of liability. It goes on and on."

I'd just finished filling out the forms for Anna so I knew what she meant. But the truth was, Sharon's family room wasn't a heck of a lot messier than it normally was. Actually, messy is probably the wrong word. In my house, rooms look messy. In Sharon's they simply look lived in. Comfortable and cozy without any of the tornado-aftermath effect I seem unable to avoid.

"You want to stay for dinner?" Sharon asked, handing me the coloring book which she'd retrieved from under the sofa. "It doesn't seem like the kind of night you'd want to be alone."

I shook my head. "Andy's coming by tonight."

"Again? He was just there a couple of weeks ago."

"That's the plan."

"Oh?"

"We're doing it for Anna."

"You going to keep this up after you're actually divorced?"

"We're going to try to. Of course with Andy you never know. By that time he may be bungy jumping in Paris or studying meditation in Tibet."

She half raised an eyebrow and gave me that look she's so good at. "What does your cop think about all this?"

My cop, as far as I could tell, tried his hardest not to think about it. He claimed he understood, but since he's childless himself, I wasn't so sure he really did. "This isn't something which involves Michael," I told her.

She grinned. "Wanna bet?"

4

I am no great shakes as a cook, and Anna is a picky eater. Since there's just the two of us most nights, I've fallen into the habit of not actually cooking a real dinner. I fix Anna an omelette or some macaroni and cheese, myself a salad, and then I nibble on her leftovers. With Andy coming over, however, I'd planned on fixing a real meal. But I'd also planned on having a good part of the afternoon for grocery shopping and preparation. Mona's death had changed all that.

So it was back to macaroni and cheese, although I made it from scratch this time instead of a box. Anna took one bite and then wrinkled her nose. "What's wrong with this macaroni? It tastes funny."

"That's because it's homemade," I explained, giving a swift elbow to the dog, Max, who seemed to think it smelled just fine. He's fifty pounds of affection and enthusiasm, but he has absolutely no manners.

"Do I *have* to eat it?" Anna asked.

Andy laughed. "Kate, you've been outclassed by Kraft."

"Do you like it, Daddy?"

"Honey, I think it's the best macaroni and cheese I've ever eaten, but that doesn't mean you've gotta like it."

Anna took a second spoonful. Then another. "I guess it's not so bad once you get used to it," she mumbled.

"You want another beer?" I asked Andy.

"Sure."

I got him the beer and then settled back to listen while Anna filled him in on the latest from the kindergarten scene. Andy listened (or at least pretended to listen—he's good at that) and then launched into a dramatic telling of a story about his own childhood. Anna found it hilarious.

Although I never had any trouble remembering why I was divorcing Andy, neither did I have any trouble remembering why I'd married him in the first place. Andy was a class act, the quintessential fair-haired boy. He could knock you off your feet with his Nordic good looks and well-tuned charm. The trouble was, he might just leave you there, bowled over and waiting for a hand up, while he trotted off on some new adventure.

"So, Kate," he said, turning his charm in my direction, "how's the picture-hanging business?" He grinned to let me know it wasn't a putdown, just good-natured fun. "You started on that big job yet?"

I set my fork down, suddenly aware that I wasn't hungry, and told him about finding Mona's body that morning.

"Sterling," he repeated when I'd finished. "She related to Gary Sterling?"

"His ex-wife."

"No kidding? Small world. Though it beats me why a dame with that much money would go and kill herself."

Andy's never bought into the belief that money can't buy happiness. And in all honesty, in his case, it probably could. "I don't think financial worries were the problem," I told him.

He shook his head in bewilderment. "From what I hear, she made out like a bandit in the divorce. Had the guy by the balls and wouldn't let go. Squeezed him but good. He's hurting still."

Anna slurped a spoon of macaroni. "Why did she want his balls, Daddy? Didn't she got her own?"

"Didn't she *have* her own," I corrected, giving Andy a pointed look.

But he just laughed. "Different kind of balls, kiddo."

Quickly, before Anna demanded an explanation, I asked how he knew Gary.

"I don't really. But I applied for a job with that new commercial development of his. Kinda combination property manager and leasing agent. Should know any day now whether I got it."

"They're hiring people already?"

"Never too early to line up tenants, especially in this market."

"What about Nutra-Pack?" I asked. Andy had only been with them a couple of months, selling vitamins and health food products. And endlessly recruiting salespeople to work under him. It had sounded like nothing more than a pyramid scheme for the nineties to me, but Andy had gone to great lengths to assure me otherwise.

"Well, that, uh, isn't quite as full-time as I'd hoped. I ought to be able to keep doing it, though, even if I get this position."

I didn't need anyone to draw me a diagram. Once again Andy had been tripped up by a sure thing that wasn't. "This new job, is it a commission position as well?"

"Jesus, Kate." Andy rocked forward, slapping his open palm against the table. "This could be the chance I've been waiting for, an opportunity to finally break into the big time. And all you're concerned about is the money."

"That's not true and you know it. I just don't like to see you wasting these years when you could be building your career."

Andy shook his head, in a slow exaggerated fashion, eyeing me as though I were the last of some ridiculous but quaint species. "You're making yourself old with all this worrying, Kate. Life is short. You ought to lighten up, learn to enjoy the moment."

That was pretty much the story of our marriage. Andy and I were like trains passing on parallel tracks. I couldn't lighten up and he couldn't settle down.

Although it was still early when Andy left, I climbed into bed anyway, risking the censure of modern American psychiatry by letting Anna climb into bed with me. It's not something I do regularly, not something Anna wants to do with any regularity anymore either, but sometimes it feels right.

When Andy and I took her to Disneyland two years ago, the thing that impressed her most, besides the soda machine outside her door, was the fact that we all got to sleep together in one big bed. This was the highlight of her trip, the thing she chose to share with the nursery school boys and girls who gathered in a circle to hear her adventures. The teacher wrote me a polite but pointed note explaining that this was a practice frowned upon by child guidance experts everywhere. In return, I loaned her my copy of *The Family Bed*, which says basically that the experts' opinion is hogwash.

Anna cuddled with her back against my stomach and was asleep in an instant. For me, sleep was a long time coming. I couldn't rid my mind of thoughts and images of Mona. Nor could I stop thinking of Libby, who though long past the age of cuddling, was now motherless.

I'd just returned from dropping Anna off at school the next morning when Sharon called.

"I have a favor to ask you," she said. "Two favors actually."

"Anything but money." Of course I would have helped out there too, if I'd thought she needed it.

"I want you to go over to Mona's with me." Her voice was thin and a little raspy. "She asked me if I'd take care of the, uh, details in the event anything ever happened to her."

"She did?" Maybe Mona had been planning to kill herself after all. "When was this?"

"Right after Gary moved out. She re-wrote her will, listed me as executrix, and made me promise I wouldn't let him get his hands on her stuff. I remember making the whole thing into a big joke. It never crossed my mind she might actually die." The sentence sort of faded out so if I hadn't known what the last word was going to be I might not have heard her. "Please, Kate. I don't want to go over there alone."

I wasn't thrilled about the idea of going over there myself, but I couldn't let Sharon go unaccompanied either. "Sure," I said, with forced cheeriness. "I'd be glad to. You want me to meet you there?"

"Might be better if I picked you up. We have to go by the mortuary too."

We? I had to admire the way she slipped that one in there.

"Can you be ready in half an hour?" Sharon asked.

"Sure. How's Libby doing? Have you talked to her?"

"She spent the night with us. The police apparently contacted the trip coordinator and they brought her here."

"Not to her father's?"

"No, she didn't want to go there."

"How is she holding up?"

"On the outside, very much in control. But she won't talk about it, won't talk at all really. Just wants to be left alone."

"Give it time," I told her. "The fact that you're there for her, that you care about her, it's bound to mean a lot even if she doesn't show it." Max began barking at the delivery truck next door. I booted him with my foot then moved to the other end of the room and put a finger in my ear. "What was the other thing you wanted. You said you had two favors to ask."

"It's probably best if I tell you in person."

"That bad?"

She laughed, a nervous laugh pitched a little too high. "See you in half an hour."

5

Sharon had decided we should swing by the mortuary first. "It shouldn't take long," she said. "Mona was quite clear about wanting her body cremated and not wanting a funeral. So it's not like we have to make elaborate arrangements."

There was that *we* again. I mumbled something generic and noncommittal.

"Although I suppose she wouldn't be too upset if we held a simple memorial service," Sharon added after a moment's thought.

I didn't bother to point out that Mona was long past being upset by anything.

Sharon parked the car near the front entrance. According to the sign above the door, Thompson Mortuary had been family owned and operated for three generations. Which was reassuring I guess, though somewhat hard to fathom. What kind of kid goes around harboring hopes of becoming a mortician?

The window to the left of the door was painted with

gold letters—Se Habla Espanol, a couple of Chinese characters, and something in an alphabet I didn't recognize; maybe Arabic. All this in one family—I was impressed. There was no mention of English. I was hoping they spoke that too.

We stepped through the double doors into a large entry hall with a vaulted ceiling and dark paneled walls. The air was cool, like the aisle by the freezer case at Safeway. Cool, I realized with a sudden queasiness, for the very same reason—preventing spoilage. The carpet was a plush magenta, a little too reminiscent of blood, I thought, to be appropriate for a mortuary. In the center of the room was a fountain that spouted a thin, bubbling stream of water, something like a large bird bath with a broken water valve.

Our eyes had barely adjusted to the dim interior light when a middle-aged man in a dark, three-piece suit emerged from behind one of the panels.

"Harold Thompson," he said, shaking our hands earnestly. "How can I be of service today?"

"We'd like to arrange for a cremation," Sharon said, and then swallowed several times in rapid succession. "The, uh, body's at the morgue but we can have it sent here when they're finished."

Mr. Thompson nodded, solemn and sincere. "My deepest condolences on your recent loss. We'll do everything we can to make this as easy as possible for you." He pressed his round face close to mine. I caught a whiff of Juicy Fruit gum. "Step this way, ladies, through that door to the right."

We followed him into a smaller room furnished with a round table and several comfortable chairs. Daylight filtered into the room through a panel of sheer drapes; the temperature, however, was still cool. I huddled in my jacket and folded my fingers into my palms.

Mr. Thompson pulled out a leather binder and flipped it open, turning immediately to the page he wanted.

"Now then, did you wish the cremains to be buried or inurned?"

"I'm not . . ." Sharon looked at me in something like panic.

"Mona wasn't clear about that part?"

"No, just that she wanted to be cremated."

"Perhaps you'd like her ashes spread at sea," Mr. Thompson offered. "We have several lovely plans available. I'm sure there would be one that would work well in whatever price range you were considering."

Sharon shook her head. "No. No boats. Mona always got terribly seasick."

Mr. Thompson opened his mouth to say something, then closed it again and cleared his throat before continuing. "If you would like a burial we could arrange for the purchase of a plot, although most of the prime locations are already spoken for."

"No, I think she meant cremated as *opposed* to buried."

"I suggest you go with an urn then." He smiled pleasantly, a nice, helpful car salesman kind of smile. "There are a number of styles to choose from, and again a variety of prices. We have a wonderful columbarium here with roomy niches, and for a flat up front fee we will provide complete and perpetual care."

How much care could a bucket of ashes take?

"I don't know . . ." Sharon mumbled, nervously fingering the hem of her sweater.

Thompson flipped the page of his binder and turned it

in our direction. "Most of the models are pictured here if you'd like to take a look."

Sharon's usual steely control had deserted her. She stared blankly at the page for a moment, then turned to look at me. Her face was drained of color. "Shit. I never thought about what she'd want me to *do* with the ashes."

"Could we arrange to have them in a paper bag or something?" I asked. "And then decide later."

Mr. Thompson's face drew up tight, like a shriveled peach. "A box," he said, "but you'll have to get a permit from the county if you intend to scatter them on private land." He pulled out a sheet of paper that looked like the order form from our local hardware store and began checking off items.

While he was writing down the information Sharon gave him, I leafed through the leather portfolio. The cover sheet listed the benefits of choosing Thompson Mortuary, foremost of which was ample off-street parking. In addition, they boasted of worldwide shipping (just like the Christmas catalogues) and an extensive selection of caskets for sale or rent. Rental caskets? I closed the book and shoved it back toward Sharon.

As soon as we were back outside, Sharon started shaking. An uneasy whimper emanated from the back of her throat.

"Hey," I said. "It's over. You handled everything beautifully."

"But what about her ashes?"

"Take it one step at a time."

"I don't know what she wanted. Not to be stuck in an urn on someone's mantel though, I'm pretty sure about that."

"What about her sister? Alice might know."

"I tried calling her, both last night and this morning. No answer, no machine." Sharon opened the car door and got in. She stared morosely at her lap, then sighed. "I suppose we've got a couple of days to figure it out."

We again. Maybe she was using the term in the royal sense. I certainly hoped so. I waited, but she seemed to have dropped the subject of bodies and ashes. I sat back and began to relax.

"About that other thing," Sharon said.

"What other thing?"

"Two favors, remember?"

I did, though I figured she'd got more than two out of me already. "What was it?"

Sharon kept her eyes on the road. "How would you feel about taking in Libby for awhile?"

"Taking her in?"

"You know, letting her stay with you."

"But I hardly know her."

"Please, Kate, just until I get everything sorted out. I don't think she spends a whole lot of time at home anyway."

"Why me?"

"Because I trust you."

Wonderful. Why did I suddenly feel like the chicken in the tale of Wily Fox?

"She refuses to have anything to do with her father. I could force her I suppose, but with everything else she has to deal with, I thought it would be better if I didn't. Although it will probably come to that at some point."

"What about your place?"

"I'd do it in a minute, willingly," Sharon explained. "But George feels kind of awkward about it. He and Gary were fraternity brothers, remember."

"Doesn't Libby have friends she could stay with?"

A feeble laugh. "None Mona would have approved of."

I felt my stomach drop. How could I take on a responsibility like that? How could I so totally disrupt my life, and Anna's? On the other hand, how could I turn away a motherless child? "Let me think about it, okay?"

"Just remember," Sharon said, "I'm counting on you."

My stomach dropped another few floors. This was far worse than the non-royal *we*.

Sharon pulled up in front of Mona's house and turned off the ignition. For a moment, neither of us moved.

"Maybe we should save this for another day," I suggested.

She shook her head. "We're here. We might as well get on with it." For a woman who's not at all puritanical, Sharon has a strong streak of old-fashioned Puritan ethic about her. "There's nothing to be gained by putting things off," she explained.

Maybe, but I was usually willing to take the chance that there might be.

While Sharon went off to gather Mona's will, safe deposit key and various bank books, I worked at cleaning up the kitchen. I ran the dishwasher, emptied the garbage, and then started on the refrigerator. We'd decided to pitch everything, even if it was fresh. The idea of eating a dead friend's leftovers seemed vaguely cannibalistic, though we conceded that our squeamishness defied logic. I dumped a grilled hamburger patty, carefully wrapped in plastic wrap, a carton of coleslaw, cheese, lunch meat, milk, eggs. Even the thick, top grade piece of filet mignon in the meat drawer, although I thought twice before adding it to the rapidly growing pile of trash. But I did set aside the almost full bottle of gin. I'd have to ask Sharon if she really wanted to toss a fifth of Tanqueray.

This whole time, I kept looking over my shoulder, turning expectantly, although I couldn't say why. Certainly I wasn't expecting Mona, not in any real sense. But there's something unsettling about being in a house where a person has died. It is more than simply empty or still, the lack of life is almost palpable. As I went about my tasks, I found myself wondering, *What was Mona feeling when she last used this glass or pot? What was she thinking when she last sat here?* And ultimately, of course, *What had been going through her mind the night she killed herself?*

I was just finishing with the refrigerator, when Sharon walked in, echoing my own unease.

"This is spooky," she remarked. "Even though Mona showed me where her papers were and went over everything with me, it feels . . . I don't know, it feels wrong." She plopped down at the table and drew in a deep breath. "What it really feels, I guess, is sad. It makes her death so real."

I sat too. "I think suicide makes it even harder to accept. There's guilt to deal with as well as loss."

Sharon picked up a rubberband from the floor and began twisting it around her fingers. "I've been thinking about that, Kate. I don't think it was suicide."

I didn't want to believe that Mona had meant to kill herself any more than Sharon did, but it seemed a more likely scenario than accidental overdose. "She'd have to have been really out of it," I said, with the weight of logic, "to *accidentally* swallow a whole bottle of pills."

"That's not what I meant."

I shook my head, puzzled. "What did you mean then?"

Sharon's eyes fixed on mine. They were a darker green than usual, the golden flecks almost nonexistent. "What I mean," she said, "is that I think Mona was murdered."

"Murdered?"

Sharon nodded.

I peered at her for a moment, trying to determine if this was some off-beat attempt at humor.

"I think someone killed her," Sharon said, "and tried to make it look like suicide."

"You're not serious?"

But she was. "Think about it, Kate. It's the only explanation that makes sense."

I thought about it, and it made no sense at all.

"Look," Sharon said, "I know you think I'm in denial or something, but I knew Mona. I'd known her for years. And I know she wouldn't commit suicide, not like this anyway. Not unless she was ill or desperately unhappy. She wasn't either of those things. And if she was going to take her own life, she'd leave a note—probably a whole series of notes. Have you ever known Mona to pass up an opportunity to have the last word?"

"But murder? Jesus, Sharon, that's going some."

Sharon twined the rubberband tightly around her little finger. "You said she was wearing her old gray sweats, right? The ones with a hole in the knee." I nodded. "And no make-up."

"That's what it seemed like anyway. I didn't take a close look at her face."

"Well?"

"Well what?"

"If you were going to kill yourself, take your soul off to

wherever it goes and leave your body behind for someone to find, wouldn't you want to at least look nice?"

"Maybe she wanted to be comfortable. I mean, who'd want her last breath constricted by tight pantyhose?"

"There's comfort and there's comfort. Mona, of all people, would care what she looked like."

That was probably true. Assuming she'd actually meant to kill herself.

"And she had a root canal a week ago. Why would she go through all that trouble if she wasn't going to be around to reap the benefits?"

Before I could answer, Sharon continued. "Another thing. Mona and I made a trip to Price-Costco last week. She stocked up on all the basics. You think she'd buy forty-eight rolls of toilet paper if she was planning on killing herself a few days later?"

"I don't know that you plan something like suicide quite as carefully as you do a two-week jaunt to the Mediterranean."

"It just doesn't fit."

"It doesn't fit that she'd lie there and let someone stuff a couple dozen pills down her throat either."

Sharon slumped back in her chair and sighed. "That's the sticky part. But maybe there's more to it."

"Like what?"

"I don't know." Sharon's brow creased in thought. "Did you see anything unusual when you got to the house Monday morning?"

I tried mentally retracing my steps, but it was all a blur. Finding Mona's body, that was the only thing I could remember. "I don't think so. Nothing comes to mind anyway." Besides, anyone who'd gone to the trouble of disguising a murder wasn't likely to leave a calling card.

"No signs of a struggle? Nothing overturned or disheveled?"

"No. I would have noticed, I'm sure. So would the police."

"Rats." She got up and started pacing the length of the kitchen. "Let's think about this logically, starting at the beginning. How did her killer get into the house in the first place? He certainly couldn't walk through the door like Casper the ghost."

Door. The word jogged my memory. There *was* something after all. I told her about the door locks. "The bottom one sets automatically when the door closes, but the top one is a deadbolt that locks from the inside and requires a key. Mona made a big deal about the fact that she always secured the house with both. But only the bottom was locked when I got here."

"Which would mean," Sharon said, slowing her stride for a moment, "that someone left the house after Mona was killed. See, she was murdered."

"It could mean that," I agreed, "but it could *not* mean that just as easily. If you're planning to kill yourself, you're hardly going to worry about keeping out prowlers."

Sharon wasn't listening; she was choreographing a murder, post facto. "Now, back to the original question, how did this creep get in? It almost has to have been someone she let in herself. A friend, an acquaintance—"

"Or someone she had no reason to distrust, like a delivery man or something." The words came out in a rush, before I had time to think about them. Was I just playing along with Sharon, or had she succeeded in planting a seed of doubt in my mind? I couldn't honestly say.

"You mentioned something earlier about Mona's having company."

I nodded. "There were two cocktail glasses next to the sink, and an ashtray." We both knew Mona didn't smoke. "And the toilet seat was up," I added, remembering suddenly my queasy episode in the bathroom.

"Don't you see, Kate? There are too many coincidences, too many things that simply don't fit."

"Maybe she wanted someone with her during her final moments."

"I can't imagine who, certainly if we're talking about a male *who*. Nor can I see her entertaining, even on the brink of suicide, without make-up and halfway decent clothes. Nothing about this makes sense."

"It's still a big leap to murder."

Sharon stopped her pacing altogether and turned to face me. "Will you talk to your cop about this, see what he has to say?"

"His name is Michael."

She made a face, squinting her eyes and wrinkling her nose in exaggerated fashion. Sharon knows Michael's name as well as her own, but she can't resist razzing me about getting involved with a cop. She finds it amusing that someone in the habit of thumbing her nose at law-and-order types and, I'm ashamed to confess, certain laws, would wind up with the law, literally, breathing down her neck. I understand the irony, but in this particular case, the breathing feels awfully nice.

"So, will you ask him?"

I nodded. I wasn't convinced the way Sharon was, but I couldn't deny that she'd raised some interesting questions.

She let out a deep breath and went back to rubberband

gymnastics. "Does the name Laurie McNevitt ring a bell with you?" she asked after a moment.

"No. Why?"

"I checked the messages on Mona's answering machine. There was the usual array of stuff—a reminder about her dental appointment, a friend calling to cancel a lunch date, someone for Libby about a history assignment—and this message from Laurie McNevitt. She sounded so . . . I don't know, agitated I guess. But she didn't leave a number. Come listen to it and see what you think."

Listening to the tape meant going into the den. I knew there wasn't going to be a ghost hovering about. Or blood, or a draped sheet, or traces of disgusting medical procedures. Yet I really didn't want to go back there again.

Sharon must have read my hesitation. "I wasn't thrilled about it either," she said softly. "But I'd like you to hear this message."

The den was at the back of the house, with a view of the garden. I tried to keep my eyes on the flowering camellia bushes so that I wouldn't have to look at the couch where I'd discovered Mona's body. It didn't work though. I focused on the couch first thing. I could see the indentation in the seat cushion where her body had rested, and in the pillow at the back where her head lolled over. For a second or two I forgot to breathe.

Finally, the machine's whirring and clicking shook me from my daze. Sharon punched a couple of buttons and a female voice came on. "Yes, uh, this is Laurie McNevitt again." There was an audible pause before she continued. "I just wanted to be sure you got my message the other day. And I wanted to, uh, I mean I hope I didn't come on too strong." Another pause. "It's just that you can't begin to imagine how hard it's been." Her voice broke on the last few words. "Like I said, you can call me any time. Please."

"See what I mean?" Sharon asked.

I nodded. It was the tone more than anything, hesitant yet almost pleading. I thought of the poor woman sitting by her phone, waiting for a call that would never come. "Maybe we should check Mona's address book," I suggested.

"I already did that. And the telephone book. No Laurie, and no L. McNevitt either. Of course there aren't all that many listings, I guess I could give each one of them a try."

"You've got enough to worry about, I'll handle this."

"Thanks." Sharon came to stand next to me and nodded at the sofa where my eyes had once again strayed. "I'm sorry you had to be the one to find her."

I nodded wordlessly. The police had taken the empty bottle of pills but they'd only moved the scotch to the bookshelf, presumably so it wouldn't get knocked over when they transferred the body.

"At least she didn't cut corners at the end," I said, pointing to the Glenfiddich label. "That's supposed to be some of the best scotch there is."

"That's the bottle?"

I nodded.

Sharon sucked in a deep breath and turned to look at me. "Mona didn't drink scotch, Kate. Only gin and wine."

6

Our silence during the ride home was as thick and gray as the sky overhead. Maybe we'd simply talked ourselves out, or maybe we'd talked ourselves into something that left us too shaken for words.

I still didn't buy into the murder theory, at least not completely. The way I figured it, there had to be any number of perfectly plausible reasons a gin-drinking woman might suddenly switch to scotch. Trouble was, I couldn't come up with a single one that satisfied me.

I was still gnawing at the possibilities when I picked Anna up from school. Mrs. Craig, her teacher, waved as Anna climbed into the car. "Look forward to seeing you tomorrow," she called out, which I thought was a nice, teacherly gesture until I realized she was talking to me rather than Anna. I'd forgotten that tomorrow was my day to volunteer in the classroom.

One of the attractions of living in Walnut Hills is the schools, which are supposedly among the best in the state. I have a hunch this has more to do with the students themselves (largely well-fed, happy kids from literate families) than any innovative teaching. Nonetheless, the schools make a big deal about the individualized instruction that sets them apart from neighboring urban schools. Parent volunteers, (moms, in other words) are what makes this possible. Generally I don't mind, unless I'm stuck with some mindless task like cutting construction paper strips. But this was one time I wasn't in the mood.

Anna buckled her seat belt, then started talking with great excitement about the class's upcoming trip to the planetarium and the dramatic production which would follow.

"We're going to be studying space," she said, practically bouncing in her seat. "We're going to learn all about the sun and the moon, and planets and stars, and the meat-eaters too. I get to be a meat-eater in the play."

"Meat-eaters?" I looked at Anna to make sure I'd understood her correctly. "Meat-eaters is a word we use with dinosaurs, honey, you must be confused."

She looked at me and sniffed. "I *know* they're dinosaurs. But there are meat-eaters in the sky too."

Was this what the highly rated Walnut Hills' schools passed off as science? "I don't think so, Anna."

"There are! Mrs. Craig said so. You can see them sometimes at night. They look like long streaks of light."

I laughed. "Meteor. You mean meteors, not meat-eaters. They're like falling stars."

Anna's face had that same crestfallen look it had when the boy down the street set her straight about Santa Claus. "You mean there aren't *any* meat-eaters in the sky?"

I shook my head. "But meteors are pretty exciting all on their own."

"Jodi's a meat . . . whatever too. I don't even like Jodi. I only agreed to be her partner since we got to be meat-eaters."

"How can you not like Jodi? She's a perfectly sweet child." Though in truth, I had to admit she showed a surprising lack of enthusiasm for *anything*. Jodi went beyond timid; she was almost listless. But I figured she was probably nice too. At least she wasn't one of the kids who got her name on the blackboard for being a pest or talking out when the teacher wanted it quiet.

"She's a dweeb," Anna said, jutting out her chin.

"Anna Austen, I will not have you talk like that about your classmates."

"Well, she is," Anna said, then turned and spent the remainder of the ride looking out the window.

Later, when Anna had finished her snack and gone off to watch her allotment of afternoon cartoons, I sat down at the phone and tried every McNevitt in the book. None of them knew a Laurie. I tried a few neighboring communities, with the same result, then gave up. I felt bad for the poor woman, but I figured she was bound to hear about Mona eventually, even without my help.

Then I called Michael at work. As usual, I got transferred and put on hold several times before I reached him.

"I need to see you," I announced.

"Ah," he said, "music to my ears. You do care about me after all."

"Of course I care about you, but that's not why I need to see you." I took a deep breath. "I want to talk to you about Mona Sterling's death."

"Oh." Michael sounded a little the way Anna had when she'd learned there were no meat-eaters in the sky. "Maybe we could kind of combine the two things. You know, you're happy to see me because I'm such a terrific guy, and then, while I'm basking in your affection I can listen to what you have to say."

"I suppose you want food, too."

He laughed. "Kate, I love everything about you but your cooking. I'll bring dinner. Seven o'clock okay?"

"Perfect."

Michael arrived promptly at seven with a large bag of Chinese food, one of the few meals Anna finds acceptable. Even so, she's picky, demonstrating a strong preference for pot stickers and fried won ton over anything that's been contaminated with vegetables. He used to put together scrumptious meals like lemon-herb chicken or stuffed sole, but he got tired of watching Anna pretend to gag. So now when we dine á trois instead of á deux, he sticks to simpler fare.

I got a quick kiss at the door and a longer one when we were alone in the kitchen. A much longer one.

"Wouldn't it be nice if I came home to you like this every evening?" Michael whispered in my ear.

"If it was every evening, then it wouldn't be like this."

He grinned. "Want to make a bet?"

Michael and I had started out hot and heavy the prior spring, after Andy moved out for the first time. Then, when Andy moved back in, we substituted long but strictly platonic lunches for the heavy stuff. The hot we couldn't do much about. Now that Andy's moved out for good, Michael is ready to move in. He has trouble understanding my hesitancy, and even more trouble believing it has nothing to do with my feelings about him.

I ignored the grin and peered into the sack. "Oh goody, you got spring rolls."

"You're changing the subject."

"You're right," I told him, blowing a kiss.

"You can't keep doing that forever, you know."

"Blowing kisses?"

"Changing the subject. We need to talk about it."

I touched his arm lightly. "I know, but not right now. Okay?"

His face turned serious. "Soon though?"

"Soon."

While I got out bowls and chopsticks, Michael opened a bottle of wine and filled our glasses. Anna made her standard five-minute appearance at the table, ate all but one of the pot stickers, half the order of fried won ton and a little broccoli chicken, sans broccoli.

"So what's this about Mona Sterling?" Michael asked when we were alone.

I explained Sharon's murder theory and the reasons behind it. Michael listened without interrupting, but he wasn't persuaded.

"Everything points to suicide," he said. "There's no sign of a struggle, no forced entry to the premises, nothing."

"Except the scotch."

"Maybe she ran out of gin."

"No, I saw a bottle in the fridge."

He raised an eyebrow. "She kept her gin in the refrigerator?"

"The freezer. She liked it iced."

"Who knows, then. Maybe she was a closet scotch drinker. I can't go to the captain based on that."

"What did the coroner's report say?"

"We only have the preliminary results, but it's pretty much what you'd expect. Looks like cardiac arrest probably brought on by an overdose of barbituates and alcohol. And it's unlikely someone held a gun to her head and made her swallow them."

"Maybe she was drugged."

"It was her prescription, Kate. She had it filled just last week."

I tried a different approach. "Sharon's not one to blow things all out of proportion. She knew Mona. If Sharon thinks it doesn't feel right, that means something."

Michael poked at his rice. "You know I'd help if I could, but I can't open an investigation just because a friend of the deceased says it doesn't feel right. I need something to go on. Something besides an absence of make-up or an abundance of toilet paper."

"Or a bottle of scotch."

He nodded. "Even that. Look, I'm not even officially involved in this. The uniforms responded to the call. Unless they see something suspicious, or unless I've got some solid reason to intervene, their report stands." He didn't need to add that this was particularly true when the uniformed cop was Jerry Watkins, petulant nephew to the captain.

Like most small communities, Walnut Hills has only a handful of detectives. Usually they work in close cooperation with the patrol officers and nobody gets too upset about territorial rights. If you go strictly by the book though, there are clear directives about who does what, and when. Jerry was a by-the-book guy, at least on those occasions when it suited him.

"If it makes you feel any better," Michael said, "the responding officers seem to have done all the right things. Jerry hasn't been able to reach her sister, but he checked with the neighbors, people who might have seen her last—nothing unusual turned up. He contacted her doctor too, and verified the prescription. In fact, it's the second time she's had it filled in less than six months. Gave him some story about losing the first bottle. Could be she was storing them up for just this purpose."

I tapped my chopsticks against my plate. On one level, I knew Michael was right. And I knew that if he had any real reason to believe Mona's death was something other than a suicide, he'd investigate—in spite of Jerry and the rules and the fact the detective division was currently shorthanded. But at the same time, I couldn't help feeling uneasy about the whole thing.

Michael leaned across the table and covered my hand with his. "I'm sorry. I know how hard this must be on both you and Sharon. I wish I could make it easier."

I nodded, trying to shake off the feeling that I was somehow letting Sharon down. Then I turned my hand over and folded my fingers through his. "So tell me," I said after a moment, "without a dicey new homicide to investigate, how did you spend your day?"

"Tearing my hair out, mostly. Sometimes I don't know which gets to me most, the snotty kids or the parents who lie to protect them."

Michael moved from the San Francisco force a couple of years ago, partly in a failed attempt to save his marriage, and partly because he wanted to feel he was making a difference—something it's hard to do in a budget-strapped urban department where the number of cases grow geometrically. He once likened it to battling a forest fire with a garden hose. Walnut Hills is different, sometimes so different it drives him nuts. He's discovered the suburbs have their own variant of the forest fire.

"Juvenile detail again?"

He nodded. "In the last week we've had three car-jackings, a couple of armed assaults, and now an arson. In all cases, we suspect the culprits are under eighteen."

"With parents who wouldn't bother to tell you even if they found a machine gun under the mattress."

Michael laughed. "That about sums it up." He stood and began clearing the table. "I spent most of my time today on this arson business. There was a fire last night at the school district office. It didn't do a whole lot of structural damage but it made a real mess of the interior. The worst part is that it may have destroyed some records."

"And you think it was arson?"

"It wasn't natural, but it's hard to tell whether someone actually intended to set the place on fire or was simply careless. An amateur job if I've ever seen one." He looked up. "You want to save these leftovers?"

I got out a plastic bowl and filled it with tomorrow's lunch.

"Probably a teen-age prank that got out of hand. They're damned lucky no one was hurt." Michael dumped the empty cartons in the garbage, then began loading the dishwasher.

I can never look at Michael without feeling some small part of what I felt that first time I saw him. It had to have been strictly physical then—something about the smile that barely raises the corners of his mouth, the easy, slow way he moves, the magnetic quality of his eyes. But I feel that same quick flush now in a way that goes much deeper. I slid up behind him and wrapped my arms around his middle.

"You tired of shop talk and ready to move on to something more interesting?" he asked.

I grinned. "Like what?"

He turned me around and slipped his arms around my shoulders. "Well, I can think of one or two things. How about you?"

I could think of a couple, too.

7

We were out of Cheerios so I fixed French toast for Anna's breakfast. Plain toast she won't eat, even with jam, but French toast ranks right up there with pancakes as an all-time favorite. It's the syrup factor that makes the difference. She'd probably eat cardboard if I let her put syrup on it.

While Anna ate, I downed a quick cup of coffee, made her lunch, then got myself dressed. I let Max out to sniff the roses, which he considers a poor substitute for our usual morning run. He gave me a long, hard look before he ambled disdainfully out the back door. I could sympathize, but the timing was tight enough as it was.

By the time I'd finished wiping the syrup from Anna's hands and face, and from the table, chair, and floor, I barely had a chance to dust a little color on my cheeks and eyelids. As make-up jobs go, mine are pretty haphazard, but the difference is enough to convince me I've reached the age where going without is no longer an option.

We made it to school just as the first bell sounded. While Anna raced off to join her friends, I made my way to the classroom, where Mrs. Craig greeted me with her usual good-natured smile, and a handful of rulers.

"We're going to be measuring today," she said, using the same hearty enthusiasm she uses when addressing her students. "We'll work together as a class, but I'll need you to wander around the room and help the kids who get stuck."

Mrs. Craig has been teaching kindergarten for close to thirty years, but she approaches each day as if she were embarking on some long anticipated adventure. She's short, probably not much over five feet, with a crown of gray curls and a face full of laugh lines. I've heard she can be a bear when crossed, but so far I've been spared that experience.

"If you'll put a ruler and one of these sheets of paper at each place," she continued, "I'll go gather the children. We have a birthday today, so they'll probably be a bit more spirited than usual."

They were certainly flying high, but then they always seemed that way to me. Kyle fell out of his chair twice, which sent the class into fits of laughter, another boy managed to drop his ruler so often I lost count, and Mary Nell's daughter, Nicole, had to be reminded more than once that talking with her friends during class was not allowed. Because of my presence, Anna was on her best behavior, but she still got a stern look from Mrs. Craig for calling Jodi a dumbbell.

Nonetheless, by the end of the lesson every child in the room had completed the assignment sheet correctly. It amazes me to see how much gets accomplished in the midst of such chaos. Mrs. Craig tells me that's because I think like an adult. She says it as though it's something I ought to be embarrassed about.

While I collected the rulers and papers, Mrs. Craig read aloud to the class, and then we moved the chairs into a circle for the birthday activities. Jodi, the birthday girl, sat in front of the large wall map and helped the teacher stick a big yellow thumbtack near Boston, her birthplace. Most of the tacks were clustered around northern California, but there were enough others scattered around the U.S. (including Hawaii) that the class was learning something about geography.

Jodi is a thin, ungainly child with unruly curls the color of burnished copper. Her manner is so consistently devoid of animation, she sometimes reminds me of a Dickens' street urchin. She was staring at her feet, mumbling something about never having been back to Boston, when Claire walked in with a tray of cupcakes. Interest in geography quickly fell to an all-time low, which is why Mrs. Craig prefers that parents bring treats to the classroom before school. Claire is one of those mothers, though, who's afraid to let go. She insists on being in the midst of Jodi's activities, even while complaining about the demands of motherhood.

"We are not finished here, boys and girls," Mrs. Craig said, "and we cannot eat until we are finished." She sent her eyes around the circle, quieting each child with her glance. "Now then, Jodi, did you bring a favorite toy or book to share with us today?"

Jodi stuck a finger in her mouth and shook her head.

"How about Special Person questions then, would you like to do that?"

This was another birthday activity in Mrs. Craig's class. The children would ask the Special Person questions about favorite food, favorite TV program, best vacation, that sort of thing. Most of the kids loved it, but I could tell the idea had no appeal to Jodi. She twisted her feet around the legs of the chair and her arms around each other. She looked at the floor and again shook her head.

Mrs. Craig put an arm around her shoulder. "Would you like to give us a news report then? Something interesting that's happened the last couple of days."

"Our landlady died," Jodi said softly. "We'll probably have to move again."

Mrs. Craig looked up at Claire who nodded and then looked away.

"Mona Sterling," I explained. "You may have read about it."

"Oh my," Mrs. Craig said, giving Jodi's shoulder a comforting squeeze. "That's the kind of excitement we can do without."

Jodi untwisted her arms and returned her little finger to her mouth.

"Well then," Mrs. Craig said, when it became clear Jodi had nothing further to add, "I think we're ready for cupcakes."

Claire and Jodi passed out the cupcakes, then we all sang "Happy Birthday." The room was quiet for about three minutes as the children ate. Once the food was gone, however, the noise level jumped considerably. Mrs. Craig began a game of Simon Says which got the class through to morning recess.

"Whew," I said, when Mrs. Craig had left to escort the class to the playground.

"Yeah," Claire agreed. "Although I think she asks for it with all this birthday stuff she does."

"Maybe, but don't you remember how special birthdays were when you were little?"

Claire shrugged. "I was raised by an aunt who didn't much go for that sort of thing."

An aunt who was undoubtedly the prototype for the grim woman Claire had become. It made me sad to think that she was passing the same qualities on to Jodi. "Did you grow up around Boston?" I asked.

She looked perplexed. "Southern Illinois. Why?"

"Just a guess, since Jodi was born there."

"Oh." A little laugh. "No, Boston was a short stay." Claire turned back to wiping crumbs off the desks. "I understand Sharon is in charge of Mona's things."

"She's executor of the will, but she doesn't inherit anything herself. It all goes to Libby."

"But she's handling all of Mona's business and . . . property?"

Claire's face looked more pinched than usual, and I sought to reassure her. "I wouldn't worry about the house. It will be a while before everything's sorted out."

She chewed on her bottom lip, clearly something short of reassured. I knew I should feel sorry for her, a woman who'd undoubtedly had more than her fair share of bad luck, but at the same time it irked me that she'd see Mona's death first and foremost as an inconvenience to herself.

Then, as if to prove me wrong, she said, "I'd be happy to help. You know, clean up, sort through things, whatever Sharon needs. I feel like I should do something, like if maybe I'd done something sooner . . ."

"I think we all feel that way."

"But I was probably home, practically within shouting

distance when she . . . she . . ." Claire swallowed. "When she did it."

That gave me an idea. "We're trying to piece together what happened over there, what might have led up to her death. It looks like someone was at the house that evening. You didn't happen to see anyone, did you?"

She frowned. "What makes you think someone was there?"

I explained about the cocktail glasses and ashtray. "Probably a male," I added. "Do you remember seeing anyone? Or anything unusual?"

Claire shook her head. "It might have been that man she's been seeing."

"Mona was dating someone?" That was news to me.

"I guess she was dating him. They went away to Mendocino a couple of weekends ago. She asked me to take in the mail and newspaper."

I remembered the grocery list scratched on Timbercreek stationery. But last I'd heard, Mona was ready to dump the entire male population. "Do you know his name?"

"No. Just that she was going away for a hot and heavy weekend. You know the way she talked." Claire glanced at the wall clock. "Oh gosh, look at the time. My supervisor's going to have a fit. She's a real stickler for making sure that things get done at exactly the same time each day. Says the patients need a routine they can count on. Truth is, though, most of them can't remember what year it is, much less what time they get their bath or their bedding changed."

Claire left for work and Mrs. Craig returned, carrying a stack of oversized colored paper. We spent the next five minutes preparing the room for an art project.

"There," she said when we were finished, "and with three minutes to spare." She checked to make sure everything was in its place, then turned to me and sighed. "That wasn't the most upbeat birthday we've had, was it?"

"It's pretty much par for the course where Jodi's concerned though."

"If her mother's been filling her head with gloom and doom about moving I can see why the poor child wouldn't feel like skipping around. I didn't realize they were the ones renting that little cottage out at Mona's place."

"You knew Mona?"

She nodded. "Though not well. Libby was a student of mine at one time and I'd run into Mona around town every so often. I hadn't talked to her in a couple of years except to say 'hi' in the grocery line. That's why I thought it odd she came by to see me last week."

"Here at school?"

Mrs. Craig nodded.

"How did she seem?"

"I didn't talk to her. I'd left early that day for a dentist appointment. The school secretary told me she'd been by." The bell rang, signaling the end of recess. Mrs. Craig stood. "I've heard that Libby's been giving her a hard time, but I don't think I could have offered much in the way of advice. Kids stop making sense to me along about the time they turn ten. Libby was the sweetest child you ever saw when she was in my class. Just like that boy she's been hanging around with, Brandon Weaver. I taught him too, a couple of years before Libby."

The students returned, putting an end to our conversation, but I couldn't help wondering why Mona would have sought out Libby's kindergarten teacher for advice.

I spent the remainder of the morning helping with an art project, and then with the cleaning of the classroom hamster's cage. I had just enough time to run home and change out of my smudged shirt and jeans before meeting Sharon for lunch.

The Peppermill Cafe is a favorite of ours. Simple fare in a quiet, comfortable setting. We slid into one of the wooden booths at the back and ordered without looking at the menu.

"Have you set a date for the memorial service?" I asked.

Sharon shook her head. "I've been holding off, trying to reach Alice. There's no answer at her home. The owner of the last place she worked says she quit a couple of months ago. The police haven't had any better luck. They apparently sent one of the Washington guys out to her place. No sign of her. I guess we'll have to go ahead without her."

"It seems strange she'd just disappear like that."

Sharon shrugged. "Alice is kind of a free spirit, or in Mona's words, a loose screw, double meaning intended. I'm not so sure she'd bother to come to the service anyway. She's always resented Mona, feels she got all the lucky breaks in life."

I'd never met Alice, but I'd certainly heard stories about her. Since my own sister and I didn't exactly see eye to eye, I could understand the demise of sisterly affection.

Sharon brushed at a loose strand of hair. "So, did you talk to your boyfriend yet?"

"Is this leading up to a question about my love life or about Mona?"

She grinned. "Let's start with Mona."

"He says everything they've found so far is consistent with suicide."

"It *wasn't* suicide."

"I'm only telling you what he said."

"What about the bottle of Glenfiddich? Did you tell him about that?"

"He wasn't impressed."

"Damn." Sharon leaned back and gave an exasperated sigh. "He won't even look into it?"

"It's not his case. And without something to go on, there's no basis for opening an investigation."

Our sandwiches arrived and we ate in silence for several minutes. "We can't let it go at that," Sharon grumbled. "We're going to have to dig around and come up with something on our own. Something that will convince your Lieutenant Stone that it wasn't a suicide."

"We?" I asked. Sharon was becoming far too fond of that particular pronoun.

"Come on, Kate. You don't want someone to get away with this, do you?"

"Well, I—"

"We're talking murder here. The intentional taking of a human life."

"But—"

Sharon drummed her fingers on the table. "Think of Libby then. The way she sees it, Mona didn't care enough about her own daughter to stick around. Didn't even care enough to say goodbye. What do you think that does to a child?"

She knew how to get to me. "Okay," I said, with a sigh. "Where do we start?"

8

"First off," Sharon said, "we know Mona had company that evening. Someone who smoked and who Mona knew well enough to have a drink with. Probably someone of the male persuasion."

"Or a woman who doesn't trust any toilet seat but her own."

Sharon gave me a look not unlike the one Mrs. Craig used to silence her kindergartners. "It seems to me that this mystery guest is a good place to start."

"So what do we do, make a list of all the males in Mona's acquaintance with sloppy bathroom habits and a nicotine addiction?"

Sharon's mouth was full of avocado and sprouts on rye so she had to make do with another icy glare.

"Sorry," I said. "It just seems like we're looking for the proverbial needle in the haystack."

"That's what cops do all the time."

Only in this particular case, the cops seemed to think there was nothing to search for. "Claire thinks it might have been the guy she was seeing," I offered.

"What guy?"

"The one she went to Mendocino with."

"The one she *what?*" Sharon picked at a sprout that was wedged between her two front teeth. "Claire is bonkers. Mona wasn't seeing anyone. If she had been, I'd have known. You know how she liked to talk."

I nodded. Mona was in the habit of giving detailed, and sometimes rather graphic accounts of her dating adventures. I thought she probably put more energy into analyzing her companions than she did into living the relationship itself.

"She had stationery from The Timbercreek Lodge," I pointed out. "She was using it for her grocery list."

Sharon shook her head. "It doesn't make sense. The last person I remember her talking about was Greg Ellis. That's the guy who gave her a sob story about being widowed on his honeymoon ten years ago, when in fact he'd been divorced four times. She dropped him right after Christmas."

"You could ask Libby. She might know."

"Speaking of Libby—" Sharon leaned across the table. "What did you decide about letting her stay with you?"

I hadn't actually decided anything, preferring to cling to the feeble hope that the matter would somehow be resolved without my participation. But apparently the ostrich approach to decision-making had once again failed me. I was back to weighing alternatives.

The prospect of having Libby underfoot, giving me those icy glares and deep, long suffering sighs of hers, was not one I approached with a great deal of enthusiasm. On the other hand, if Anna were suddenly motherless, wouldn't I want someone to reach out to her?

Besides, Sharon had asked me, as a favor, and Sharon

was a friend. A double good turn, then. Sharon and Libby. Maybe it would help balance out my big account in the sky, which was, I feared, somewhat more weighted with selfish acts than I would like.

"I'm not making any long-term commitment," I said finally, "but she can stay with me at least until we get Mona's affairs sorted out."

We. How had that crept in there?

Sharon smiled, a wide smile that dimpled her cheeks. "Thanks, Kate. George isn't any too happy about my involvement in this. And when George isn't happy, well . . ." She rolled her eyes to the heavens.

"It has to be what Libby wants though."

"Oh, it is. Absolutely."

"You already asked her?"

The smile turned sheepish. "I knew you'd come through so I didn't see the harm in mentioning it." She gave my arm a gentle squeeze. "And I appreciate it. Really, I do."

I took a moment to consider whether I'd been had or commended, and decided on the latter. But it was a close call.

"Now, back to this business of Mona's death," Sharon said, pushing her empty sandwich plate aside. "I think we should start by going through Mona's things at the house. Her calendar, address book, files, stuff like that. See if something turns up."

"Like a threatening letter, signed with full name and return address?"

Sharon regarded me coolly.

"Or maybe compromising eight by ten glossies of some powerful political figure."

She sighed loudly. "Are you going to help me with this or not?"

"I said I would, didn't I?"

"Such enthusiasm."

"You didn't ask for a cheerleading squad." But I smiled a truce at the same time.

Sharon smiled back, then plunged ahead with the business at hand. "You free tomorrow morning?"

Although I'd hoped to use the morning to paint, I didn't exactly have paying clients lined up, and I knew that's what she meant. Besides, I'd already given into this "we" thing. There was no point dillydallying about.

"I'm free," I told her.

"Good, we'll get started as soon as the kids are at school." Sharon reached for the bill. "My treat," she said, dismissing my protest with a wave of her hand. "Oh, and I'll bring Libby over later this afternoon. What time would be good for you?"

My previous dealings with Libby had tended to be brief, and largely one-sided. Apparently the prospect of moving in with me hadn't much warmed her to the notion of conversation. She arrived that afternoon with a couple of heavy suitcases and an equally heavy scowl.

"You really want me here?" She made it sound like an accusation.

"Sure," I replied, hoping my voice betrayed none of the doubt I felt. "As long as you feel comfortable about it."

She shrugged. "It doesn't really matter much where I live. Just as long as I don't have to live with Mr. I'm-so-cool Sterling."

Libby's hair, which had been unnaturally blond the

last time I'd seen her, was now an equally unnatural red.
Not chestnut or auburn or even copper, but bright, brilliant red, a color more suited to spray paint than hair.
The lids of her eyes were red too. Red and purple and
green, lined so heavily in black it looked as though she'd
used a laundry marker to do the job. At least we wouldn't
have to worry about whose make-up was whose.

"You may have to move in with him at some point," I
reasoned. "After all, he's your father as well as your legal
guardian."

"Well, I won't go." Her voice rose several decibels and
her mouth, which was a deep dead-rose shade of red,
grew tight. "That's final. He can't make me."

Here we were, not five minutes into togetherness and
already I'd managed to make her angry. Not an auspi-
cious beginning.

"Well," I said, seeking to smooth the waters, "it may
not come to that. And I'm sure your wishes will be taken
into account. Come on and I'll show you to your room.
It's kind of a catch all now, but I'll empty the closet and
help you fix it up."

I took one of her suitcases and led the way down the
hall. Libby plopped onto the bed and let her eyes roam
the room. It was the smallest of the three bedrooms in
the house, and the darkest. Andy had used it as an office,
and when he moved out I'd started putting stuff there
just to get it out of the way. The only reason there was
even a bed in the room is that I'd started sleeping there
during the time it took Andy to find a place of his own. It
was quite a contrast to Libby's own bedroom, which was
large and airy, with a view of the garden, and filled with
the memorabilia of childhood sliding into young adult-
hood. I could imagine what she must be feeling.

"It won't take long to spruce it up," I said, sitting on the bed next to her. "We'll get started tomorrow."

Libby bit her bottom lip and said nothing.

My heart ached for her. "I'm so sorry about your mom, honey. She was a wonderful woman. Funny and bright, and kind. I know how much you must miss her."

Libby fixed her eyes on the large, black spider making his way around the perimeter of the ceiling.

"I lost my father when I was twelve," I told her. "It shook my whole world. I didn't think I'd ever get over it. But somehow you do. Not get over it really, but get through it."

Libby took off her shoe, stood on the bed and whacked the spider, pulverizing him against the faded green wallpaper. "I'm not twelve," she said, stepping down and slipping back into her loafer. "And don't go making my mother into a saint, because she wasn't."

9

By the time I returned to the kitchen, Anna had finished nearly half the chocolate cookies I'd bought by way of atonement. Not that a sugary treat would make up for having some stranger horning in on your life, but I'd thought it might soften the transition.

Anna had been delighted with the cookies, and not at all put out when I told her about Libby. Of course, I don't think she understood the difference between a boarder and the more familiar concept of baby sitter, whose sole job was catering to Anna's wishes. I was pretty sure we'd need more than cookies when the truth finally sank in.

"How about some milk to wash down all that chocolate?" I asked.

"Chocolate milk?"

"Plain milk. The stuff that makes your bones strong and your eyes sparkle."

She shook her head. "I'm not thirsty."

I clenched the fistful of Tootsie Roll wrappers I'd found as I was cleaning out her lunch box and waved them at her. "I'm surprised you were hungry, even for cookies. Where'd you get these anyway? Claire didn't bring them to school, did she?"

Anna grabbed another cookie before I could snatch the package from the table and hide it away. "Oscar gave them to me."

Oscar? I mentally scanned the names of boys in her class. There was no one named Oscar. Sneaky. "You mean Oscar the Grouch?" I asked.

"Oscar the Grouch isn't real!" She raised her chin and sniffed, "He's for babies anyway."

"Then who is Oscar?"

"A man at school."

"A teacher?" Walnut Hills Elementary was strictly a Mr.-Mrs.-Miss kind of place, all the way down to the custodian, but occasionally some progressive, young substitute made his way into the classroom and shook things up a bit.

Anna swallowed the last of her cookie and hopped down from the chair. "He wasn't a teacher, just a man. On the playground after school. He likes talking to kids and giving them treats."

Her words reverberated for a moment inside my head. Along with a few other words. Child molester. Kidnapper. Drug pusher. Lunatic. I felt a chill work its way down my spine.

"Anna," I said, trying to stay calm, "haven't I told you never to talk to strangers. And certainly never to take things from them. Remember how we discussed what might happen, how people who look and act nice, sometimes aren't?"

"He was at school," Anna replied, as if that were reason enough. "And besides, all the kids talked to him, not just me."

"All?" Maybe he was the school psychologist or something.

"A lot of them anyway."

Then I remembered the fire. Perhaps he was an arson investigator or someone from the insurance company. I relaxed just a little. But I thought it wouldn't hurt to mention the matter at school either.

While Anna lay on the floor, nose to nose with Max, fluffing his fur and crooning over him as though he were a three-month-old baby instead of a five-year-old dog, I started dinner.

I hadn't expected Libby to move in with us quite so immediately so I hadn't given much thought to preparing for the event. But I figured this first meal would probably be the hardest on all of us, and I wanted to make it something a little special.

My cupboards, however, held nothing the remotest bit special. Not even ingredients that would make up into something special. Finally, I settled for tried and true. Pasta with some homemade meat sauce Michael had stuck in the freezer the last time he made a double recipe. Anna would balk at the meat, but if I hid it under the noodles instead of on top, she might get down a couple of bites before she figured it out. I made a salad too, and set the table with my good place mats and the more expensive brand of napkins I usually saved for company.

I'd just put the noodle water on to boil when the doorbell rang. Anna went to answer it, then called to me in a voice that would give a rooster a run for his money. "Mommy! Someone's here."

Someone was male. Late teens, early twenties. He had

thick black hair, heavily greased, and shaved close to his head at the sides. I counted three earrings straight off, but on closer examination discovered two others, small gold posts high up on his left ear. He had a long, thin face, full mouth, and narrow, deep-set eyes which he kept partially closed.

No clipboard though. No handful of brochures or clear glass jar with a prominent display of generous donations either.

He ran a hand over his chin, which was dark with a day's growth of whiskers. "Libby here?" he asked.

When I nodded, he looked at me expectantly.

Finally, he said, "You gonna get her or should I?"

What now? Sharon hadn't given me a list of operating instructions.

Before I could say anything though, Libby herself appeared in the entry hall. She'd changed from the oversized painter's overalls she'd worn that afternoon into a black spandex crop-top and an unevenly hemmed skirt that looked like a Goodwill reject. A collection of mismatched bracelets circled her left arm.

"Brandon," she cooed, gliding past me and draping herself against the young man. What ensued was the most X-rated kiss I have ever seen off the big screen. And it went on forever.

Anna watched, gaping with an open mouth. She took her eyes off the exhibition only long enough to cast a quick, curious glance in my direction. I cleared my throat loudly, and was about to send Anna for the garden hose when they parted.

Or part of them parted, anyway. But it was enough.

"Would you like to introduce your friend?" I asked Libby.

She mumbled something, but I would never have picked out his name if I hadn't heard her speak it a moment earlier. I thought Brandon might be in the same boat.

I held out my hand. "Kate Austen," I said.

Brandon's hand touched mine briefly, then he shoved it in his back pocket, as though I might have designs on keeping it.

"Won't you come in? We're going to eat soon, but you're welcome to stay and join us." I laughed my sprightly, hostess laugh. "Nothing fancy though, I have to warn you."

"No dinner for me," Libby announced. "I'm going out with Brandon." She dragged him into the house and thrust him onto the living room sofa. "I'm not ready yet though. Every time I go to look for something I discover I left it home."

Brandon tugged her arm and she fell onto the sofa next to him. Actually, it was more like on top of him. But after she looked up at me, she slid off his lap and onto the seat cushion. Her hand remained draped across Brandon's thigh.

Damn Sharon anyway. What were the rules here?

"Are you sure you won't stay for dinner? I've got really good spaghetti sauce. Homemade. By a friend of mine who's a terrific cook."

If I'd been the one listening to this Donna Reed imitation, I'd probably have puked. Brandon just shrugged.

"Well, I'll give you two a moment alone to discuss it." And maybe in the interim I could place a quick call to Sharon.

I did, but Sharon was no help at all.

"It's your house, Kate, you set the rules."

"But what did Mona do? I don't want to come down on Libby like the wicked witch of the north. The poor girl has just lost her mother after all. She probably needs to be with someone who's familiar and, uh . . ." I searched for the right word. "Comforting."

"So let her go."

"But you told me Mona thought this guy Brandon was a good-for-nothing." A piece of shit, was the way Sharon had put it. But with Anna hanging on my every word I had to temper my description.

"Well, she wasn't any too pleased about the fact that Libby was involved with him. And I know she once threatened to call the police if he didn't get out of her house. But I don't think she actually tried to prevent Libby from seeing him."

Great. "But did she have rules, curfew, that sort of thing?"

"Beats me. Look, whatever you decide," Sharon said, "it will be okay. It's not like she's Anna's age, you know."

I did know, and that was the problem.

When I hung up, I could hear voices coming from the other room. Mumble, mumble, and then a long quiet spell before another mumble. My mind was able to fill in those empty spaces with disquieting ease.

"I don't know," Libby was saying. Mumble, mumble. "Not tonight."

Another interlude of quiet. Then Brandon said, "Come on, it's not like your old lady is breathing down your neck anymore. We'd have the whole place to ourselves."

"Uh-uh," Libby said. "Let's just go get a pizza or something."

There was some more mumbling and another long silence, then Libby said, "Pizza or nothing. What'll it be?"

Yea, Libby! Way to go.

Brandon must have settled for pizza because I heard Libby head off to finish dressing. A few minutes later Brandon sauntered into the kitchen, an unlit cigarette dangling from his lips.

"You got a match?"

"Sorry," I said, "I don't allow smoking inside the house."

He eyed me disdainfully through lowered lids and slouched into the nearest chair. The metal studs on his jacket scraped against the table.

"You a good friend of Mona's?" He said her name with a sneer, but maybe it just came out that way because he was trying to talk without removing the cigarette.

"We were—"

Before I could finish, the doorbell rang again.

"Shit," Libby screeched, running down the hall in her stocking feet. "Don't answer it."

But I already had.

Although I'd never actually met Mona's ex-husband, I'd seen his picture in the paper on several occasions. There was no mistaking the fleshy, ruddy-faced man in front of me.

"I understand you've got my daughter," Gary bellowed, leaning forward to close the space between us. I expected to feel a finger jabbed against my chest any minute.

"You must be Gary," I chirped. "I'm Kate Austen." I didn't offer my hand because I was afraid of what he might do with it. Not that Gary had been physically abusive to Mona as far as I knew. Emotionally abusive certainly, and a first-class jerk. But he was in a foul mood and I wasn't taking chances.

He humphed. "I want to see Libby."

"I'll see if she's available." I started to close the door, but Gary stuck a foot just inside.

"Get Libby down here, now. You give me any trouble and I'll haul your ass into court so fast you'll drop your drawers. Do I make myself clear?"

Holy Hannah, what had I gotten myself into?

While I was trying to come up with a response, Libby appeared behind me, clutching Brandon's hand. "This isn't your night," she said coolly, and with a poise that astounded me. "I don't have to see you until Friday."

"That agreement don't mean shit anymore."

"Says who?"

Gary turned on a smile meant to charm. "Libby, sweet pea." His voice dropped a couple of decibels and took on a saccharine tone. "I know how terrible this must be for you. I just want to help, that's all. Daddy worries about his little girl."

"I'm doing fine."

"But we should be together at a time like this."

Gary stepped forward as if to touch Libby's shoulder, but Brandon wedged himself between them.

"Fuck off, man. Can't you see she doesn't want you around?"

Surprisingly, Gary stepped back. "Who are you?"

"See," Libby wailed, still clutching Brandon's hand tight in her own. Her bracelets clinked as they brushed against his jacket. "All this hot air about how important I am to you, and you don't even know who my friends are."

"He's a *friend*?"

"A really *good* friend," Brandon answered. "We're like, you know, in synch. Spiritually and otherwise."

It was my guess that the *otherwise* far surpassed the spiritual part. From the look on Gary's face it was clear his thoughts followed mine.

A smirk pulled at his mouth. "Well, least you aren't an ice maiden like your mother."

"Just because she wouldn't sleep with *you*, that doesn't mean anything."

"There you go, shutting me out. How am I supposed to know who your friends are when you won't even talk civilly to me?"

"Words," Libby replied. "Words, words, words. That's all you're ever good for."

"And the paycheck part," Gary said bitterly. "Don't forget that."

Brandon squared his shoulders. "She's got her own money now. Her own house too."

Gary glared at Brandon. "That so?" Then turned to me, his tone surprisingly reasonable. "May I come in? Just for a moment?"

I looked at Libby, who shrugged.

Now that anger wasn't contorting his face, Gary looked almost stately. He wasn't handsome, although at one time, many years and even more pounds ago he might have come close. But he had that prosperous, accustomed-to-being-in-charge look that can make you look twice at a man you otherwise wouldn't.

"Why don't you all go into the living room," I suggested. "I just have to run and check on dinner, and then I'll bring out something to drink."

Gary had started for the other room when Libby screeched again, pointing her finger through the open door. The bracelets jangled, like an ill-constructed wind chime. "You brought *her?*"

Gary turned to look. "She's my fiancée, sweet pea."

A curvy blond in a red leather mini-skirt and fringed, high-heeled boots flounced up the walkway, and smiled. Broadly. "Gary, honey," she whimpered, "I'm lonesome sitting in the car all by myself."

Libby made a high-pitched noise something like a cat late at night.

I took Anna and fled to the kitchen.

Again, the voices drifted in from the other room. Only this time there was no mumbling, and no long silences.

"I won't stay with you," Libby yelled. "You just try to make me and see what happens."

"But we're family."

"Not Miss What's-her-name. She's not family."

"Maybe not technically, but you're going to have to get used to the idea that Bambi is part of my life. Now that your mother's dead, we're the only family you've got."

"You're glad she's dead, aren't you? No more calls from her lawyer. No more support payments. Now you and Bimbo can stop complaining about the money you have to shell out."

There was a dainty little squeal which I presumed was Bambi's response to being called Bimbo, but it didn't get the attention she undoubtedly hoped it would. Gary stayed focused on the money issue.

"It was my money, damn it."

"It wasn't *your* money," Libby said. "It was community property. She had just as much right to it as you did."

"Listen, young lady, I built that business. I worked hard, kissed ass, and shook my buns building Sterling En-

terprises into what it is. And she stole it from me. Don't
you go telling me what I can and can't do."

"Kissed ass?" Libby said dramatically. "That's certainly
one way to characterize it."

Gary's voice was low and hard. "You don't know what
you're talking about."

"I know more than you think."

"Let's go," Bambi whined. "All this shouting is giving
me a terrible headache."

"Your mother was a desperate, warped woman," Gary
said, ignoring Bambi. "She tried her best to turn you
against me from the very beginning."

"She didn't have to do that," Libby sniffed. "You did it
all yourself."

By the time I'd worked up my courage to leave the
kitchen, Gary and Bambi were on their way out the door.
"I'll talk to you later," he said. The *you* was terse, and I
couldn't tell whether he was talking to me or Libby.

Brandon was headed out as well, leading Libby by the
wrist. "Come on, we're out of here too."

"Don't wait up for me," Libby said, with a look in my
direction. "I've got the key you gave me."

"But this is a school night," I protested.

She shrugged. "Don't I qualify for bereavement leave
or something?"

Before I had a chance to respond, Brandon yanked her
out the door. I heard a motorcycle start up, gun its en-
gines, and take off at warp speed.

I dropped into the nearest chair and took a long, deep
breath. Anna threaded her way under my arm and into
my lap. I hugged her tight and kissed the top of her head.

"It's going to be okay, honey. Change is always a bit
rough in the beginning."

Anna leaned back, resting the full weight of her body against my chest and began swinging her legs. She raised her left arm as though it were laden with bracelets.

"This is fun," she said gleefully. "I sure hope Libby comes back tomorrow."

10

"You owe me," I told Sharon as I climbed into her car the next morning. "You owe me big." We were headed over to Mona's to begin our search for *The Clue*, but I was pretty sure she realized I was talking about Libby rather than the Nancy Drew stuff.

"Come on," she said, backing out of the driveway. "It couldn't have been that bad. What did Libby do, come home drunk?"

I snorted.

"She *did* come home, didn't she?"

"That's not the problem. Not the whole problem anyway."

Libby had actually come home earlier than I expected. And with none of the lingering-at-the-door kisses I'd anticipated either. She'd barrelled into the house, grunted in my direction, and then gone straight to her room, turning out the lights almost immediately.

"Brandon wasn't the worst part," I said. "Gary showed up too."

"Oooh." Sharon's voice trailed off, something like the whistle of a departing train.

"The guy's weird."

She nodded. "I'm sorry you had to deal with him right off like that."

"What if he shows up again? Libby doesn't want to live with him. She doesn't much want to see him, in fact. But legally, can she refuse?"

"That's something the attorney is trying to work out. Mona and Gary fought this battle during the divorce, though I guess things are different now with Mona dead." She paused. "Gary's getting married soon, maybe that will take his mind off Libby."

"And in the interim?"

"Just do the best you can. I'll try to get this whole thing straightened out as fast as I can."

I cringed as she whipped by a double-parked truck, oblivious to the threat of oncoming traffic. Sharon drives as though she learned on the bumper cars at Playland. Every minute I spend in the car with her takes hours off my life.

"On some level," I said, once we were safely back in the righthand lane, "it's nice Gary wants her around. You read about divorced fathers who never see their kids."

Sharon snickered. "I don't know about now, but when they were battling this out earlier, Gary's interest was strictly financial. The more nights Libby spent at his place, the less child support he had to pay."

It was stuff like this that gave me a renewed appreciation of Andy. Whatever his faults, he adored Anna and wasn't the least bit mean or vindictive. Of course he wasn't the least bit prosperous either, so maybe that made it easy.

As we jolted to a stop at a red light, Sharon reached into her purse for a sheet of paper. "Here, take a look at this." She dropped it on my lap as traffic started to move.

"What is it?"

"A checklist." She floored the accelerator and made a sweeping left turn from the righthand lane. "For finding Mona's killer."

I looked at the sheet in front of me. It was actually more of a grid than a checklist. It reminded me of the graphs and charts I'd run into on the college entrance exams. The ones I invariably skipped over.

"I listed possible motives on the left," Sharon said. "I think I covered most of the main ones. Financial gain, revenge, love, insanity—"

"I think we can probably scratch the wandering maniac theory."

She shook her head. "You don't have to be loony to be insane."

Of course on some level you did, but I figured it wasn't worth arguing about. Besides anyone who commits premeditated murder has to be a little off his rocker to begin with.

Sharon squeaked through a light that was more red than yellow. "I left space at the top," she continued, "so we can list possible suspects. I haven't put down any names though."

"Well," I said, getting into the spirit of things, "there's always the spouse. Or ex-spouse. That's usually the first person the cops think of."

"Gary?" She looked at me as though I'd suggested Mona had been killed by aliens. "I'm not fond of the man, but he *is* one of George's oldest and dearest friends. I can't believe he's a killer. And I can't imagine Mona inviting him in either. She was adamant about not letting the guy set foot in the house."

"Maybe he disguised his voice, kind of like The Big, Bad Wolf."

Sharon didn't laugh. She didn't even acknowledge she'd heard me.

"He's got a motive too," I continued. "With Mona dead he no longer has to make those hefty support payments you told me he always groused about." I held my breath as she rounded the corner straddling the yellow line. "Why did he agree to the plan anyway, if he found it so unfair?"

"Who knows?"

"Andy says Mona had something on him, something she used to put the squeeze on him in the divorce."

Sharon shrugged. "Like I said, I'm not fond of the man. But I'd put Bambi on the list before Gary. I've suspected all along that she's more interested in his pocketbook than his soul—or his body. What's more, I don't trust anyone who signs her name with a heart."

"Bambi does that?"

"It's how she dots the 'i' at the end of her name. Sometimes even in a different color ink."

"Overly cute, but hardly criminal."

"I was thinking," Sharon continued, "that maybe we should put that man who lives down the street from Mona on the list. You know, the one who wanted to remodel his one-story ranch style into a four-story villa with twin spiral towers. Mona wrote a protest letter to the planning commission."

"So did everyone else on the block." In fact, so had a sizable percentage of the town's residents. Walnut Hills takes the planning approval process seriously.

"For some reason though, he decided it was Mona's fault his plans were turned down."

"So four months later he walks down the street and knocks on Mona's door. She not only invites him in, she sits there cooperatively while he pours a bottle of pills down her throat?"

Sharon gave an exasperated sigh. "If I had all the answers, Kate, we wouldn't be here."

I refolded Sharon's grid. When you stopped and really thought about it, the list of possible killers was almost endless. It could have been some guy Mona cut off in traffic, or a disgruntled student. Or maybe she'd unknowingly witnessed some crime and had to be silenced. It could be about money, love, anger, even some perverted sense of justice. And I knew, from my association with Michael, that without some solid evidentiary clue, cases sometimes remained open indefinitely.

"Mona told me she had something she wanted to talk about," I said. "She'd asked if we couldn't get together over the weekend but I put her off till Monday. Do you think what she wanted to tell me might be significant?"

Sharon swung into the driveway causing me to grab the door handle for support. "You know Mona, she always had something she wanted to say. Besides, no offense here, but why *you*?"

"You're right." Mona and I were friends but hardly bosom buddies.

Sharon parked, missing the potted daffodils on the left side by a narrow margin. She took a deep breath, steeling herself for the task ahead, then dug into her purse for Mona's keys. "You remember which key fits the top lock?"

"The rounded one I think."

We headed up the walk, Sharon jangling the keys loosely in her palm. As it turned out, they weren't necessary. The front door was already ajar.

"Good Lord, look at this," Sharon wailed, pushing the door fully open. "Someone's been here."

The house wasn't a shambles, but it was clear that someone had indeed been there. And it wasn't the cleaning lady.

"I think we'd better call the police," Sharon said.

I nodded agreement.

"I'll stay here by the door while you call. That way if there's still someone in the house, I'll be able to go for help."

I turned. "Thanks a bundle."

"One of us should stay here, and you've had more experience at . . ." She paused. "At these things."

Encounters with killers is what she meant, and to my mind experience didn't buy you much in that regard. But arguing hardly seemed worth the effort. I stomped noisily down the hall, giving fair warning to whatever intruder might be lurking about. And for the second time in less than a week I used Mona's phone to call the police.

"Call your friend too," Sharon yelled after me. "Maybe this will convince him that Mona's death wasn't suicide."

It wasn't, strictly speaking, Michael's kind of case. But in light of Mona's recent death, I thought he might be interested. More to the point, I *wanted* him to be interested.

Michael was, as usual, away from his desk. I left my name and Mona's number, then called the dispatcher, reported the burglary and rejoined Sharon by the front door.

The police pulled up in less than ten minutes. Our local tax dollars at work. While the big city folk in San Francisco and Oakland have to contend with 911 lines that ring busy and a police force so overworked it sometimes takes days to write up a burglary, those of us in elite enclaves like Walnut Hills get real service for our money.

Or fast service anyway. The two officers who'd arrived so swiftly didn't exactly set any records for zealous investigation once they were there. The older and heavier of the two meandered from room to room, kicking at the clutter on the floor and mumbling variations of, "Yep, looks like they got to this spot too." The younger man trotted along behind, notebook in hand.

"What's missing?" the older man asked.

"We don't know," Sharon said, and then explained why we were there in the first place. "All the big stuff—television, VCR, stereo, it all seems to be here."

"What about jewelry?"

"She didn't have any."

The cop raised an eyebrow.

"Well, she had some but she kept it in the safe deposit box."

"She was divorced," I explained, because the eyebrow was still raised. "Most of the jewelry had come from her husband and she didn't want it around."

The man humphed. "Loss undetermined," he muttered and the younger man again scratched in his notebook.

The phone rang and I went to answer it, leaving Sharon to sort out the details of police forms and procedures.

As usual, Michael's voice sent a lovely tingle down my spine.

"It's always such a pleasant surprise to find your name in my stack of message slips," he murmured. "To know you've been thinking about me."

"Someone broke into Mona Sterling's house," I replied, before he could steer the conversation into the I–thou arena.

Michael was silent.

"Doesn't that seem suspicious?"

He cleared his throat. "You and Sharon didn't cook this up yourselves, did you, just so I'd be more inclined to investigate Mona's death?"

"What?" I pulled myself up straight. "You don't honestly think I'd do that, do you?"

"No, I honestly don't. But I wouldn't be doing my job if I didn't ask."

"So, will you come take a look? See if there's anything here which could lead you to Mona's killer?"

There was another moment of silence followed by a long sigh. "It's not unusual for houses to be broken into after someone has died, you know. Burglars read papers just like everyone else. An uninhabited house, a distracted family, it makes for a pretty good target. It takes weeks before anyone can figure out what's actually missing. Sometimes there's never a complete list."

"But Mona didn't just *die*. She may have been murdered."

"We've been over this, Kate. There's nothing to suggest foul play."

"The thief didn't take anything though. Nothing obvious anyway. It's more like he was looking for something."

"Could be the guy got scared off before making his haul."

Logic can sometimes be a most exasperating quality. "Does that mean you're going to let it drop?" I asked.

"It means we'll treat it like a burglary. For now, anyway. There's nothing I could do there that the cops on the scene can't do better, and I'm up to my eyeballs in this arson case. Now that the district's offered a reward, half the kids in town seem to recall seeing or hearing something." He sighed wearily. "Why don't you let me talk to whomever's in charge there."

I went and got the older officer, who grunted into the phone for a couple of minutes before handing it back to me. "The lieutenant needs another word with you," he said, and ambled off.

"They're going to take extra prints," Michael explained. "And photographs. And I'll review the report personally, though I have to tell you, the chances of finding anything meaningful are pretty slim."

"You want me to look around too? I might see something the cops wouldn't, because I knew her, I mean."

Michael grunted. "You and Sharon are going to do that anyway. Whether I ask you to or not." His voice dropped then, turned soft. "How about I come by this evening? You can fill me in on the details of the crime while I nibble on your neck."

"That's probably not such a good idea. The dropping by part I mean." I told him about Libby.

"Nice going." He didn't sound any too happy about the arrangement.

"How about Friday night instead? I'll get a baby sitter and we'll go out to a movie or something." The "or something" usually won out. We had a long list of movies we'd never gotten around to seeing.

"Friday's the day I leave for Santa Barbara. The criminology conference, remember?"

I hadn't.

"Will you miss me?" he asked.

"You know I will."

"So much that you'll throw yourself at me the minute I'm back?"

I laughed. "The very minute. You want to try for the airport lounge or shall we wait for something more comfortable?"

"Ah, Kate." That was all he got out before the line clicked and he turned serious. "I've got another call. I have to run."

I hung up with an odd little hollow spot in my heart. Truth was, I *would* miss him. More than he realized. More than I cared to admit to myself.

For the next forty minutes, we followed the two officers from room to room, peering through doorways as they dusted for prints and snapped pictures. A couple of times Sharon ventured closer to offer a word of unsolicited advice, which was never received with more than a grunt.

"They didn't seem particularly interested in any of it," she huffed once they'd gone.

"That's probably because they know there's not much chance of finding the perp. Very few residential burglaries are ever solved."

Sharon raised her brow and regarded me with amusement. "My, my. You've become intimate with the law in more ways than one."

I shrugged. "You pick up stuff without thinking about it."

"This wasn't a simple burglary though. I'm sure it's related in some way to Mona's death."

Michael's indifference aside, I was inclined to agree

with her. "The trouble is, we're too late. The thief has probably already made off with the give-away clue we were hoping to find."

"We'll never know unless we look. Come on," Sharon said, gesturing impatiently. "We've wasted enough time already, twiddling our thumbs while those buffoons in blue sleepwalked their way through department procedure."

We started in the den, on the theory that since Mona had died there the room might offer evidence about her death. It was a pretty dumb theory since the paramedics, the police, the coroner's office and the killer, as well probably as the burglar, had all been there before us. But we had to start somewhere.

We went through closets, cupboards, and drawers, then moved onto the kitchen and the bedroom, repeating the procedure. Though I'm an incurable snoop, and have been known to peer into the medicine chests of people I barely know, there is something about going through a dead friend's things which is more than a little unsettling. It left me feeling nervous, depressed and guilty all at once. I kept waiting for Sharon to decide that we'd done enough, but when Sharon sets her mind to a task she doesn't easily give it up.

"Have you found anything?" she asked finally, plunking herself down on Mona's bed.

What I'd found was that Mona's monthly Mastercard bill was higher than my mortgage and that her phone bill was nothing to sneeze at either. I'd learned that Mona wore white cotton panties and no nonsense bras, but that she had a scarlet silk teddy from Frederick's of Hollywood that had little holes in all the places I'd want to be sure were covered. I knew that she washed her hair and face with products from France, that she wore a night guard to protect her teeth from grinding, that despite her minimalist tendencies in decor, she was a pack rat at heart.

"Nothing that points to murder," I told her. "How about you?"

She shook her head. "Zip."

The doorbell rang just then and we both jumped. Jumped, exchanged nervous glances, and immediately started speaking in hushed tones. You'd have thought we were a couple of school girls in the midst of telling late night ghost stories.

"Go see who it is," Sharon whispered. "I'll stay by the phone, just in case."

"Why me?"

"What's the problem?" she mouthed. "The killer is hardly going to ring Mona's bell in broad daylight."

I leaned closer and mouthed back, "Then what makes you think you need to stay by the phone?"

In the end we both went, peering out through the side window before unlatching the door. But we'd raised our blood pressure and taken minutes off our lives for nothing. It was only a UPS delivery man.

"You gotta sign for it," he said. "It's insured."

Sharon signed and took the package, a small, lightweight thing from Union Square Jewelers in San Francisco. "You think we should open it?"

"I don't see the harm. You're going to have to inventory her entire estate anyway."

She peeled away the shipping wrap and opened the box. "Cufflinks," she said, bewildered. "And a tie tack." She examined the receipt. "It must be something Mona ordered."

Sharon handed me the box. The cufflinks were burnished gold ovals, each set with a diamond and engraved with an ornate cursive monogram. The tie tack was a larger diamond rimmed in gold. Even before I looked at the receipt I could tell they must have cost a bundle.

"Why would she buy cufflinks?" I asked.

"As a present, most likely."

"Men wear cufflinks these days?"

Sharon took the box and looked at me with mock disdain. "Maybe not in your circle, Kate. But among the upper crust, they are still very much in vogue." She pulled out one of the ovals and examined it. "The lettering is so fancy it's hard to tell, but it looks like an 'S'."

Stanley? Steven? Sebastian? I tried to think of men I knew whose names began with S. "Sterling! Do you think she bought them for Gary?"

"She couldn't stand the guy."

"Or so she said. Maybe they were working toward a reconciliation and she was too embarrassed to admit it."

Sharon shook her head. "No way."

"Her father-in-law?"

"You don't give something like this to a father-in-law, especially an ex-father-in-law. Besides, Harry wouldn't know what to do with a long sleeve shirt, much less one with French cuffs." She put the cufflink back in the box and snapped the lid. "I hate to admit it, Kate, but you may have been right about Mona seeing someone. The weekend away, this present, it all fits. I just can't figure out why she never mentioned him."

"Maybe he's balding, four-foot-four and weighs two hundred pounds."

She laughed.

"Or he could be famous. Sylvester Stallone, Bruce Springsteen, Steven Seagal, Telly Savalas—"

"Telly Savalas is dead."

"Okay, we'll forget about him. How about Steven Spielberg, Sidney Sheldon—"

"Enough. We obviously aren't going to find the guy based on his initials. Maybe Libby knows."

"Speaking of Libby." I checked my watch. "I want to run out to Macy's and see if I can't get some pillows or something to brighten up her room. You think we've done enough here for today?"

"I guess. I don't know where else to look anyway."

We were on our way out the door when the phone rang. "Let the machine pick it up," Sharon said.

But it's almost impossible to walk away from a ringing phone without finding out who's calling. We waited until the machine clicked on.

"This is Laurie McNevitt again." The voice was thin and tentative, as it had been earlier. "Please, even if you don't know for sure, I'd like to talk . . . to maybe, uh . . ." She paused, started, then stopped again. She exhaled deeply, abruptly. "I'm sorry. I shouldn't keep bothering you."

I rushed for the phone but she'd already hung up.

"Oh dear," said Sharon. "The poor woman sounds so . . . so disheartened."

"If she'd only leave her number. Did you check the tape to see if she called during the last few days?"

Sharon nodded. "There were only a couple messages. Nothing important."

She dropped me off at my house where I picked up my own car and headed for the mall. With luck I'd be able to find something that was cheery and bright, but not frilly or overly cute. Or expensive. In some ways it didn't much matter what I found. Anything would be an improvement.

The rain, which had only threatened earlier, was now coming down in earnest. And the wind had not let up. I was cold and wet by the time I'd made it across the parking lot to the entrance. Just inside the door was a window display featuring slim, smooth-skinned bodies in bikinis. Never mind that I hadn't looked that good even at twenty, and that I wouldn't now be caught dead in anything other than a sturdy one piece, the image of sunshine and warmth was unbelievably tantalizing—and unmercifully taunting. Who was responsible for thinking up these displays anyway? And why couldn't they stick to hawking meaningful merchandise like umbrellas and galoshes.

I wound my way to the bedding department, then through the displays of posh designer sheets, cases, and matching everything else. I didn't even allow myself to slow down as I passed. I'd once taken a peek at those price tags and been sure that the printer had misplaced the decimal. It hadn't.

On the sale table in the back corner I found a perfectly serviceable blue and white striped comforter and a set of pillow shams which almost matched. Unfortunately, on my way there I'd spotted a fuchsia and lavender print which I liked a whole lot more. Question was, did I like it thirty dollars more?

I was trying to evaluate that question, which is something you really can't do with much precision, when Susie Sullivan, now Lambert, called to me from across the aisle. Her arms were laden with a whole boudoir-set from

Ralph Lauren. Color coordinated pillows were already waiting for her in a pile by the cash register.

"Have you seen this newest collection?" she gushed. "Every design is exquisite. I've had the hardest time choosing."

Susie has recently remarried, for the third time. I know she redid the whole house before the wedding, but given the way she drools over her new husband, it didn't surprise me to learn they'd already worn out the sheets.

She set her load by the register, handed the saleswoman her charge card and moseyed over. "You won't be happy with this fabric," she said, fingering the stripe. "It's much too stiff."

"Well, the price isn't."

She smiled weakly, acknowledging my attempt at humor without applauding it. "It's not really your style anyway, Kate."

"It's for Libby Sterling. She's staying with me until things get sorted out."

"I'd heard that. How's she holding up?"

"Hard to tell. She's not about to let anyone see her pain, that's for sure."

"Teen-age girls," Susie said dramatically, "they are impossible to deal with under the best of circumstances." Susie dealt with her two by sending them to an eastern boarding school during the year and sailing camp for the summer. Her son, who was a classmate of Anna's, got the nanny treatment instead. "It was really awfully good of you to take her in," Susie added, as an afterthought.

"What's sad is that Libby feels totally rejected. The way she sees it, Mona didn't care enough about her to stay alive. Didn't care enough even to leave a note."

"Mmm." Susie held out her left hand and studied her

newest diamond, a rock so big I thought she might have trouble lifting her arm. "That's basically what happened though."

"Maybe not. Sharon has a theory Mona might have been killed."

"You mean, *murdered?*"

I nodded.

"Goodness, what makes her think that?"

I explained, then waited for Susie to dismiss the idea as absurd.

Instead, she drew her brows together in thought. "Well, it certainly makes sense," she announced after a moment.

"It does?"

"Mona called me Saturday."

"What did she want? Was she upset?"

Susie shook her head. "She left a message on our machine. Early evening some time. Stephen and I were away for the weekend and didn't get back until late Sunday. There was a whole string of messages. I went through them rather quickly so I can't remember exactly what she said, but the gist of it was that she wanted to reschedule our Monday afternoon tennis game. Apparently something unexpected had come up and she couldn't make it."

"Did she say what?"

"No. It was a quick message. I hardly paid any attention at all. But it's been bothering me since, trying to remember what she said. It doesn't make sense that she'd call to reschedule if she was planning on killing herself an hour or two later."

I had to agree, it didn't.

"So, do they have any leads?" Susie asked.

"If by 'they' you mean the police, the answer is no. 'They' don't even buy into the murder theory." Because Michael was part of the "they" and I didn't want to sound critical or disloyal, I took a moment to explain the official position. "From their point of view, suicide's a logical conclusion."

"Hmmm," she said, laconically. "I wonder."

"Mary Nell's convinced that Gary's upcoming wedding sent her into depression."

Susie laughed. "Hardly." The sales clerk motioned and Susie started for the register. "I wouldn't expect Mary Nell to understand, but some of us weather divorce just fine. And I certainly don't think Mona went off the deep end over Bambi. As I recall, they even had lunch together a couple of months ago."

"Mona and Bambi?"

Like politics, divorce makes for strange bedfellows, but I was still surprised. Never in a million years would I have imagined Mona and Bambi sharing the same room, much less a table. What could they possibly have found to talk about?

12

In the end I decided on the lavender print, then went all out and bought a dust ruffle and pillow shams as well. I threw in a heathery cotton area rug to cover the bare spot in the carpeting and a couple of inexpensive, decorative pillows in matching shades. After leaving the mall, I stopped by the hardware store and bought a can of paint for the dresser, an ugly brown thing Andy and I had picked up at a garage sale soon after we were married. We'd had plans to paint it then, but as was typical of so much of our life together, the good intentions had remained fallow.

I made it to school just as Mrs. Craig was leading the children down to the pick-up spot at the far corner of the playground.

"Was that man here again today?" I asked Anna. "The one who gave you the Tootsie Rolls?"

She shook her head and started to hand me her backpack. Anna would do well with a cortege of personal servants to anticipate her every need. Instead, she has to make do with a mother.

"What am I," I asked, glancing at the backpack, "your own private sky hook?"

By way of an answer, Anna grabbed my hand and gave me one of her silly, winning smiles. I carried the backpack.

"Where are we going?" she asked, as I led the way to the office.

"I want to have a word with Mrs. Sommer about that man who was at school yesterday."

Mrs. Sommer ran a tight ship so I figured the man was either tied into the arson investigation or one of the auxiliary teachers the school sometimes brought in for special classes. But I wasn't taking any chances. It seemed lately that nearly every news report I encountered had something to say about an abduction or molestation. And only last month a ten-year-old girl in a nearby town had disappeared while riding her bike to school. No place was safe anymore, not even the relatively sheltered neighborhoods of the suburbs.

Mrs. Sommer shook her head when I told her about the man named Oscar who'd been giving away candy. "No, we didn't know," she said, her brow furrowed, "and that's not the way we would handle a special inquiry in any case." She turned to Anna. "Did this man talk to lots of children?"

A shrug.

"More than just you?"

Anna nodded. "He had a whole bag of Tootsie Rolls to give away."

"He gave them to anyone who wanted one?"

Anna nodded again.

"All kindergartners, or were there older children too?"

Anna had that look on her face, like Tootsie Roll or not, she was beginning to wish she'd never mentioned the episode in the first place. "Mostly kids in kindergarten," she said, kicking the carpet with her toe.

"Just girls, or boys too?"

"Girls mostly."

"What did this man look like?" Mrs. Sommer asked. An anxious tone had crept into her voice.

Anna's foot grew still and she puckered up her face in thought. "A fairy," she said at last.

"A *what?*" My face grew red with embarrassment. Walnut Hills wasn't exactly a hotbed of liberalism, but we were close enough to San Francisco that words like "fairy" and "faggot" were rarely used, in public at any rate. And they certainly weren't part of my vocabulary. I looked at Mrs. Sommer with an expression that I hoped said something like, *where do kids come up with these things?*

Mrs. Sommer, however, with over thirty years experience in elementary education, understood what Anna meant. "Kind of like an elf?" she asked.

"Except he wasn't tiny like that. He was tall." Anna thought for a moment. "Tall and shiny."

"Shiny?" Apparently even Mrs. Sommer had trouble with that one.

Anna nodded. "But not silvery."

"I see. What kind of things did you talk about?" Mrs. Sommer asked, apparently having decided the description route was going nowhere fast.

"Nothing much," Anna said.

"Can you remember anything?"

"He just asked us our names, and about our families and stuff." Anna shot me one of her it's-all-your-fault looks and went back to shuffling her feet against the carpet. "He was just being nice," she muttered. "He didn't have to share his candy, you know."

Mrs. Sommer patted Anna's hand. "It's just that we like to know what's going on out on the playground. If you see him again, will you come tell me?"

Anna nodded.

"Right away. It would be such a big help to me if you could do that."

By the time we left, Anna was sufficiently pleased at the prospect of helping Mrs. Sommer that she forgot about being irritated with me. And being a firm believer in the efficacy of sleeping dogs, I decided to skip a second lecture about talking to strangers.

Libby didn't roll in until almost five, which had given me a chance to spruce up the room a bit. I remade the bed with the new cover, spread out the area rug and removed the pile of junk from the closet floor. I didn't get around to repainting the chest, of course, but I did move a framed Boulanger print from my bedroom to Libby's, and then picked a bouquet of iris for the night-stand. It wouldn't have made *Architectural Digest,* or even one of those women's magazines that feature low-cost decorating tips, but I thought it was pretty nice. And a vast improvement over the room Libby had left that morning.

Not that any of it would make up for the fact that she'd lost a mother. Or begin to make her forget, even for a moment.

She let herself in with the key I'd given her, nodded in my direction, then went straight to her room and shut the door. Half an hour later she was still in there. I got together a snack of cookies and milk, then switched the milk for a Pepsi, and knocked on the door.

"What?"

"Can I come in? I brought you some cookies."

Libby mumbled something which I took to mean I could enter.

She was lying on the bed, arms crossed over her chest, staring at the ceiling. "I'm not hungry," she said, without so much as a glance at the plate.

"You don't have to eat them."

Silence.

"Is there something else you'd rather have? An apple maybe, or some toast?"

She sat up abruptly and gestured to the room. "You didn't have to do this, you know." Her tone was flat, but I thought I caught a flicker of something in her expression.

"I wanted to," I said gently, touching her arm.

She yanked it away. "It's not like I need special treatment or anything. And I don't need you to go feeling sorry for me either."

"I've been meaning to do something with this room ever since Andy moved out. I just never got around to it before." I sat on the bed, wanting to hug her tightly and make everything right. If only it could be that easy. "How was school today?" I asked instead.

She shrugged and stared silently at the wall dead ahead.

"I hope you didn't feel I was forcing you to go. Going back for the first time after . . . after something like this, it's got to be hard."

Libby kept her eyes focused on the wall and said nothing.

"Were the other kids . . . um, understanding?"

"What's there to understand?"

"I guess I mean, did they treat you okay?"

"You think they were going to point their fingers and laugh out loud?"

The tone of her voice bothered me more than her words, but I didn't know where to go with it. We sat in silence while Libby glared at the wall and I wracked my brain for inspiration. "There are counselors who specialize in helping people deal with grief," I told her finally. "It might help if you talked to one of them."

She raised her chin and regarded me coolly. "I don't need a shrink."

"I wasn't talking about a psychiatrist necessarily. And it's no reflection on you. The death of someone you love, it's a pretty terrible thing for anyone."

"I'm fine."

She wasn't. But it hardly made sense to sit there and argue the point with her. I made a mental note to call the school, maybe someone there could help. "Think about it, okay? And let me know if you change your mind."

"I won't," she said, turning back to address the wall.

I started to leave, then thought of something. "Does the name Laurie McNevitt mean anything to you?"

"No, why?"

"She left a message on your mother's answering machine."

Libby shrugged. "I didn't keep up with my mom's friends."

It wasn't the most opportune time or place, but since I'd started down this particular road I thought I might as well finish. "How about men your mom was seeing. Any names come to mind?"

"I told you, I wasn't interested in her friends."

"Was she seeing anyone in particular?"

Another shrug.

"She spent the weekend in Mendocino not too long ago. She go with someone?"

"Probably." Libby snorted. "She spent enough time choosing what she was going to wear. Plus she had a facial and a body wrap right before she left. But at least she spared me the *Do as I say and not as I do* lecture."

I returned to the bed and sat down next to her. "I know that as much as anything else right now, you're angry with your mom. That's normal. As are the jumble of other emotions you're feeling. But she loved you, Libby. We used to talk about mothers and daughters, and I know for a fact that you were the most important thing in her life."

"Yeah? Well I guess it wasn't enough, was it?"

The hurt in her voice made my own throat ache. I thought about telling her that Mona's death might not have been a suicide. Was it fair to raise that prospect without more proof? Would it do anything but confuse Libby further?

Before I had a chance to respond, she reached for her backpack and started pulling out binder and books, effectively cutting off further discussion. "I've got to get started on my homework."

"Libby, I—"

"Please, I've got a ton of work here."

I hesitated, then stood. "Tomorrow is the memorial service," I told her on my way to the door. "Is there anything in particular you'd like to have included?"

"Whatever you and Sharon want. It doesn't matter to me, I'm not going."

She opened a book and sprawled out on the bed facing away from me. My heart ached for her but I could think of nothing more to do. I closed the door quietly and reminded myself that time is a great healer.

I waited until later that evening to tell Libby about the break-in, knowing that it would be somehow added to the list of wrongs for which Mona was responsible. I debated telling her at all since her mood had improved slightly by dinnertime. She'd offered to set the table, and then shown remarkable patience when Anna insisted on helping. Although Libby hadn't talked during the meal unless prompted, she made an effort to be attentive. She'd even laughed at Anna's description of the yard teacher, Ms. Wright, nicknamed Ms. Wrong, who never got anyone's name straight, confused the fire drill with the lunch bell and the pizza line with the hot dog line, and couldn't see well enough to know whether the kids she benched actually ended up there.

When Anna went off to get her bath, I related the story of the break-in to Libby. She listened impassively, eyes fixed on the jagged crack in the linoleum.

"It's hard to tell what was taken," I said. "None of the obviously valuable stuff is missing."

"What valuable stuff?" Libby asked bitterly. "She let my father have it all."

It was true that Gary had taken the bulk of household furnishings, but that was because Mona hadn't wanted them. "I think your mother wanted a fresh start," I explained. "Something that was uniquely hers."

Libby pushed back her chair and stood. "She might have asked me what I thought. It was supposed to be my home too."

The phone rang just then, and Libby stalked off toward

her room. I considered following, then thought better of
it.

"Did I catch you at a bad time?" Sharon asked, responding no doubt to the frustration in my tone.

"Not at all. Libby and I were just having a riotous and
uplifting conversation about familial love." I drew in a
breath. "I feel so bad for her and I don't know what to
do."

"Just be there for her," Sharon said, repeating the advice I'd given her days earlier. "I don't know there's
much else we *can* do. Look, I'm at one of George's client
dinners so I can't talk long, but I have some interesting
news."

I waited, knowing she would continue without prompt-
ing on my part.

"After I left you this afternoon, I started going over the
stuff I'd picked up at the bank. What's interesting is that
Mona withdrew three thousand dollars Saturday morning, in cash."

"Cash?" I tried to imagine what that amount of money
would look like. "Why would Mona want that much
cash?"

"I don't know, but I bet it's got something to do with
her death."

"You think she was killed for the money?"

"We certainly didn't find that much cash lying around
anywhere."

"But the killer would have had to know about it. And
why would he leave the sixty-five dollars we found in her
wallet?"

Sharon gave an exasperated sigh. "If I had answers,
Kate, you'd be the first to hear them."

Three thousand dollars, cash. What had Mona been planning?

I pondered that question for the next hour or so, and found the possibilities were almost endless. But none of them made any sense.

13

After a good deal of wavering, Sharon had decided to hold the memorial service at the mortuary. The other logical choice was the community church, but for reasons I didn't quite understand, it wouldn't have been available until late the following week. And then, only in the event the services of the minister were called upon as well.

Sharon was convinced Mona would find the mortuary's fake waterfall and polyester-clad ushers less offensive than an hour's sermon by Philip Chapman, with whom she'd almost come to blows over censorship in school libraries. Chapman had wanted to protect the youth of Walnut Hills from such filth as *Lord of the Flies, Huckleberry Finn,* and a long list of other books which he'd never read but nonetheless knew to be a corrupting influence. That he'd ultimately lost the battle hadn't softened Mona's feelings toward him in the least.

The service was scheduled to begin at eleven, but Sharon had gone over early to deal with any unforeseen snafus that might arise. I arrived almost on the hour, accompanied by Libby, who'd decided at the last minute to come along after all, and then decided that she really needed to wash her hair first.

By the time we arrived the chapel was practically full, but there were two, nearly empty pews down front. Gary and Bambi sat at the end of one, Sharon and George at the end of the other. As I started down the aisle, Libby grabbed my arm.

"No way," she whispered. "Especially not with Bimbo there."

"We'll sit behind them, next to Sharon."

But Libby had already turned and headed for one of the spare chairs at the back. With a shrug to Sharon, I followed. We'd barely gotten ourselves seated when the string quartet at the front started playing a Bach concerto I recognized as one of Mona's favorites.

As the music ended, Sharon stood and walked to the podium at the front. "We are here today," she began, "to say a final goodbye to Mona Sterling. We are here to share our sadness, and our joy too, at having known such a fine person." She went on to speak with feeling and a touch of humor about the friend she would dearly miss. There was nothing maudlin in her tone, nothing sappy about her account of their evolving friendship. When she finished, she invited others to come forward. For almost an hour, a steady stream of people made their way to the podium and told of the ways in which Mona had touched their lives.

Gary spoke the longest, for almost ten minutes. He acknowledged the divorce but didn't dwell on it. His manner was relaxed, infused with the easy assurance of a man used to being in command. In spite of all the negative things I'd heard about the guy, I was impressed. He might be an arrogant and vengeful bastard, but he was also a master at playing the moment.

Throughout it all, Libby sat motionless in her chair, back straight, head up, eyes fixed on the spot at the front of the room where the roof slanted down to join the wall. Her eyes remained dry and her breathing even. But out of the corner of my eye, I saw the fingers of her left hand digging hard into the palm of her right.

When the last person had spoken, the quartet started up again and we filed into an adjoining room for refreshments. Sharon had kept things simple; tea and coffee, muffins and fruit. The table was set with several lovely, and most un-funereal, mixed spring bouquets. The musicians, who'd moved into the reception hall once the chapel was empty, struck up a medley of old Beatles' songs. At first, people stood silently in tight little clusters, subdued by awkwardness as much as grief. But gradually, as the groupings grew more fluid, quiet murmurs gave way to the flow of spirited conversation.

Libby made one silent, hawklike sweep of the area, then ducked into the ladies' room and wouldn't come out, even when I went in after her.

"Why should I?" she asked, from behind the closed door of the stall. "You think I want to hang around and listen to a bunch of old busybodies talk about how wonderful my mother was?"

"She had a lot of friends. They're going to miss her."

"La-di-da. They'll survive."

"And so will you, Libby." It tore at my heart to think of how alone and miserable she must feel. "This is a terrible time for you right now, but you're strong and bright and capable. You'll get past it."

"There's nothing to get past. I just don't want a bunch of people staring at me and feeling sorry for me is all. It was a stupid idea to come to this thing in the first place."

At some level, I could sympathize with what she was feeling. "You don't have to go out there and mix with people. I just wanted to make sure you were okay."

"Couldn't be better," she answered sarcastically.

"I'll take you home whenever you want. Let me know when you're ready."

She opened the door a crack and peered through. "Brandon should be here soon. I'm going to go with him."

"Why didn't he come to the service?"

She laughed harshly. "Are you kidding? The way my mom treated him, I'm surprised he agreed to show his face here at all."

"She didn't like him?"

Another laugh, which passed for an answer. "Last week she even threw a frying pan at him. Screeched like a banshee too. It was one of their worst fights ever."

I opened my mouth to ask more, but Libby shut the door in my face, with a solid bang. "Let me know when Brandon gets here, okay?"

Back in the reception hall I ran into Stan Lundy, divorce attorney for the rich and famous. And me, but only because Mona had steered me in his direction. He greeted me with an affable hug.

Stan is short and round, with a moon face, a thin, scratchy voice and almost no hair. He's as aggressive and tenacious an advocate as anyone could hope for, but he definitely doesn't fit the image.

"It was nice of you to come," I told him.

He shook his head sadly. "After all Mona and I went

through, I can't believe it comes down to this. And that one there," Stan threw a glance in Gary's direction, "he walks off like a bandit, just the way he was trying to all along."

"Not quite, thanks to your efforts."

Stan acknowledged the compliment with a quick smile. "But the ex, he still comes out ahead. Especially now that Mona's share of the business reverts to him. That was one of the issues we really banged heads over." Stan rubbed his jaw. "That sounds crass, doesn't it? Here poor Mona's dead, and I'm fretting about seeing my hard-fought efforts go down the tubes. It's no wonder lawyers have the reputation they do."

I patted him on the arm. "You don't have that kind of reputation, Stan. Everybody knows you're a teddy bear at heart."

He grinned. "Not everybody, Kate. And I wouldn't want that rumor to get around. But I'm glad you think so."

"Mona did too."

"She was a hell of a woman. I can't believe . . ."

His words were cut short by the approach of his son-in-law and partner, Paul Simms. The two men couldn't have been more different. Paul was tall, fine boned and debonair, every inch of him so well-manicured that the merely well dressed looked rumpled by comparison. He wore the air of success as easily as he did his gold Rolex.

Stan greeted Paul, then introduced me. Paul shook my hand, smiled politely and mumbled some vague form of pleased-to-meet-you. I'd actually met him once before, at the fall back-to-school night for parents, but he obviously didn't remember, and I didn't bother to explain. Men of his ilk rarely remember meeting women of mine.

"I know your wife," I told him instead. "In fact, we're on the school auction committee together."

Laurelle was on so many committees I wasn't sure Paul even tried to keep them straight, but the connection got me past the awkwardness that often follows an introduction. And since Laurelle was Stan's darling daughter and only child, I thought the comment showed a bit of the social savoir-faire I usually lack.

Paul nodded absently, running his long fingers through a head of silky blond hair. Then he did a sort of mental double take and I thought maybe he'd remembered meeting me after all.

"Austen," he said, focusing his attention in a way he hadn't earlier. "You're the woman who found her, right? The decorator who found Mona Sterling."

"Art consultant," I corrected. It was a mistake people made pretty frequently.

He blinked, looked puzzled.

"I'm an art consultant, not a decorator."

"Right," he said, though I wasn't sure he understood the difference. "But you're the one who was at her house that morning?"

I nodded. Laurelle must have mentioned the canceled committee meeting.

Stan looked in my direction with an expression of concern. "Good grief, Kate. I didn't realize that was you. How awful." He started to say something more, but a heavyset man who was apparently an old friend clasped his shoulder just then, and Stan excused himself.

Paul fidgeted uncomfortably for a moment, no doubt looking for some graceful way to follow suit. He must have decided, however, that good breeding dictated another round of conversation, because he turned his full attention my way, his brow creased with evident feeling. "It must have been quite a shock, finding a, uh, a body like that."

I nodded. "It was. It still is." A mental picture of Mona, slack-jawed and stone-still, had etched itself somewhere not far from the surface of conscious thought. At moments when I least expected, it would break into full-frame focus and leave me weak in the knees.

"Could you tell right away what had happened?"

"More or less. I could tell she was dead. And with the empty bottle of sleeping pills on the table next to her, well I guess I sort of knew before I really even thought about it."

Paul's lower cheek twitched. "I understand there wasn't a note or anything. Nothing that explained why she might have done it."

"Not that anyone's discovered."

He rubbed the cheek. "Do you suppose there's any chance it might have been accidental?" I couldn't tell if Paul was actually interested, or if he'd merely reached for the most convenient topic of conversation.

"It might have been," I told him, swallowing the urge to mention a third possibility—murder. "But it's unlikely. You know how meticulous Mona was."

"I didn't," he paused slightly, "know Mona, that is. At least not well. She was Stan's client." He paused again. "I do mostly tax work and a little commercial litigation." He straightened his tie, checked his watch, then held out a hand. "I'm going to have to run, I'm sorry. It was a pleasure meeting you."

Paul moved on and I grabbed a cup of coffee and muffin. Libby had emerged from the rest room and was now slouching against the wall on the far side of the hall. Her face was set in a scowl, her eyes fixed on the floor. Every so often, she'd raise her head and let her eyes drift around the room, searching, no doubt, for Brandon. I started in her direction, then thought better of it. The last thing Libby wanted right then was to be smothered with well-meaning kindness.

Instead, I began scanning the room too, looking not for Brandon but for Mona's nameless paramour. Certainly, I thought, he would have come to her memorial service. There wasn't a face anywhere in the crowd which seemed remotely plausible, though at one point, I thought I might have been onto something.

The guy was movie-idol good looking, with broad, muscled shoulders and the kind of soulful eyes you see in aftershave commercials. He was closer to Libby's age than Mona's, but I thought that might explain the fact that she'd kept the affair quiet. He didn't look like the type to wear cufflinks either, unless he'd chosen the polo shirt and khaki pants as some kind of private statement, but I was willing to overlook what I saw as a fairly minor detail. He stood off by himself, to the side of the door, looking lost and vulnerable.

In the few minutes it took to squeeze through the crowd, I'd concocted a full-blown, wonderfully touching tale of their romance. He'd been her student, a young man who'd had to make his own way in the world from an early age. But he had maturity beyond his years, sensitivity unheard of in the male species, and the soul of a poet. Though the attraction was instantaneous and intense, they'd managed to fight it until, finally, the passion had simply swept them off their feet and clear to Mendocino. In my mind, I could picture the warm glow of firelight against their skin as they stretched out, sated with love, in front of the old stone hearth in the cottage at Timber-creek.

Just as I made it to the other side of the room and si-dled up next to the young man, primed to tell him I un-derstood everything, Stan's gentleman friend approached.

"We ready?" he asked.

"Yes, sir," the young man said. "The car's out front. I got it washed and polished, just as you asked."

"Did you manage to get by the cleaners as well?"

He nodded. "The suit will be ready by four."

"Very good, let's be on our way then."

With that, young Adonis donned the blue cap I'd missed seeing earlier. Stan's friend and his driver left, and I returned, privately red-faced, to scanning the room.

The only other possible prospect I encountered was a lanky, ashen-haired man who'd been drifting around the perimeter of the room since I'd first spotted him. He was more unusual looking than attractive, although his pale coloring, high forehead and bright, electric blue eyes held a certain allure. He wasn't really Mona's type, but this guy was about as different from Gary as one could be and still qualify as male. I thought that would have been a big plus in her book right there.

And, he smoked. I'd seen him step outside for a ciga-rette while I was talking to Stan. The other thing that struck me was that he seemed not to know anyone else at the service. He'd slide past a cluster of Mona's friends, now engaged in loose banter which had little to do with death, stand awkwardly with his hands in his pockets, and then move on, edging past another group.

Before I could make my way across the room to him,

Mary Nell materialized at my side, followed immediately by Claire.

"I heard about yesterday's burglary," Claire said, her face pinched with anxiety. "You were lucky you didn't walk in while the guy was still there."

"Burglary?" Mary Nell's voice had that damsel-in-distress tone she uses when confronted with the unpleasantries of living in California.

As I explained about the break-in at Mona's, she punctuated my recitation with breathless little gasps.

"Oh my, poor Kate," she said when I'd finished. "You've had a horrible week, haven't you?"

Not nearly so horrible as Mona's, I thought. But it's difficult to find fault with Mary Nell because it's so obvious she means well.

"Did they clean the place out?" Claire asked. "That happened to my aunt after her husband died. They did it while she was at the funeral. Came in and took everything."

"I don't know what they took. Nothing obvious. It's more like someone was searching for something if you want to know the truth."

Claire did her own version of the distress gasp. "What would they be searching for?"

That was the question I'd been asking myself. And I didn't have a clue. I shook my head and shrugged.

"Oh my," Mary Nell said. And then said it again.

Claire hugged herself and chewed on her lower lip. First Mona's death, then the break-in. Both events right there in her backyard. I could imagine the icy trepidation which was no doubt rolling through her.

"Why would they be looking for something?" she asked again, with an expression more dour than usual.

She looked at me and then at Mary Nell, as though we were deliberately withholding information. Then she glanced at her watch. "I'd better get going," she mumbled, "I'm already late for work."

"That woman is the sourest creature I know," Mary Nell said when Claire was beyond hearing.

"I gather she's had a pretty hard life. Her parents died when she was young, and then she was widowed even before Jodi was born."

"Widowed," Mary Nell sniffed. "It's a good story, but if you ask me, there never *was* any husband. She doesn't have a single picture of him, you know."

I'd heard Mary Nell's opinion of unwed motherhood before. I didn't believe it applied to Claire, but I didn't actually care if it did, either. Dan Quayle and Mary Nell could snub their noses all they wanted, I wasn't going to be a party to it.

I looked around again for the lank, blond-haired man, spotted him heading in Libby's direction, took my leave of Mary Nell and followed. Libby was still slumped against the wall, but her eyes now worked the room nonstop. I could tell by the expression on her face that Brandon had not appeared as promised.

The man chose a spot about three feet to Libby's left, leaned against the wall and gave her a fleeting, sideways smile. Libby either didn't notice or didn't care. Her scowl stayed locked in place, not softening, even for a moment. And when she glanced to her right, it grew positively fierce. I let my gaze follow hers, lighting as she had, on the fast approaching figure of her father. And Bimbo.

Bambi, I corrected myself, afraid that if I let it slide mentally, I'd make the same mistake when I addressed the woman in person. Not that I had any intention of seeking her out. In fact, if possible, I wanted to avoid the Gary-Bambi-Libby storm altogether. I turned to head in the other direction, but Libby called my name.

"Kate," she said a second time. "You said you'd give me a ride?" Gary had positioned himself so that Libby was sandwiched between his own bulk and the wall. She had to crane her neck and peer over his shoulder to see me.

"Are you ready to leave?" I asked.

Gary turned and glowered. "There's no need. I'll take Libby home."

"I'd walk first," Libby said with a sneer. "In fact, I'd crawl if need be."

"Libby, please. I'm only trying to help."

"Cut the Mr. Nice Guy act. You don't care about anyone but yourself. You'll do anything to get your own way."

"Please," Gary said again, lowering his voice almost to a whisper. "This is a terrible time for both of us, we should be together."

"Then what's *she* doing here?" Libby spat the "she" at Bambi as though it were a poison-tipped arrow.

Bambi, looking far from offended, tossed her head and smirked at Libby. "Why shouldn't I be here? I'm part of your father's life and it's time you got used to it."

"You're not part of *my* life," Libby screeched. "And you never will be."

Bambi looked at Gary with a helpless little shrug.

"Especially after what you did to my mother."

Libby's voice had been rising steadily. Most of the people nearby were trying hard to ignore the scene being played out virtually under their noses, but a few stopped talking and turned to watch.

"What *I* did to your mother?" Bambi sniffed.

"I don't know why you called her Friday afternoon, but it got to her."

"Me? I didn't call your mother. Why would I do a thing like that?"

Tears filled Libby's eyes and ran down her cheeks. She wiped at them with the back of her hand. "It's all your fault," she screamed. "Wasn't it enough that you ruined her marriage? Did you have to butt in again and destroy her life?"

"Libby, honey—" Gary placed a hand on Libby's shoulder.

She twisted away angrily. "Don't you see?" she sobbed. "The phone call is what did it. She was so upset. It must have pushed her over the edge." She turned toward Bambi, her face twisted with rage and grief. "It's like you killed her. You're a murderer as well as a whore!"

In a rush, she pushed past Gary and Bambi and stumbled through the door.

"I didn't call Mona," Bambi said haughtily, to no one in particular. "I can't imagine where Libby got the idea I did."

14

By the time I made it outside, Libby was nowhere in sight. I looked around the side of the building, then checked the car, thinking she might have gone there to wait for me. No such luck. I was heading back to the entrance of the mortuary when a motorcycle roared past on my left, Libby's bright red top knot whipping about wildly in the breeze. Brandon, it appeared, had finally surfaced.

"Jesus," Sharon said, joining me on the front steps.

"Yeah, well, I tried to tell you."

"I swear, Kate, I didn't have any idea how bad it was. You've got to believe me."

I believed her. Not that it made matters any easier.

"I mean, I knew she didn't particularly want to live with her dad, but I thought it was just, you know . . ." Her voice trailed off. "But I guess it isn't."

"Right, it isn't."

"She acts like she really hates the guy."

"Right," I said again. Heavy, dark clouds were blowing in from the west. I tucked my hands into my folded arms to keep them warm. "How did she and Gary get along before the divorce?"

"They were never particularly close, but I don't think it was anything like this. Gary always wanted a son. He never let Libby forget she didn't quite measure up."

"Geez."

"Yeah. It got worse, the older she got. Probably some sort of misplaced male insecurity, but he was always coming down on her about something."

"He's the one pushing for togetherness though."

Sharon shrugged. "Control maybe. He's the kind of man who likes to win. The kind who thinks primarily in those terms. That's part of the reason the divorce was so difficult. Why he's still so resentful. Gary wanted to feel he'd come out on top."

And he hadn't. Not only had Mona ended up with above-guideline support, she'd walked away with part of his business. But if he was so unhappy with the settlement, why hadn't he pushed to fight it out in court?

Sharon hugged herself against the icy wind. "We should be finished here soon. You want to go out for lunch afterwards?"

"I can't, sorry. I've got an appointment. Dr. Martha Caulder." I paused for emphasis. "Psychiatrist."

Sharon turned, eyes wide. *"A shrink? You?"*

I grinned. "A client. She liked what I did with Dr. Riley's office."

"Riley? He's a veterinarian."

"She doesn't want the same pieces, for heaven's sake. It was the concept she liked. Understated and unobtrusive."

Although, in truth, I was having a hard time figuring out what about the concept actually appealed to her, since Dr. Caulder was one of those people who speak largely in negatives. She didn't want paintings that dominated the room, but she didn't want her office cluttered with a series of small pieces either. She didn't like romanticized landscapes or seascapes; she didn't like bold colors, geometric abstracts or pictures of people; and she absolutely could not have anything which evoked strong emotion and might therefore be upsetting to her patients.

I thought maybe a nice off-white wall would be her best bet, but in the interest of building my clientele I was willing to give unobtrusive art my best shot. I'd pulled together a couple of prints, a grainy, sepia-toned photograph and a watercolor in subdued grays and greens. Once I got her reaction to those, I'd have a better idea what to look for.

"I'm trying to develop the commercial side of the business," I explained. "There's a lot more opportunity there than in residential."

"Well, that's good then." Sharon's face didn't mask her disappointment. "It's just that I was thinking after lunch, we could pay Mona's neighbors a visit. Ask them if they saw anything unusual Saturday night."

"The police already did that."

"So?"

"So I don't see what—"

She cut me off. "Michael's a sweetheart and all, but I don't have the same faith in law enforcement you do. Besides, we knew Mona. We might pick up on something they wouldn't." She looked at me, pausing for a deep, dramatic sigh. "Guess I'll just have to manage without you."

It was my turn to sigh. "My appointment's in Concord," I told Sharon. "I could stop by the college on my way back and take a look through Mona's office. Maybe there's something there that would help us. Who knows, I might even find the three thousand dollars stashed in a pencil box."

Her peevishness gave way to a grin. "Terrific idea," she said, suddenly full of enthusiasm. "Ask around too. Maybe you can find someone who's got answers we don't."

Wouldn't that be nice? Especially since I was having trouble even formulating the questions.

My appointment with Dr. Caulder took all of five minutes. It was a resounding *no* on all fronts. "I cannot have things like this on my walls," she proclaimed. *Things* came out like *dteengs* and it took me a minute to figure out the word wasn't some esoteric psychological term for *crap*. Because that's what the tone implied. Disheartened but not defeated, I set up another appointment for the following week. "Plee-se," she said as I left, "bring me some *dteengs* I like this time."

If only I had some clue as to what that might be. On my way to the college I wracked my brain for ideas, and came back once again to the simple white wall. Maybe I could suggest some kind of textured paper or stippled paint in place of actual art. Unless her patients were crazy enough to find Rorschach meaning in texture, in which case she'd have to stick to a flat latex.

Fifteen minutes later I was at the college. I'd never been to Mona's office before. In fact, I'd never been on the campus, though I frequented the parking lot during summer months when the local farmers used a portion of it for an open-air market. There was usually a lively crowd then, but now, on a gray mid-winter Friday afternoon, the place was practically deserted. I had no trouble finding a parking place right by the main gate.

Finding Mona's office wasn't difficult either, but finding anything of interest *in* the office proved to be more of a problem. It was a small space, outfitted with metal desk, bookshelf, and one extra chair. The bookshelf held a single row of books and a box of tissues. The drawers were empty except for the basic tools of the profession and the inevitable collection of pennies, odd buttons, and dusty Lifesavers. It was clear Mona used the room for mandatory office hours and little else.

Seated at the desk, I drummed my fingers on my knees, surveying the room for a second time. Since I was sleuthing, I figured I might as well go at it like the pros. I rolled back the chair, pulled out the wastebasket and was nose deep in orange peels and pencil shavings when the office door flew open with a crash. The man who stood in the entrance, practically snarling, was shorter than me, and wiry rather than muscled. But all the same, he had the look of someone you didn't want to mess with—kind of like a scruffy and ill-tempered alley cat. His nostrils flared and his black eyes narrowed. He stepped forward, baring a front tooth of bright gold.

I held onto the wastebasket as though it were a shield, and prepared to scream.

"It's some dame," the man yelled to an unseen companion. "Rooting around in the garbage."

A moment later, a gray head poked through the door frame. A friendly, female gray head. We recognized each other at the same instant.

"You're Mona's friend," she said, her face relaxing

into a smile. "We met this morning, at the memorial service."

I nodded. It had been one of those meetings in passing and I couldn't remember her name, but I did remember that she was one of Mona's colleagues in the English department.

Flustered, I stuffed the wastebasket back under the desk. "I came for Mona's things," I stammered. "Her personal effects, that is. The friend who's handling the estate asked me to stop by."

The woman, who'd apparently missed the part about my rooting around in the garbage, looked as embarrassed by the situation as I was. "It's okay, Luis," she said. "Thank you for being so attentive, but this is a friend of Mrs. Sterling's."

Luis scrunched up his face, cast a suspicious eye at the wastebasket, and then at me. Finally he shook his head, befuddled, and left.

"I'm so sorry," said the woman, "but we didn't know who was in here. Luis heard sounds, and then we saw that the light was on . . . and well, after what happened a couple of weeks ago I've decided you can't be too careful. I hope he didn't frighten you."

I mumbled something that I hoped glossed over the fact that Luis hadn't been too far off the mark.

"He's the maintenance man," she explained, "but he's sort of taken on the role of watchman too. Unofficially of course."

She apologized again. I apologized. We re-introduced ourselves. Jean and Kate. And then we apologized to each other for having forgotten the earlier introduction. We talked a bit about Mona and the service and how much we would miss her.

Jean peered into one of the open drawers. "Did you find everything you came for?" she asked.

"I was just checking to make sure nothing important got left. There doesn't appear to be much here."

"No, most of us don't keep anything in our offices except what we absolutely need. The security around here is simply awful. And the students . . . well, things aren't what they used to be."

I nodded sympathetically, wondering if I'd chatted long enough to make a graceful exit. I started to rise.

"Take that episode a couple of weeks ago," Jean said. "It's a sure sign how bad things have become. The secretary down the hall actually called the police. Though by the time they got here, he was gone."

"Who was gone?"

"That man, the one who was badgering Mona."

I dropped back into my seat. "Badgering her?"

"Goodness, it was awful. He was yelling and pounding his fist. Kept talking about how it was all her fault and how he was going to get even."

"Get even for what?"

"He looked like such a mild-mannered guy too, not one of these glassy-eyed crazies. But I'll tell you, he was angry. He had us shaking in our boots."

I tried again. "Why was he so upset?" For a woman trained in communication, Jean was taking a rather long time getting to the crux of the matter.

"I didn't get the whole story until afterwards, of course. But apparently the man's wife was one of Mona's students. Children grown and gone, the old empty nest syndrome. Anyway, she decided to take some classes. That was last fall. Well, one thing led to another and she decided to go for her degree. This spring she enrolled as a full-time student."

"I take it the husband wasn't pleased."

Jean nodded. "What really got him going apparently, was that his wife was too busy with school work to fix home-cooked meals and do his laundry. The poor woman had probably been waiting on him hand and foot for years. He, of course, blamed Mona. Said she'd filled his wife's head with feminist lies and teachings of the devil. He talked like that—devil, wrath of God, woman's place. I could hear him all the way down at the other end of the hall."

"What did Mona do?"

"At first, she tried reasoning with him. When that didn't get her anywhere, she asked him to leave. She stayed really cool. Cooler than I would have been. He didn't actually hurt her, but we were afraid he might. That's why we called the police."

I leaned forward a bit, the rush of discovery pounding in my chest. A man who'd been angry at Mona. A man who'd threatened her. Maybe I'd stumbled onto something after all. "Do you know the man's name?"

Jean shook her head. "No. His wife's name is Eve though, I remember that. I thought there was a certain irony in the whole thing. Eve and the Tree of Knowledge all over again."

"Do you think anyone in the administration might know?"

"Maybe, but they've all left for the day." She rubbed her temples, lost for a moment in thought. "We ought to be able to figure it out easily enough though."

I looked up. "How?"

Jean pulled open the bottom left desk drawer. "Class

lists," she said, hauling out a half-dozen manilla folders.
"There can't be very many Eves."

In fact, there was only one. "Eve Fisher," she said, closing the last folder. "She's enrolled in Mona's re-entry
tutorial too, which means she's an older student. That's
got to be it."

The name sounded vaguely familiar, but I couldn't
quite place it. "Does it list an address or phone number?"

"Just the phone number."

I pulled an old Safeway receipt from my purse and
wrote the number on the back.

"Why are you interested in all this anyway?" Jean
asked. And then, while I was deciding how to respond,
her eyes grew wide and she came up with an answer herself. "You think this has something to do with why Mona
killed herself?"

"I don't know what to think," I said truthfully.

I sat in the car debating my next move. I could tell the
story to Michael, who'd listen attentively, knit his brows,
and then point out that Mona would hardly have welcomed a hot-head like Eve's husband into her home,
much less sat still while he force-fed her sleeping pills. I
could tell Sharon, who might go after the guy herself in a
fit of rage. Or I could look into it further before I said a
word to anyone. The choice seemed pretty clear.

I got out of the car again and found a pay phone. Only
what I really wanted was a phone book, and it was missing. I've never been able to understand why anybody
would want to steal a phone book, though given the fre-
quency with which I encounter cut cables in phone
booths, there is clearly an attraction there I'm missing.

Across the quad I found another phone booth, book attached, and checked the listings. There were lots of Fishers, but I got lucky and found one which matched the number Jean had given me. What's more, it was one of the increasingly rare listings which included an address.

Anna wouldn't be out of school for another hour. I had plenty of time to drive over to the Fishers, and hopefully to speak with Eve. About what, I wasn't exactly sure. But I've never been one to let the lack of a clear-cut plan stand in my way.

Ike and Eve Fisher lived on the outskirts of Concord in an older subdivision of small, look-alike stucco homes. It was one of those neighborhoods that had faded along with the fresh paint and newly planted lawns which had once been its main attraction. The kind of place where women had run next door to borrow an egg or lend an ear, where men had called out to one another over the whine of the lawn mower and children's playful babble. The streets were quiet now, the residents off on some solitary endeavor or holed up alone behind closed drapes.

The Fisher's house was among the better maintained. Freshly painted trim, a green lawn, and a border of daffodils set it apart from its neighbors. I tried the doorbell, which played a cute little tune but generated nothing by way of response. Ike was undoubtedly at work. I figured Eve might be in the library, frantically working to finish a research paper. Or, if Ike had been forceful enough, she might be upstairs frantically ironing his shirts and ignoring the doorbell. In either case, it appeared I was out of luck.

I climbed back into the car and headed off to retrieve Anna, newly appreciative of the fact that I had a young child and seemingly countless years before I faced my own empty nest.

And that's when I remembered why Eve's name had seemed familiar.

Hers had been the paper I'd seen by Mona's phone, the one about a woman haunted by memories of her child. The one, I recalled contritely, I'd thought so melodramatic and overwritten. It's funny how knowing a bit of background will change your perspective. I wished now I'd read more of the story, could remember more of what little I had read. I'd probably still find it too sappy for my tastes, but now that I knew something of Eve, her loss touched me in spite of her words.

Had she been writing metaphorically about her now grown children? Or had she actually lost a child? I thought of the empty house, the callous husband. I could imagine the loveless void at the center of Eve's life, and I mentally crossed my fingers, hoping she'd chosen the library over her husband's shirts.

It wasn't until I was almost to Anna's school that I thought to wonder why Mona had set that particular paper aside. Certainly not because of its fine style or perceptive insights. But probably not because it was so appallingly bad either. Had she singled it out because of her dispute with Eve's husband? But why? Had she maybe pulled the paper out to show it to her visitor Saturday evening? And again, why?

Stopping the car at the first pay phone I found, I called Eve and left a message.

15

"How was school today?" I asked Anna, later that afternoon.

"Fine." She licked a thick smear of raspberry jam from her finger. Bagel with jam was what I'd offered her; jam with bagel was what she'd concocted for herself.

"Was that strange man there again?"

She ignored me.

"You know, the one who looks like a . . . fairy."

Anna gave me the kind of withering look I thought only teenagers knew. "Why," she asked airily, "are you making such a big deal out of this?"

Because, I thought, everywhere I look these days I run across another account of a kidnapping or attempted abduction. Just that morning the paper had run a story, "String of Attempted Abductions Worries S.F. Parents." True, that was San Francisco, but it wasn't all that far away, and each of the girls had been stopped near school. And only last week an Oakland boy had barely managed to escape from a man who tried to lure him into a car with cookies and candy. I had reason to be worried. On the other hand, I didn't want Anna to live in constant fear, to grow up to be someone like Claire, who worried incessantly and often without reason. It was a fine line and maybe in this instance I'd crossed it. I decided to pull back.

"Just curious," I told her.

Anna washed down her snack with a glass of orange juice, then wandered off in the direction of the television. I fed Max the jamless piece of bagel left on her plate, wiped the table, and took a couple of Advil. What had started earlier in the day as a dull, almost imperceptible heaviness at the back of my head, had grown into a throbbing pain. I pulled out a magazine and tried to read, but found myself instead fretting about Mona's death, Libby's happiness, Anna's safety, and my abysmal failure with Dr. Caulder that afternoon. The worst part was, I couldn't come up with a solution for any of it.

Libby rolled in just as I was setting the table for dinner and wondering whether to lay out two places or three. Actually, stormed in is more like it. She slammed the door, threw her jacket onto a chair with such force it scattered the napkins, yanked open the refrigerator and tossed in the six-pack of Coke she'd apparently acquired since motoring off with Brandon after the service.

Anna licked the peanut butter from her fingers and watched with wide-eyed interest. Max positioned himself between the peanut butter and the fridge, watching with a different sort of wide-eyed interest.

"Did you and Brandon have a nice afternoon?" I asked, mostly to provide an alternative to the stomping and slamming.

"Yeah, terrific." This in a tone which suggested it had been anything but. Kicking off her shoes, she retrieved one of the soda cans from the fridge and popped the tab. "The guy's a fucking asshole sometimes."

Anna stopped her licking. Her eyes grew wider.

My own narrowed disapprovingly.

"A total dick-brain in fact. My mother gets so shit-faced she kills herself and he's like, whoopee, serves her right. The guy's about as supportive as a flea."

In my head, compassion and irritation were staging a major battle. My mouth, however, engaged without waiting for the outcome. "If you're going to stay in my house," I said coolly, "even for a short while, I expect you to follow a few basic rules. One of them involves language."

Two pair of eyes blinked in my direction. Anna was clearly intrigued. Libby had that vacant *come-again?* look which seems genetically programed into puberty.

"I also expect you to let me know where you're going, with whom, and when you plan on returning. And I hope you will ask rather than announce."

"Well, *ex-cuse* me."

The voice dripped with adolescent sarcasm, but I caught something of the little-girl-lost in her expression. For the moment anyway, compassion got the upper hand. My tone softened. "Your whole life has just been turned inside out. I understand that and I want to make things as easy for you as I can. But Anna and I have a life too. You can't live here and go on as though we don't exist."

Libby shrugged, studied her Coke can, looked over at Anna and then back to the can. "I'm not used to having younger kids around."

"It's not just that."

"So you wanna ship me off to live with Mr. High and Mighty and his whor—" She caught herself. "His, uh, fiancée."

I shook my head. "That's not what I meant."

"Well, I won't go. Nobody can make me."

That was Sharon's battle not mine. I picked up the scattered napkins and placed them back on the table. "That reminds me," I said, "he phoned and left a message on the machine. Wanted you to call him when you got in."

Gary had left two messages really. One for Libby: *You'd better call me, young lady, and you'd better apologize like you mean it.* A second for me. The words were a little different, but the tone was identical. I was no more inclined to return the call than I assumed Libby was.

She glowered at me for a moment, then picked up her jacket and headed for her room. "If Brandon calls, tell him I'm out."

"We're going to be eating in about ten minutes," I called after her.

"I'm not hungry," she yelled back, then shut her door with a loud thud.

I swallowed two more Advil and poured myself a glass of wine. In a moment of black humor, I thought I understood what might have driven Mona to suicide.

Anna and I had an unusually subdued dinner. No silly stories or long, winding chronicles of the latest cartoon episodes. No *whys* or *how comes*. And I didn't push it. But I did read an extra two chapters in *Ralph S. Mouse* and agree to stay around for part of the *Wee Sing* tape which was her current favorite. Then I filled the tub with water and prepared to take a long, hot bath.

I'd got only as far as removing my shoes when the

phone rang. I was tempted to ignore it, especially when I considered there was a high probability it might be Gary. But there was also a chance it might be Eve Fisher, and she was someone I did want to talk to.

Instead, the caller was Brandon.

"Libby there?" he mumbled.

"Um, no. She isn't."

"Yeah?"

"Yeah."

"You tell her I'll be here for about ten minutes more, then I'm splitting. She wants to come along she'd better give me a call sooner rather than later." With that, he hung up.

Ever the diligent hostess, I went to relay the message to Libby, then stopped outside the door. Her sobbing was muffled and barely audible, but so tortured it made my own throat ache. I knocked softly.

"Go away."

"I want to come in." I entered before she had a chance to protest again. The room was dark but I could see enough of her face from the hall light to know she'd been crying for hours.

"Go away," she said. "Just leave me alone."

"Not until I'm sure you're okay." I sat on the edge of the bed and ran a hand down her back. She rolled from her stomach onto her side, away from me. "Brandon called. I told him you weren't here, but he said he'd be home for a bit longer if you wanted to reach him."

"Never."

"I take it you two had a fight."

"He's such a jerk. Turns out my mother was right about him all along."

"You want to tell me about it?"

She shook her head and made a sound that was somewhere between a choke and a hiccup. Then she rolled over, sat up, and buried her face in her hands as a fresh round of tears overtook her. "I'm such a horrible person," she sobbed. "I made my mother's life miserable. It's no wonder she hated me."

I hugged Libby tight and rocked her. This time she didn't resist.

"I miss her so much, Kate."

"I know you do, honey, but you've got it all wrong. You didn't make your mother's life miserable at all. She understood what it was like to be your age. She worried about you, of course, but she never stopped loving you, even when she was angry."

"No, you don't understand." Libby's whole body shook with the tide of tears. "You don't know how awful I was sometimes. I'm sure that's why she killed herself, because I was so awful and mean."

Once again, I considered raising the prospect of murder, and once again I decided to hold my tongue. What did we really have anyway? A bottle of scotch, a burglary, and a rescheduled tennis date. It didn't seem fair to play with Libby's emotions like that when there was still the chance Mona's death had truly been suicide.

Libby continued sobbing and I continued rocking, my own chest tight with the depth of her anguish. Max joined us after awhile, resting his chin in Libby's lap and whimpering plaintively along with her.

Eventually, Libby's tears subsided. I made her a sandwich, which she devoured with record speed while protesting that she wasn't the least bit hungry. When she finally went off to bed, I let the now-cold water out of the tub, took another two Advil and climbed into bed myself.

I thought about calling Michael, but the night was young still and I knew he wouldn't be back in his hotel room for at least another hour. As much as I wanted the comfort of his voice, I wasn't up to lying awake, waiting, while the demons ran circles in my mind. I'd call in the morning.

As it turned out, Michael called me. At quarter to seven.

"You're up bright and early," I said, trying hard to disguise the fact that I was not.

"I've got a seven o'clock breakfast meeting."

"Mmm." I rolled over and propped the pillow under my head in anticipation of the sweet nothings Michael does so well.

There were no honeyed words this morning, however. "Have you seen yesterday's *Sun?*" he asked.

Had I? I tried to remember. The *Walnut Hills Sun* is published on Tuesday and Friday afternoons. It's strictly a local paper, focusing on community news, events, and personalities. I usually glance through it when it arrives, then toss it. Sometimes though, it gets lost for weeks in the stack of magazines and catalogues piled in my "must read" corner.

"I'm not sure," I said finally.

"Maybe you should."

"Now?"

"You otherwise engaged?"

I mumbled something I thought best left unintelligible, then set the receiver down and went to get the paper. I brought it back to bed with me and started scanning as I picked up the phone. "You're not calling about the Mayor's plan to renovate the duck pond?" That seemed to be the lead story. There was a nice piece about the upcoming school auction too, but I thought that even less likely.

"Second page," Michael said. "Top left."

I opened the paper. There, right where he'd directed me, was a two column article by Susie Sullivan Lambert. *Foul Play Suspected in Recent Death.* I read it quickly, with a horrible, sinking sensation in the pit of my stomach. *Mona Sterling's death this past week is being treated by police as a suicide, but her closest friends feel the authorities are overlooking important and obvious evidence to the contrary.* It was all there, everything, including my name and the information Michael had told me in confidence. She'd quoted me accurately, except for the part about police incompetence and cover-up, but she'd changed the whole thrust of our discussion.

For a moment I could think of nothing to say. It was like being whacked between the eyes by a two-by-four and not knowing exactly what had happened. "Michael, I'm sorry," I said finally. "I did talk to Susie, but I didn't say anything about the police not doing their job. And I didn't 'give her a story' or whatever it's called. We were just talking, in the bedding department at Macy's."

"Not real smart, Kate." His voice was so low and soft I could barely make out the words. It gets that way when he's angry or upset.

"No, in retrospect it wasn't."

"Thought you knew to be careful dealing with the press."

"But she writes the *Around Town* column. Promotions, engagements, local celebrities. I wasn't thinking of her as a reporter when we had our conversation."

Michael sighed heavily. "That's fairly obvious."

How could Susie have done this? Not only using what

I'd told her without asking, but deliberately distorting my words. I wanted to give her a good swift kick in the rear end, but that was nothing compared to the pounding I wanted to give myself. Short circuit of the mouth-brain synapse, it was a condition I'd never managed to outgrow.

I dropped the newspaper onto the bed. There was no way I could look at it any longer. I swallowed hard and tried to find my voice. "How did you see this already, down there in San Diego."

"The captain faxed me a copy last night."

My throat grew tighter. It was worse than I'd imagined. "I take it he wasn't exactly pleased."

"That would be one way to put it. Among other things, he thinks I ought to 'keep you on a shorter leash.' His words, not mine."

"Great. The captain's going to have a heyday rubbing your nose in this."

Michael grunted. "Probably."

I shut my eyes and gave myself another round of mental lashings. "I feel so bad about this. I've caused such trouble for you . . ."

Michael cut me off. "Nothing I can't handle."

"The flak you're going to get . . ." I cringed, imagining the position I'd put him in.

"I can take care of myself," he said softly. "It's you I'm worried about."

"Me?"

"If Mona Sterling's death was actually a homicide, you've just sent her killer an invitation with your name engraved on it." His words rolled out slowly. "I want you to be careful, Kate."

I was momentarily stunned. Michael was more worried about me than his own neck. I've always known that he's a nice person, deep-down rare and genuine nice, but he still surprises me sometimes. "You're not mad?"

"I'm not mad; I'm worried."

Had not it been for the overriding message of potential peril, his words would have been, as the saying goes, music to my ears. As it was, they were more like the rumble of thunder. "You really think I might be in danger?"

"The article implies you know things about Mona's death, things that suggest murder rather than suicide. Things that just might point to a particular person. Now I'm not saying there's even a killer out there, but if there is, and if he's gone to the trouble of disguising Mona's death as a suicide, he's not going to like your meddling."

I took a moment to digest this, wondering just how a killer's displeasure might manifest itself. I had no trouble coming up with possibilities.

"I'm not trying to scare you, Kate. I just want you to be careful."

I promised I would.

"You haven't crossed anyone in particular over Mona's death, have you?"

I had a feeling I wasn't on Gary's list of favorite friends, but I hadn't actually crossed him. "Not that I'm aware of."

"Good. It might not be a bad idea to drop this murder idea altogether."

"Now? But there are too many unanswered questions."

I could hear the sigh, and the expression on his face was easy to imagine. "Such as?"

"Well, there was the break-in."

"We've been over that."

"And the three thousand dollars." I realized I hadn't

told Michael about that. "The day she died, Mona withdrew three thousand dollars from the bank. In cash. And it's not in her wallet or the cookie jar either."

"Interesting." Michael paused, his tone thoughtful. "But it doesn't necessarily spell murder. She may have wanted to settle some private obligation before she died. Or to make a bequest outside of her will."

"Or she might have intended the money for a bribe, or a payoff of some kind."

"You got any theories along those lines you'd like to share with me?"

"I could probably come up with a couple if you give me some time."

He laughed. "I'm sure you could."

"There's also someone who recently threatened Mona." This was the kind of lead cops like so I took my time, punctuating my news with appropriate pauses. "The husband of one of her students. He apparently created quite a scene with his accusations and stormy temper. It was so bad the department secretary called the police."

Michael went back to sighing. "You talking about Ike Fisher?"

My bubble burst. "You know about him?"

"He's on a Caribbean cruise, Kate. Left three days before Mona Sterling died."

Damn. I'd really thought there was a connection there, particularly with Eve's paper being the only one on Mona's desk. "Did he take his wife with him?"

"Probably, though I don't know it for a fact. Is that important?"

"No, not really." I couldn't imagine what motive Eve

would have for killing Mona. "How do you know all this stuff about Ike Fisher anyway?"

"His name was in the computer. Concord sent us a copy of the police report since Mona was a Walnut Hills resident."

That didn't explain what Michael was doing running a check on a case that didn't officially exist. "You just happened to find his name there among the millions of megabytes, or whatever the heck they're called, floating around in your computer system?"

This time the sigh was different. Michael sounded mildly embarrassed at having been found out.

"You've been 'meddling' too, haven't you?" I chided. "You've been poking around about a simple suicide, just on the off chance it wasn't?"

"It's strictly unofficial. Though I have to tell you, Kate, I haven't turned up anything I could take to the captain."

"That means you've found something, though?"

He hesitated. After the way I'd handled Susie I didn't blame him. "It's probably nothing," he said. "But there was some out-of-town private eye who called the station a couple of days ago inquiring about Mona Sterling's death. Wanted to know if we'd found anything suspicious about it."

My pulse skipped a beat. "Did he say why he wanted to know?"

"Nope. And the guy who took the call didn't think to ask. But you can see why I want you to be careful."

Unfortunately, I could.

$$\boxed{16}$$

In the wake of Susie's story, murder was going to be a hot topic all over town. Any reservations I might have had about telling Libby were beside the point. Since she was bound to hear about it sooner or later, I thought it best that she get the story straight from the start.

I raised the issue over breakfast, going through the list of oddities about her mother's death one by one, then reminded her that it was still just a theory. As I'd predicted, the news was something of a mixed bag. The murder scenario certainly eased the hurt and guilt, but it opened the door to a whole host of new emotions. I watched them play out on her face.

"Who would want to kill my mom?" Libby asked when I'd finished.

I shook my head. "I've no idea. Did she ever mention any kind of dispute or trouble?"

Libby thought about it for a moment. "Not that I remember."

"How about the name Ike Fisher. Did she ever mention him?"

"No. Who is he?"

"The husband of one of her students. He blamed your mother when his wife decided she preferred the classroom to the kitchen."

"Not much of a choice," Libby snorted.

"Depends on how long you've been in the kitchen," I told her. Of course, if Ike was in the middle of the ocean somewhere he could hardly have killed Mona anyway, but I couldn't let go of the thought that there had to be a connection. "His wife's class paper was on your mom's desk the night she died. Any ideas why she'd have set it out?"

Libby shrugged. "Mom graded papers all over the house. I'm surprised she never lost any. She spilled coffee on a bunch once. Made a real mess of them."

Grading papers. It certainly made sense. Maybe I was making a big deal out of simple coincidence. In fact, if Eve Fisher had actually dropped out of school, which looked to be the case, Mona might have set the paper aside knowing it no longer needed grading.

But in that case, we were back to ground zero in terms of motives and suspects.

I tapped my fork against my plate. "More waffle?" I asked.

"No thanks. I'm not used to eating breakfast."

I handed the remaining square to Max who preferred it from someone's plate, with syrup, but would make do without when he had to. Though Anna and I had finished eating long before Libby got up, I'd somehow found myself nibbling a second breakfast while she ate.

"Yesterday at the service you said something about a phone call that upset your mother."

Libby nodded. "It was Friday evening, early. We hadn't eaten dinner yet."

"What made you think the caller was Bambi?"

A shrug. "It was a woman, I know that. I could hear her voice from a couple of feet away so she must have been talking really loud. And my mother's face got all blotchy the way it used to when she'd talk about Bimbo."

"But you don't know for sure that's who it was?"

"No, not for sure. I heard my mom say something about 'divorce' though." Libby pushed a fork around in the puddle of syrup left on her plate. "She'd been in a real snippy mood for a couple of days, and I know my dad was late getting the check to her that month. I just sort of assumed they were all tied together. Bimbo's always complaining about how unfair it is that *we* get paid, even when my dad's short on cash."

Like an actor who'd been waiting for his cue, Gary chose that moment to call.

"Kate," he said, as though we were old friends. "I was hoping we might be able to get together this morning. Any chance you're free for breakfast?" His delivery was smooth as silk.

"I've already eaten."

"How about lunch then?"

"What's this about anyway?" I was fairly certain Gary hadn't taken a sudden interest in making sure I got three meals a day.

"Oh, nothing in particular. I just thought it might be a nice idea if we had a chance to talk, get to know one another a bit better." He paused to give me a chance to agree. When I didn't, he continued. "Libby staying with you and all, it seemed like a good idea."

"Sorry, I can't make lunch."

"What's good for you, then?"

Was this the same guy who'd snarled at me only a few days earlier? "It's kind of hard," I told him. "I have to find a baby sitter for my daughter."

Libby caught my eye and mouthed, "I'll watch her for you."

"It's your father," I mouthed back, covering the mouthpiece with my hand.

She made a retching sound. "You really want to go?"

Actually, I didn't. But my curiosity got the better of me. "I'll have coffee," I told Gary, "while you eat breakfast. Where shall we meet?"

"How about Park West, in half an hour."

Park West is no Denny's. No Berkeley-style muffin and latte place either. It's the main dining room of the Park Manor Hotel, Walnut Hills at its most posh. Gary was already seated when I arrived, but he rose to greet me.

"I'm so glad you were able to make it," he said, helping me with my jacket and then my chair. "Would you like something to drink? I've ordered a Bloody Mary for myself."

"Just coffee thank you."

He smiled. "I took the liberty of ordering a croissant and small omelette for you. I'd feel like a boor eating when you had nothing."

That was quite a liberty since I'd been clear about having already eaten. But I kept my mouth shut. His drink arrived and the waiter poured my coffee.

"I'd like to start by apologizing," Gary said. "For the way I jumped on you the other day. Mona's death has been more of a strain on me than I realized. I'm afraid

I'm not my best when I'm under stress." He gave me the kind of smile that was supposed to wipe the slate clean.

I didn't return it, but I was tempted. The guy was good.

"It's been . . . just awful really. People think because you're divorced something like this doesn't affect you, but it's not that simple. I still had deep feelings for Mona."

I'd heard about some of Gary's feelings. They were not, apparently, the ones to which he alluded.

Gary took a long, slow swallow of his drink. "And, of course, she was the mother of my only child. That's a bond which can never be severed, as I'm sure you must understand." Another smile, this one tinged with a shadow of sadness.

I was beginning to feel like Dorothy talking to the Wizard of Oz. I didn't have the slightest idea of the man behind the voice. I gave a noncommittal nod and was saved from the necessity of further comment by the arrival of our food.

My "small" omelette would have fed a starving family of four, and my croissant was actually in the plural. The breakfast was small only by comparison with Gary's. Mine fit quite nicely all on one plate while his took three.

He started with the sausage. "Tell me," he said casually, before popping a large half-link into his mouth, "whatever got you started on this murder idea in the first place?"

Ah, so that's what it was. The getting-to-know-one-another routine was just a ploy. "You're talking about the article in Friday's *Sun*?"

He nodded. "It was one of those maddening pieces which whet the curiosity without imparting anything concrete."

"It's also one of those maddening pieces which isn't entirely accurate. And the reason there wasn't more substance to the article is that there's nothing substantive to report."

A charitable smile. "But you obviously didn't pull this theory out of thin air."

"No, not entirely." I broke off a piece of croissant and stuck it in my mouth.

Gary waited, his expression questioning.

"It's mostly that Mona didn't seem the kind of person to commit suicide. She wasn't depressed that any of us were aware of. There was no note. She left Libby all a—" I bit off the word "alone," sure that Gary wouldn't see it quite that way. "She left Libby to struggle with making sense of her mother's death. I can't imagine she would do that. And the bottle she'd supposedly been drinking from was scotch. Sharon says she never drank scotch."

"Sharon?" Gary's eyebrows shot up, then he laughed hollowly. "I should have known she was part of this."

"Part of what? The article was a mistake. I happened to be talking to the woman who wrote it, going on the way people do after someone's died, and the next thing I know she's turned my words into a commentary on conspiracy."

He leaned back with an understanding nod. "You can't be too careful when dealing with newshounds. Believe me, I speak from experience."

I broke off another bit of croissant. "I think I've learned my lesson."

"Of course," he continued, "there was also this burglary the paper mentioned. A burglary in which apparently nothing was stolen. I take it that part is accurate anyway?"

I nodded.

"They have any leads, any idea what the thief might have been looking for?"

"What makes you think he was looking for something?"

Gary shrugged. "That was the general idea, wasn't it? Nothing obvious was missing, and you think it's somehow tied in with Mona's death." He scooped up a forkful of scrambled egg. "With her murder, in fact."

"The police don't see it that way. They think it was more like a routine break-in. Apparently that's not uncommon after someone has died."

"What else don't they see your way?"

I shook my head. I'd learned my lesson with Susie; I wasn't going to be tripped up a second time. "Nothing else."

He looked up from his plate. "That's it, then? The article implied there was more."

"That's it. More woman's intuition than hard fact." Unless you counted the phone call from the private investigator Michael had mentioned, but I wasn't breathing a word about that.

"Interesting, all the same." Gary paused, lost for a moment in thought. "Sharon's right about the scotch, you know. The stuff gave Mona a headache. Though I suppose under the circumstances, she might not have worried about that."

"No, I guess not." But if she normally drank gin, why would she select something different for her final nightcap?

Gary had finished the sausage, eggs, and hash-browns, and moved onto the pancakes. He took a bite and chewed intently for a moment. "I wish you'd spoken with me first. We might have been able to look into the matter discreetly, avoid all this publicity.''

"Publicity?"

He made a dismissive gesture. "Attention then. It's upsetting. And it causes trouble, business-wise. With talk of murder, there's bound to be someone nosing around. That stuff's a real pain in the ass for a person in my line of work."

"Yeah, well, being murdered is kind of a pain too."

Gary shot me an appraising look. "You're right," he said, managing to look contrite. "I guess I'm just a little sensitive about this current project of mine." He hailed the waitress and ordered a second Bloody Mary. "Sure you won't join me?"

I shook my head, then declined a second cup of coffee as well. Despite my intentions to the contrary, I'd somehow managed to finish off one whole croissant and make a sizable dent in the omelette as well. Three breakfasts in one morning was something of a record, even for me.

"You want my opinion," Gary said, leaning back in his chair, "it sounds like you and Sharon are having a hard time accepting Mona's suicide. That's understandable, we all are. But if the police are satisfied, there doesn't seem to be much point in beating your heads against the wall. I'm afraid all this talk about murder is going to do more harm than good."

"Business-wise," I added.

His face tensed for a moment, then relaxed into amusement. "Not just that. I'm worried about the effect it will have on Libby." He finished his meal, wiped his mouth with a napkin, and folded it neatly across his plate. "I was thinking about taking her away on a short trip, just the two of us. I've a little time before the wedding and, it appears, a rather large fence to mend. What do you think?''

"What I think doesn't matter. You'll have to ask Libby what she thinks."

"Yes, well . . ." His smile was resigned. "I guess I have a pretty good idea how she's going to react."

At least the guy wasn't stupid.

His second drink arrived. He took a long swallow. "Libby always was a mommy's girl."

"I got the impression she gave Mona plenty of grief too."

He nodded. "That's part of the problem. Mona was too liberal with Libby. Let her get away with all kinds of crap, which meant it fell on me to be the bad guy. Never mind that Libby lives like a princess because of my blood and sweat; the minute things don't go just her way, she flies off the handle and blames me. And I'm sure Mona encouraged it. Probably put her up to it half the time." Gary paused for another gulp of Bloody Mary. "I'd like to think now that there's just the two of us, we'll be able to forge a better relationship."

I wasn't going to be the one to tell him he was off to a lousy start.

"Mona was the one who turned this divorce into open warfare, you know. Kept pushing me for more. She wound up with enough to live like royalty while I have to bust my ass for every penny."

"But you agreed to it."

He looked at me over the top of his glass, then shrugged. "Bambi was anxious to get things settled, to get on with our lives. I told her the money was ours, hers as well as mine, but she insisted that putting the past behind us was worth the price. Shows you what a genuinely lovely woman she is.''

Given that Bambi had been whining to Libby about their finances, I thought Gary's tribute was probably off base. But being smitten with someone will do that.

He finished his drink, then signaled the waiter for the check. "Well, I'm glad we had a chance to get to know one another a little better. Maybe we can do it again some time." A playful wink accompanied his smile. "And let's see if we can't drop this murder business." Another smile. "For everyone's sake."

At various times during our conversation I'd come close to experiencing a touch of compassion for the man, but his last remark erased any lingering good feelings.

I ignored the smile and looked him straight in the eye. "For your sake, is what you mean."

"I think all of us who knew Mona are experiencing a sense of loss."

"But you didn't *lose* anything. In fact, it worked out pretty well for you. You don't have to pay alimony anymore, you've got full control of your business once again. And you've got Libby, more or less."

Gary leaned across the table. His ruddy, slack-skinned face was only inches from mine. "Are you suggesting that *I* killed Mona?"

"Did you?"

He laughed. "In my dreams many times, but never in the flesh."

17

Libby was reading to Anna when I returned home, a worthwhile endeavor which would have been more worthwhile had she been reading something other than *Cosmopolitan's* "Thin Thighs by Summer."

"You got a bunch of calls," Libby said. "I let the machine pick them up. I hope that's okay."

"It's fine." Preferable actually. One of my pet peeves as a caller is finding myself stuck trying to leave a message with some well-meaning human when I know there's a perfectly good answering machine available. Humans write slowly, demand that everything be spelled twice, and then usually get it garbled anyway.

"What did my dad want?" Libby asked.

"I'm not sure really."

"I bet he yelled and cussed a lot though, right?" She lowered the magazine and looked at me.

"He seemed to be trying a gentler approach this time."

"You mean he gave you the 'Libby is my only child, I

care about her deeply and it pains me that we aren't closer' line?''

I laughed in spite of myself. "More or less. It sounds like you don't believe it."

"Why should I?" she muttered, returning to her magazine. "It's pure crap."

A large part of it no doubt was, but I thought there might be some truth there as well. How to separate the two was something I couldn't have begun to figure out.

I gave the rail-thin model gracing the cover of *Cosmopolitan* an envious glance, then left to change clothes. After my brunch with Gary I was in need of something with a looser waist.

I did indeed have a number of calls. The little red light blinked so frantically I gave up trying to count how many. The first message was from Mary Nell, who spent a good sixty seconds offering apologies and sympathy before getting around to asking about the article in the *Sun*. She would love to hear the details, but only if I felt like talking of course, and if there was anything she could do, please let her know. There were similar calls from Jane Myers, Patricia Heafy and Judy Wiggins, women I usually spoke to only in grocery lines and on class field trips. They didn't offer as much in the way of apology and sympathy, but they each found their own way of beating around the bush, diplomatically tying the call into something besides Mona's death.

Laurelle Simms had called as well. As far as she was concerned, Monday morning was an absolutely terrible time for the rescheduled auction meeting. She would have to move her tennis lesson to the afternoon which meant that she couldn't get her nails done until Tuesday. But since time was running out and everyone else had been contacted first, it seemed she didn't have much choice. And would I please call and tell her why in the world I thought Mona had been murdered.

In addition, there was a brief message from Sharon, two from Brandon asking Libby to call him and, finally, a message from Andy. He'd landed the job with Sterling Development.

As I brushed my teeth and ran a comb through my hair, I found myself wondering how long this new job would last, or more realistically, how long Andy would last at it. It wasn't that he was stupid or lazy, he was far from being either, but he tended to lose sight of the fact that he was no longer a twenty-year-old kid with the world on a string and an endless stretch of tomorrows. And he didn't take well to being reminded of the fact either.

I headed back to the living room. Though Libby was no longer reading aloud, her face was still buried in the magazine.

"Brandon left a couple of messages," I told her.

"Good for him." She didn't bother to look up.

"If he should happen to call again, I take it I'm to tell him you're otherwise engaged."

"Tell him I've joined a nunnery and taken a vow of silence. On Jupiter."

"I know about Jupiter," Anna said, pulling herself from a slouch that mirrored Libby's. "It's the biggest planet in the solar system."

I gave her a glowing smile. Mrs. Craig's unit on space was paying off.

"But it's pretty far away," Anna continued, "so you'd have a hard time getting there and back in time for dinner."

Libby laughed, Anna looked pleased, and I was left

wondering whether my daughter had missed some important part of the lesson or was on her way to developing a sophisticated sense of humor.

There were only two calls I planned on returning. I tried Andy first.

"Congratulations," I told him.

"You sound surprised. Didn't think I'd get the job, did you?"

"I've told you for years, you've got a tremendous amount going for you."

He gave a half laugh. "But I lack focus, follow through, and ambition, right?"

I hadn't called to fight. "We have different styles is all."

This time his laugh was real, and good-natured. "That we do, Kate. That we do."

"I wanted to ask you something. The other day you implied that Mona had some kind of leverage she used to force Gary's hand in the divorce settlement."

"That's the rumor."

"Do you have any idea what it was?"

"Nope, and I don't particularly care either. Any time you get into development and politics there are a lot of gray areas. It's best not to poke too deep."

"You think it was something to do with his business then?"

"There we go again, Kate, different styles. I don't know what was going on with the Sterlings' divorce, and I'm not interested in knowing."

I understood Andy well enough to realize I wasn't going to get anywhere by pushing the issue. We talked a bit about his new job and about Anna, then I hung up and returned Sharon's call.

"I take it you saw the paper," she said.

"Unfortunately, so has everyone in town."

"Good thing your friend's away."

"Michael? He's the one who called me about it first. Seems the captain faxed him a copy."

"Uh-oh."

"I think that does a fair job of summing it up."

Sharon groaned. "Oh dear, and I was the one who got you into this in the first place." She paused for a moment of penitence. "Still, romantic interests aside, it was an interesting article."

"It was totally misleading."

"Not totally. And it might help us."

"How?"

"You know, stir things up a bit. We certainly haven't found anything going about it the way we are."

"Michael said the same thing, only he thinks what we'll stir up is trouble."

"Trouble for him, you mean."

"Believe it or not, he seemed less worried about himself than danger to us."

"Well," she snipped, "if the police were doing their job, this wouldn't be an issue."

There was no way I could leave it at that. "I think Michael's keeping an open mind," I said, carefully sidestepping any mention of the unofficial investigating he'd done.

Sharon laughed. "Sorry, I didn't mean to insult your boyfriend. The real reason I called was to see if you were free this afternoon. I thought we might take the kids somewhere. George is in New York and Kyle is driving me crazy."

I looked out the window at the heavy gray sky and the

trees whipping about frantically in the wind. "Doesn't look very hospitable out there."

"It's downright dreary, and so is my mood. That's why I want to get out. Libby can come too, if she's interested."

We tossed ideas around and finally settled on the Hall of Science, largely because it's an easy drive and requires nothing in the way of advance planning. We thought we'd head out later in the day and maybe go out for dinner as well.

Libby looked at me like I had rocks in my head when I suggested she might like to come along.

"Let me know if you change your mind," I told her. "We won't be leaving for a couple of hours."

She was busy stretching her mouth in an odd way I finally determined was some sort of beauty exercise, and only nodded in response. Anna and I left to do errands, stopping off first at the library. I settled her in the children's corner, then spent nearly an hour with the computerized newspaper index and rolls of microfiche looking for mention of scandal in connection with Sterling Development.

There'd been protests by neighborhood groups and the slow-growth coalition; there'd been a challenge to the EIR, and heated debate about the rezoning of a tract of farm land; there was even some discussion having to do with financing and restructured debt, but nothing I found hinted at corruption.

Anna was getting impatient and I'd run out of ideas so we moved onto Payless for construction paper, foil leaf, star stickers and the fluorescent markers Anna had been eyeing for some time. I didn't see the need for fluorescent color in a space poster, but Anna insisted. And although I was pretty sure I saw the ploy for what it was, I didn't want to dampen her enthusiasm for learning either.

We picked up toothpaste and shampoo first, then headed to the aisle of art supplies. Claire was at the other end, frowning into the construction paper.

"Great minds and all that," I said, falling into place next to her.

She jumped and stifled a little yelp. "Goodness, Kate. I didn't hear you sneak up on me."

"I didn't sneak up, Claire, I wandered up, which is something people tend to do in stores. It's just that you've got your head in the stars, so to speak."

She either didn't get it or didn't appreciate my attempt at humor, because she continued frowning. "These projects are a pain in the you-know-what. Does Mrs. Craig think parents have an infinite amount of time and money to spend on this kind of stuff? At least you're artistic. For the rest of us, it's just one more unnecessary chore."

"I don't think it needs to be elaborate."

"It won't be," she grumbled. "I try to be a good mother, really I do. But it's not easy."

I murmured sympathy.

Anna, who'd been tugging impatiently on my sleeve, stopped suddenly. "What happened to your hair?" she shrieked, peering at a nearby child.

I had to look twice, and even then I'm not sure I would have recognized Jodi if Anna hadn't. The loose, bouncing copper curls were gone, as was most of her hair. It was cut short, so that it hugged her head in a tight cap. It seemed darker too, and not nearly so red.

Claire answered before Jodi had a chance. "We cut it," she announced. "Such a bother getting all those snarls out each morning. This will be so much easier, won't it?"

Jodi nodded, though not with a great deal of enthusiasm.

Anna, who fought me each morning while I fought her snarls, stepped away, as though short hair might be catching. It was clearly a condition she wanted to avoid at all costs. "You look like a boy," Anna announced.

"She does not," I countered. "It's very chic, Jodi. You look like a model." Or more accurately, I told myself, like a mannequin, since I was sure a model would have to smile once in a while.

"It's a little short right now," Claire said encouragingly. "But it will grow out before you know it. And it does look nice, doesn't it?" She patted Jodi on the head, then picked up a package of multi-colored foils. "How in the heck are we supposed to make a planet? And look at these prices. This whole project is nothing but a bother."

Claire can work herself into a funk faster than anyone I know. It annoys me and, at the same time, makes me feel sorry for her. "I've got an idea. Why doesn't Jodi come to our house this afternoon? Anna's got more of this stuff than she can use, and I'd be happy to help both girls."

Anna glared at me.

"That's awfully kind of you," Claire sputtered.

Anna bumped against my arm in case I'd missed the frosty glare.

"But I'm afraid we've got a full schedule," Claire said. "Thank you for offering though."

Anna relaxed and started gathering her purchases. Now that the threat of Jodi's company no longer loomed, she was amenable to a friendly overture or two. She dragged Jodi off to examine the shiny stickers which she wanted to use for stars.

Once they were beyond hearing, Claire turned to me

and whispered, "That was quite a piece in the paper. The idea of murder had never even crossed my mind, and now that's all I can think about." Her face seemed more pinched than usual, but her voice had none of its customary hesitancy. "In Walnut Hills too. I didn't think things like that happened here."

"They don't often, though this is by no means the first. Why just last spring—"

Her hand flew to her mouth as recognition dawned. "I remember hearing about it. You were involved in that one too, weren't you?"

She made it sound as though I'd committed the crime myself.

"I wasn't really involved, I just—"

She drew in a quick breath of air, no doubt thankful she hadn't been sucked into letting Jodi spend the afternoon in my company. "This wasn't at all what I expected when we moved to Walnut Hills."

"It's really not like that—"

But Claire had already grabbed Jodi's hand, storming off at a brisk pace in an effort to elude the epidemic of local crime.

"I'm *not* getting my hair cut," Anna said after they'd left.

"Nobody said you had to."

She looked at me sternly. "I just want to make sure you don't get any ideas."

When we got home, Brandon's motorcycle was blocking the driveway. As I headed up the path, I heard voices coming from inside the house.

"Did you?" Libby's tone was harsh.

"Hey, Lib, it's over. What's the big deal?"

"It matters to me is what."

"*It matters to me*," Brandon mocked. "Jesus you act more like your old lady every day."

"Maybe it's you that's the problem, ever think about that?"

"Kiss my ass. I got better things to do than hang around and be insulted by some prissy fifteen-year-old. When I'm rich and famous don't even think of coming around, sniveling about how sorry you are."

"You—rich and famous?"

He laughed, a mirthless sort of bark. "Right, and sooner than you think."

Anna and I were nearing the front door as Brandon stormed passed. We didn't even rate a grunt by way of greeting.

"I take it you and Brandon haven't managed to patch things up," I said to Libby.

"Brilliant," she muttered, and stormed passed in the opposite direction toward her room.

18

Lawrence Hall of Science, set high in the Berkeley hills, offers a panoramic view of the bay and the San Francisco skyline beyond. Even on a cold, wet, ugly day like today, the vista is impressive. It is not, however, what draws the teeming crowds to the site.

Run by the university and designed by some of the top minds in science, Lawrence Hall is billed as providing an opportunity for hands-on-learning about science. Although it more than lives up to its promise, I sometimes think the real draw, at least on dreary winter days, is not the pursuit of scientific knowledge but the open expanse of indoor space where children can run free. I know from experience Anna isn't the only one to studiously avoid any exhibit which doesn't do a good job of disguising itself as a video game.

Because rainy days attract a particularly large crowd, both the main and auxiliary lots were full. As a result, we were forced to park a fair distance up the road, which is narrow and twisty and not made for walking. We went single file, the children between us and firmly in our grip. Once inside, they immediately broke free.

"One room at a time," Sharon cautioned. "You come get us before moving into another area. We'll be over there." She pointed to a bench near an Early Artifacts display, which offered nothing in the way of moving pieces or gimmicks, and was thus largely ignored.

When we were settled, Sharon reached into her purse and pulled out the sheaf of papers I recognized as her murder compendium. She spread them flat against her lap, smoothing the crease with her hand. "Now that the memorial service is over, we can concentrate on our investigation."

I ignored the papers. "It was a nice service," I said.

Sharon was quiet a moment. "Yes, it was."

I gazed out the glass doors to the open patio where the rain pounded against the pavement in heavy sheets. We'd made it inside just in time. "What have you decided about Mona's ashes?" I asked.

"I haven't."

"Don't you have to—"

She cut me off. "Please, Kate. I've got enough to worry about already." Without looking at me, she shuffled her papers. "Now, did you get a chance to stop by Mona's office?"

I told her about Ike and Eve Fisher, and the fact that they were on a cruise when Mona was killed.

"He could have set it up," Sharon said. "You know, hired a hit man or something."

"You're forgetting our first assumption, that Mona knew her killer. That it was someone she not only let through the door, but may well have had a drink with as well."

"The guy could have arranged it so they would meet somehow. Maybe he picked her up at a bar, all friendly like, then took her home and killed her."

"Pretty fancy hit-man to be working for a guy like Ike Fisher."

"It's possible," Sharon insisted.

I looked at her through half-open eyes. "Possible, but not likely."

She frowned, tapped her pen against her chin, then drew a line through something on her list. "I called the Timbercreek Lodge," she said. "The guy acted like I was asking for national defense secrets. Wouldn't tell me a thing."

"What did you expect?"

"About what I got, but I figured it was worth a try. I'd certainly like to know more about this mystery man of hers."

"Ditto."

Sharon examined her chart again. "Another thing that bothers me is Alice. Nobody's been able to locate her. What if she's dead as well? Two sisters killed within a short period of time, that's got to mean something."

"Bad karma is a family trait?"

Sharon shot me a withering glance. "I was thinking more along the lines of a family secret. Something that both women knew and the killer wanted kept quiet."

"It would have to be a pretty powerful secret."

"How about incest?"

"I thought her father was dead. Her mother too for that matter." If we were going to get kinky, we might as well go for gold.

"Could have been an uncle or a cousin."

"Did she ever mention anyone like that?"

"That's the point, Kate. It was a secret."

"But why wait until now to kill her? I mean, she's had a lot of years to talk about it."

Sharon rolled the pen between her fingers. "You've read those accounts. Women who've repressed what happened to them as children, then years later they suddenly remember."

It made sense up to a point. "Somehow, though, I can't imagine Mona repressing much of anything."

Anna buzzed over to grab our hands and yank us into the next room. The one available bench had been taken over by a group of young girls who were using it as a horse, so Sharon and I stood off in the corner, next to a wall-high chart of periodic elements. At a console in front, children who wouldn't know helium from hay took great delight in pushing buttons and lighting up the squares. I was willing to bet most of them thought they were playing Jeopardy.

"The way I see it," Sharon continued, picking up where we'd left off, "Mona doesn't suspect a thing. She invites this guy in, they have a drink or two, he slips something into her glass and that's that."

"Wouldn't he have washed the dishes afterwards? I mean, why leave two glasses in the kitchen and make it obvious she wasn't alone. That doesn't make sense."

Sharon made a face. "Have you ever known a man to wash a dish he didn't have to?"

Could someone, even a male, really be that stupid? Probably. Especially if that someone was nervous. "I guess that might explain the scotch too. If that's what the killer was drinking it would be kind of second nature for him to set it up the way he did."

"You're right," Sharon said excitedly. "We may be on to something." She checked her list. "This is what we've got so far. Killer known to Mona, male, drinks Glenfiddich, smokes."

"And doesn't make a habit of washing dishes." It didn't sound as though we'd narrowed the field much. "Does Gary smoke?" I asked.

She nodded. "Though he tries to give it up at least once every six months." She scribbled something else, then looked at me with a sigh. "He may well drink scotch too, but we've been over this. Mona wouldn't have let him in her house, much less fixed him a drink."

"And besides," I added pointedly, "he's George's buddy."

"You don't really think he's capable of murder do you?"

"I don't know. I think we ought to at least consider the possibility."

Just then Anna and Kyle appeared and announced that they were hungry. We fought our way through the crowd, down to the cafeteria. I held a seat while Sharon got soft drinks and cookies.

"You know," I said while the kids blew straw wrappers at one another, "there's the three thousand dollars to think about as well. I hate to think ill of a friend, but we have to consider the possibility that Mona wasn't squeaky clean herself. Most people simply do not have that amount of money in cash. Not unless they're involved in something unsavory."

"Three thousand was not a lot of money to Mona."

"Sharon, three thousand dollars *cash* is a lot of money to anyone."

She sighed heavily.

In truth, I too had trouble imagining Mona involved in anything shadier than jay-walking. She had a strong, almost self-righteous sense of morality. Still, people sometimes find themselves backed into situations that aren't of their choosing. "I think you should at least make note of the possibility on that chart of yours," I said.

"Mona was my friend. We'd known each other since college."

"And if she got herself in trouble of some kind, would that make her any less of a friend?"

Sharon's eyes met mine briefly, then she looked past me. "No," she said, barely audible. "I guess not." But she made no effort to retrieve the paper from her purse.

We stared out the window in a gloomy silence. The sky was dark, the clouds low and thick. The rain was coming in torrents, as though someone had opened a large spigot in the sky.

"Do we brave the elements," I asked finally, "or wait for it to let up?"

Sharon looked at her watch. "They'll be closing soon. And it doesn't look like the storm's about to blow over."

When the kids had finished their snack, we wound our way up the narrow road to the car. It was rough going because the shoulder was muddy and we had to stay on the pavement. I was worried that oncoming cars would have difficulty seeing us in the dusk and heavy rain.

"Whose idea was this anyway?" Sharon mumbled.

"Yours," I told her.

"I was afraid of that."

Finally, drenched and spattered with mud, we made it to the car.

"Look at that," Sharon said in disgust. "You've got a flat."

I looked, and then looked again.

What I had was four flats. And an uneasy, sick feeling in the pit of my stomach.

19

My misgivings were confirmed half an hour later by the man from the auto club.

"Looks like they was slashed," he said, removing a fat, slimy cigar from his mouth. "No-account vandals are getting the upper hand, if you want my opinion. We ought to lock 'em all up and throw away the key." He turned off the flashlight he'd used to check the damage, then stuck the cigar back into his mouth. "Can't do nothing at this point but tow the car. Don't imagine you'll find a place to fix 'em at this hour though. You called the police yet?"

I shook my head, pulling back to avoid a cloud of foul-smelling smoke.

"Better make a report, for insurance purposes. I'll put in a call for you. We'll give 'em fifteen minutes, then I got to take the car or leave. Sometimes the cops come out on these things, sometimes not. Depends."

He tramped off to his truck and I joined Sharon and the kids in the car. All of us were wet, but I was soaked clear through, and shivering. I turned the ignition and threw the heater on full blast.

"I'm bored," Anna complained.

"I have to go to the bathroom," Kyle said.

"I can't believe this," Sharon muttered, "I really can't."

A police car pulled up less than ten minutes later. Either it was a slow day for crime or the guy had been close by when the call came in. In either case, I was grateful. The man was thickset, with a jowly face and almost no neck. He took my name and license number, looked at his watch and wrote down the time. He didn't even peek at the tires.

"Aren't you going to dust for fingerprints?" I asked, when it became evident he considered his job complete.

"This isn't the movies, lady."

"But somebody did this intentionally. It's not like I ran over a set of steak knives, you know."

"Hey, I'm sorry about your car and all, but there's no chance we're going to find these goons. Stuff like this happens."

Sharon leaned over so she could speak through the open window. "This isn't simple vandalism," she said. "Kate's name was in the newspaper, in connection with a murder."

The man didn't even blink.

"I don't mean as a suspect," Sharon hastened to add. "But she's investigating. This thing with the tires could be related. You know, the killer trying to scare her off."

The man leaned closer to peer at Sharon. Water dripped from his hat onto my lap. "We get this kind of vandalism on a daily basis, ma'am. We got no shortage of murders either, and I can't recall a case where they were connected."

"He could have at least tried," Sharon grumbled after he'd left.

"Yeah," Anna and Kyle muttered in unison. I was sure they hadn't the foggiest notion what they were agreeing with since they'd been too busy accusing each other of hogging the heater vent to have listened to our conversation.

Sharon folded her arms across her chest. "Stuff like that is what gives cops a bad name."

All things considered, I was just as happy the guy hadn't put on a big production. The chances of anything turning up were pretty slim, and we'd have been stuck there in the middle of a cold, wet nowhere for hours.

As it was, we didn't get home until well past dark.

The man from the auto club gave us a ride downtown where we caught BART back to Walnut Hills. We took a taxi from the station to Sharon's, and then Sharon gave me a ride to Mona's so I could pick up her car to use until mine was back in service. Although a Jag XJ12 is a bit pretentious for my tastes, I thought I'd probably be able to adjust.

Sharon wanted me to spend the night at her house, but what I needed more than company was a hot bath and the comfort of my own bed. I didn't want to uproot Libby again either. Besides, I found simple, random vandalism the most logical explanation for what had happened. Hadn't the policeman said he took similar reports daily?

That line of thinking held me until I got into bed, where it crumbled abruptly in the liquid facelessness of night. What started as a small spark of worry, grew rapidly to full-fledged panic, and I didn't fall asleep until the sky began to grow light the next morning.

The telephone woke me. I reached for it on the third

ring, but Libby had already picked it up. When I recognized Gary's voice, I placed the phone noiselessly back in its cradle. Why court trouble?

By the time I dragged myself into the kitchen some time later, Anna and Libby had finished eating. Libby had made pancakes, although from the looks of the kitchen I had to assume it was something she didn't do regularly. She was reading the Sunday comics, oblivious to the mess around her, while Anna licked the last of the syrup from her plate and Max watched with practiced patience.

Libby looked up from the paper long enough to announce that she'd be spending the afternoon with Gary. "It's his Sunday," she explained, sounding bitter and resigned all at once.

The sharp-edged fear of the night before had dulled into a sort of murky dread. I wondered briefly what Gary had been doing late yesterday afternoon. In all honesty though, I had trouble imagining him crouched in the rain and mud, clutching a knife.

Libby left a little before lunch, subdued and unenthusiastic but less reluctant than I would have expected. The two-Sundays-a-month routine was apparently so well ingrained she didn't question it. The fact that Gary had promised it would be just the two of them, without Bambi, was probably something of a selling point as well.

Though the sky was still heavy and gray, and the ground damp, the rain had finally let up. I took Anna on her bicycle, and Max on his leash, and headed for the park. Anna rode while Max and I jogged along beside. It wasn't the most efficient form of exercise, especially because Anna stopped peddling every time she started to talk, and Max preferred sniffing to trotting, but it was enough to partially clear my mind and raise my heart-beat. I was still breathing hard by the time we reached home.

Bambi was coming down the front steps as we headed up.

"Oh, you're back," she said. Her words were accompa-nied by a breathless and indecipherable laugh. "I just stopped by with a little something for Libby."

I yanked at Max, who seemed determined to wipe his muddy fur on Bambi's white wool slacks. "She's not here right now," I said.

Bambi laughed again. "I know. I thought it might be better if I dropped this off when she wasn't around. It's not much really, just a couple of tapes. Groups she likes."

She handed me a small package, then shifted her weight to her other foot and began twisting her engage-ment ring.

Max was pulling at his leash and Bambi showed no sign of moving on. "Would you like to come in?" I asked fi-nally.

"Well, maybe. Just for a minute."

I wiped Max's feet with an old towel I keep by the door for that purpose, then shut him in the kitchen. When I came back, Bambi was sitting on the couch, hands folded primly in her lap. Her eyes, however, were surveying the room as though she thought there might be a Rembrandt hidden amidst the clutter.

"Would you like some coffee?" I asked.

"No thanks. I just wanted to . . . you know, do some-thing for Libby. I thought maybe it might help us be . . . like, friends." Bambi had unnaturally long lashes and a small, Kewpie doll mouth that was set in an habitual pout.

She turned toward me, jutting her bottom lip out even farther. "Libby doesn't like me much I think."

"Under the circumstances that's not too surprising."

She nodded. "I know. I'm sure Mona never said one nice thing about me in her entire life."

I cleared my throat. "That's not quite what I meant."

"But I never phoned her on Friday," Bambi continued, oblivious to my attempt to set the record straight. "Really. I don't know where Libby got the idea I did."

I shrugged. "It's not important. There was apparently something about the conversation that made Libby think it was you."

Bambi's flawless white skin grew paler. "Mona mentioned my name?"

"No, it was more an impression Libby got."

"Well, it wasn't me." Bambi drew in a breath, swallowed, bit her lower lip. "Libby certainly didn't mince words, did she? I've never been so humiliated in my life."

The woman reminded me of the way Anna gets when she's in one of her snippity moods. "No one actually blames you for Mona's death," I said. "Libby was upset. It was her mother's memorial service after all. She needed to lash out at someone and you were the easiest target. In fact, if anything, I think she blames herself for her mother's suicide."

"Of course, it may not have been suicide at all." Bambi's fingers tapped silently against her purse. "The paper said you had proof that it was murder."

Damn Susie anyway. Damn me and my big mouth. "Not proof. There were just a few considerations the police may have overlooked."

Bambi sat back, folded her hands and studied them. "I

see." She ran her tongue over her bottom lip. "What kind of considerations?"

"Little stuff. The article is completely misleading."

"I see," she said again. A long pause. "There's nothing concrete, then?"

"Right."

"Nothing which might imply a motive?"

"No, nothing like that."

"And no list of suspects?"

"No list of suspects."

Bambi's eyes drifted from her hands to a spot over my shoulder. She hugged herself and gave a little laugh. "I guess it's really no concern of mine anyway. It's just that I hate to see Gary upset. And then with the wedding so close . . . well, all this talk about murder is bound to put a damper on things." She stood. "I guess I'd better be going."

"I'll make sure Libby gets the package."

Bambi looked at me blankly for a moment, then nodded. "Oh that, yes. Thank you."

I headed out to the street with her to pick up the mail. As we walked down the driveway, she eyed the Jag. "That's Mona's car, isn't it?"

"Mine was . . ." I started to explain, then thought to wonder where Bambi had been late yesterday afternoon. It was even harder to picture her crawling around in the wet and muck than Gary, but anything is possible. "Mine's in the shop," I said.

Bambi nodded, her eyes still on the Jag. "She bought that car right after the divorce, you know. Raked Gary over the coals, then couldn't wait to dangle her riches in front of his eyes." The doll-like mouth grew tight. "Mona ended up with a lot more than she deserved."

"He went along with everything though. It was an out-of-court settlement, so he must have found it acceptable on some level."

Bambi turned and looked at me, then she shrugged. "Yeah. It would have cost a bundle to fight it out anyway."

Later that afternoon, Michael showed up, unannounced, at my door.

"You back already?" I asked, reluctantly extracting myself from a kiss that showed no sign of coming to an end.

"I caught an early flight out."

"Good." I pulled him into the house. "Just let me put these paints away and wash up." The picture I'd envisioned was not the one taking shape on canvas anyway.

"I can't stay. I just stopped by on my way to the station."

"So you didn't come back early in order to rush into my arms?"

He grinned. "I came here first, didn't I?"

"Yeah, but you're planning on rushing off again." I was teasing him but I also felt genuine disappointment, which I tried my best to disguise. "Maybe you can come back later." I gave him a sly smile. "For dessert."

"God, Kate, I love it when you beg."

I threw my paint rag at him and went to wash out my brushes. Michael followed. He leaned against the wall and tickled Max behind the ears.

"How come you have to go into work on Sunday?" I asked.

"I have an appointment with the captain."

I turned around, spraying water across the counter. "Oh, no. He's angry about the story, after all."

Michael shook his head. "No. I mean he was, at first. But it turns out you may have been right."

"About what?"

"All of it. We did a routine dusting for prints after the burglary. Got a couple of good partials and a clean thumb print from the glass by the door. We don't have a match yet, but if we ever nail down a suspect we'll be able to run a comparison."

"Great." Though the news hardly seemed enough to make the captain forget the biting words Susie had so publicly put in my mouth.

"I had the guys take extra prints too, if you'll remember. And what's really interesting is that the bottle of scotch and glass were completely clean."

I shrugged. "I'd hardly expect the burglar to take time out for a drink."

"That's not what I meant. Most objects are covered with smudged prints. Very often we can't get a clear one, but there are signs the thing's been handled. The bottle and glass had nothing. They'd been wiped clean. And short of evidence pointing to a compulsive, overly fastidious cleaning lady, that usually means someone is trying to eliminate evidence. I'm not talking about the burglar either."

My breath caught in my throat. "You really think Mona was murdered?"

"Looks like a distinct possibility. The lack of prints isn't conclusive, but I've got the go-ahead to open an investigation. I'm hoping to prod the coroner's office along too."

Until now Mona's murder had seemed somewhat abstract. I'd tossed ideas around with Sharon, made a mental list of suspects even, but somewhere in back of my mind the notion of murder had seemed pretty far-fetched. Now, it hit me straight on, with the impact of an icy ocean wave. And then, before I had a chance to catch my breath, another thought rolled over me. If Mona had actually been murdered, and if my tires had not been an act of simple vandalism, then odds were, Mona's killer had his eye on me. It was not a comforting thought.

"What's the matter?" Michael asked, catching the look on my face. "I thought you'd be pleased."

I leaned against the counter and started to tell him about my car. I hadn't even got as far as the parking lots being full when I burst into tears.

$$20$$

Michael did finally make it back to my place that night, but quite late. He rolled into bed, draped an arm across my middle, dug his chin into my back and fell asleep. Still, it was nice. I lay awake awhile, drifting in the pleasant, padded warmth of half-sleep, my mind freed for the moment of worry about tire slashers and killers.

Morning came much too soon and passed in a flurry of disjointed mumbles and grumbles. Most mornings when Michael stays over, we share a quiet, early-morning cup of coffee before he leaves for work. This morning, however, Libby was already up and firmly entrenched at the kitchen table. I made the necessary introductions, which accounted for a good part of the mumbling on both parts. Michael decided to skip the coffee, grabbed a Pop Tart instead, gave me a perfunctory kiss on the cheek and a not so perfunctory warning about being careful, then left.

"That your boyfriend?" Libby asked, as the door shut.

I nodded. It was as good a description as any.

"He's cute."

I laughed. Leave it to a teen-ager to cut to the heart of the matter. "Yeah, I think so too."

"Is he in trouble?"

"Trouble?"

"Like someone's after him or something. You know, trouble."

I shook my head. I had no idea what she was talking about.

"I thought maybe that's why he was carrying a gun."

"Ah, that." She had a good eye, but her logic was scary. I shuddered to think that this was the morality we were passing onto our children. "He's a cop," I explained.

"A cop?" She looked at me as though my forehead had sprung a leak. "Doesn't it kind of choke you up having him around?"

Did it ever. "Sometimes," I told her, smiling to myself, "but not in the way you mean."

She shook her head and went back to the newspaper. "Weird."

I made myself coffee and toast, then joined her. "How did it go with your dad yesterday?"

"Okay," she said, giving a half-hearted shrug. "We visited some friends of his, then went to the Warriors game. As if I give a damn about his friends or basketball. The tickets were expensive though. He made sure he told me that about a hundred times."

I sipped my coffee. "You don't like him much, do you?"

"It's mutual. He doesn't like me much either."

"What makes you—"

Libby cut me off. "It's too early in the morning for a lecture, okay? And you'd be wrong anyway." She dumped her dishes in the sink, caught the look I gave her, reconsidered, and put them in the dishwasher instead. "I gotta run. Make-up chem lab at seven sharp. And remember, if Brandon calls tell him I said to get lost."

"I know it's none of my business, but it might help if you two talked things out. With all that you're going through, this is a lousy time to cut yourself off from a friend."

"Some friend!" Her voice dripped with loathing. "He cheated on me, lied to me, treated me like dirt, and then he expects me to kiss his feet."

"Maybe if you—"

"My mom always said he took things. Money, drugs, beer. Every time something was missing, she'd accuse Brandon. I thought she was making it up because she didn't like me hanging around with him."

"Well, I'm sure she—"

"She didn't know the half of it! All those times I defended him too, and now he has the nerve to laugh about it. He's a slimy, two-timing lowlife." She picked up her backpack and headed for the door. "If I never see him again, it will be too soon."

I wasn't about to twist her arm. In fact, telling Brandon to get lost might be the highlight of my day. "I'll give him the message," I called after her.

I was on my way to Sharon's for our rescheduled auction meeting when the loose end of a thought tickled my mind. I turned around and headed for the high school instead.

"Can you tell me where I'd find Libby Sterling?" I asked the office attendant.

She was a middle-aged woman with a pinched face and

heavily wrinkled skin that spoke of too many hours in the sun. She didn't bother to look up from the stack of pink squares she was busily sorting into smaller stacks. "Libby's in class."

"What I meant is, which class?"

The woman raised her eyes. "That's not information we give out. You from the press too?"

"Too?"

"There was a man here the other day looking for Libby, going to do a story about being the child of a suicide victim, if you can imagine. Poor girl has enough to worry about without feeling like a zoo animal."

"I'm not from the press, I'm a friend." I introduced myself and explained that Libby was staying with me.

"Then you ought to be able to talk to her this afternoon."

"She forgot her lunch," I said, grabbing at the first thought to come to mind. Anna forgot hers at least once a week.

The woman gave my empty hands a hard look.

"Money," I amended. "Lunch money."

"You want to put it in an envelope? I'll see that she gets it."

"Actually I need to talk with her too. Just a quick word about her afternoon plans."

"You couldn't have asked her this morning?"

"No. I mean, I could have but I didn't. Please, it won't take but a minute."

The woman must have decided I was too much of an airhead to be someone worth worrying about. She looked up Libby's schedule. "Room 310," she said. "The bell rings in about five minutes. You can catch her on her way out. I don't advise interrupting class, the teacher is a bear.''

"Thanks." I turned to leave, then turned back. "Did Libby ever talk to that newsman?''

"She was absent the day he came, but we wouldn't have allowed it anyway.'' The woman twisted a rubberband from her wrist, securing a stack of pink cards. "I said I'd have Libby get in touch with him if she was interested, but he didn't want to leave his name. Funny guy, not my image of a journalist.''

I headed down the south hallway, following the numbers in sequence from 300 to 308, where they stopped abruptly. A young man in a varsity jacket pointed me in the other direction, down the north corridor, where sure enough, 309 picked up right on the other side of the library, which was designated as Room 4. The architect was either dyslexic or a product of this new math I'd been hearing so much about. I got to room 310 just as the bell was ringing. Libby was the first one out the door.

"What's wrong?'' she asked, without stopping.

"Nothing. I just wanted to ask you something.'' We were weaving our way through a horde of students coming from the opposite direction so conversation was difficult. It apparently hadn't occurred to them that the rules of the road could also apply to foot traffic. "This morning you mentioned that Brandon took things from your mother, like beer and drugs.''

She nodded.

"What kind of drugs were you talking about?''

Libby spun her head in my direction. "Hey, not those kind. Just pain killers, tranquilizers, that sort of thing.''

"Sleeping pills?''

"Yeah, that too. My mother should have bought stock

in the local pharmacy. She gave them enough business."

The guy to my left swung his arm unexpectedly and I ducked. The football he was trying to catch bounced at my feet. I gave him a dirty look, which apparently made no dent at all since he retrieved the ball and tossed it back the length of the crowded corridor.

I did a little two step to catch up with Libby. "At the memorial service you mentioned your mom and Brandon had a big fight a couple of days before she died. Do you remember what it was about?"

"The usual stuff."

"Did she accuse him of taking her pills?"

"Among other things. She found a bottle that was practically empty. Claimed she'd just had the prescription filled. She went totally ballistic."

I whistled softly under my breath. "Brandon cleaned out practically the whole bottle?"

"The guy's a toad," Libby said, slowing her stride to address me directly, "but that's no reason to make a federal case of it. Shit like that happens all the time. It's not worth getting him in trouble over."

"It's not that. Just an idea I had. I'll tell you later."

The timing fit. So did the rest of it. The prescription for sleeping pills had been filled on Monday. A few days later Mona had found the bottle nearly empty. Which meant there couldn't have been enough left to kill her on Saturday.

I found a pay phone in front of the school, called Michael and told him what I'd learned.

"That's proof she didn't kill herself," I said.

"Not proof exactly, but interesting. If it's true." Michael took down Brandon's name. "I'll have someone talk to him today."

"Can you keep Libby's name out of it?"

"We'll try." He paused for a moment, then asked, "You have time for lunch or something?"

"What do you mean 'or something?' " In the early days of our relationship, we'd more often than not used lunch as an excuse to satisfy appetites of a different nature.

Michael laughed. "I meant salad, sandwich, taco, maybe just a cup of coffee. Unfortunately, that's all I have time for."

"Look what's happening to us," I sighed, heavy with the melodrama. "The spark is gone already."

"Speak for yourself, lady. My spark gets any hotter, I'll be the first documented case of spontaneous human combustion."

I laughed and checked my watch. I needed to swing by a couple galleries in my search for Dr. Caulder, but if I skipped the rest of the auction meeting, which was now more than half over, I could manage that and still have time to meet Michael.

We settled on a coffee shop close to the station. It offers little in the way of inspired cuisine, but gets good marks for dependable, quick service. Then I spent the rest of the morning trekking through galleries searching for bland, emotionless art.

The restaurant was nearly full, but we found a recently vacated booth near the window. Because my waistline was still feeling the effects of brunch with Gary, I settled for a small fruit salad and a glass of water. Michael, who can eat like an eighteen-year-old quarterback and never gain an ounce, had a bacon cheeseburger, fries, and a bowl of minestrone. We'd learned from experience not to order the coffee so he had a Coke instead.

"Did you reach Brandon?" I asked, dipping my spoon into Michael's soup. It was heavy on the fat and salt, but quite tasty.

"Turns out there's no hurry. The coroner's report came in right after you called. Lab analysis shows a fairly high concentration of alcohol in her blood, but no evidence of barbituates. No trace of any medicines in her stomach at all."

He paused to watch me dip into his soup a second time. "What did show up," he said after a moment, "was a high concentration of morphine."

"Morphine?"

He nodded. "My best guess at this point is that Mona Sterling died of an intravenous overdose."

I don't know exactly what I had been expecting, since she obviously hadn't died of a gunshot or a stab wound, but the news was still something of a surprise. "An accidental overdose?"

Michael shook his head. "I don't think so. A self-administered IV injection is pretty tricky under any circumstances. In this case, the puncture mark is in her neck, which is probably why it wasn't obvious straight off. On the right side of her neck in fact. So unless she was left handed, extremely agile, and close to double jointed, it seems pretty unlikely."

He waited for a minute for my reaction. "She wasn't left handed," I told him.

"Besides, the business with the scotch bottle and pills doesn't make sense unless it was set up to mislead us. Make something look like a suicide that wasn't."

Frowning, I reached for another spoonful of soup. "You were the one who pointed out awhile back she wouldn't have let someone pour a bottle of pills down her throat. You think she'd be more receptive to a needle and syringe?''

''No, but an IV is something you can manage without a person's cooperation, swallowing isn't. Mona could have been tied up, knocked out, held down—any number of things.'' He saw me eying his soup again, and pushed the bowl across the table. ''Here, you can finish it if you want.''

''You sure?''

''That's why I order so much food when you're with me. I know I'll never get a chance to finish it myself.''

I gave him a dirty look, but I took the soup. ''So, who do you think did it?''

''You're the one with all the ideas.''

I doubled the dirty look.

''I'm serious, Kate. I was hoping you might be able to help me out here.''

''Well, I do have a few ideas.''

''I thought you might.'' His expression was serious, but his voice held a trace of amusement.

The waitress brought my salad, such as it was, and Michael's burger and fries. He offered me the first bite, which I declined.

''Let's start with the ex-husband,'' Michael said. ''You've met him?''

I nodded. ''We're practically old buddies by now. And I'd certainly put him high on my list of possible suspects. First off, he's got an obvious motive. Mona got an interest in his business as part of the divorce settlement. When she died, it reverted back to him. He doesn't have to pay out support anymore either.'' I paused for a bite of salad. ''Of course, he says he didn't do it.''

''He just happened to volunteer this?''

"I asked him."

Michael's eyes narrowed. "You *asked* him if he murdered his ex-wife?"

"More or less."

"And what, exactly, did he say?"

" 'In my dreams' were, I believe, the words he used. He doesn't try to hide the fact that he's bitter about the settlement. Andy says the rumor is that Mona had something on Gary, sort of a blackmail type thing, and that's why he went along with her settlement proposal. My guess is he pulled something shady with his taxes, or maybe with the permits for his new project."

Michael swallowed with that pained expression he gets whenever I mention Andy's name. "For a couple in the midst of a divorce, you two sure talk a lot."

"We talk," I said. "That doesn't mean we're not serious about the divorce." I reached for a french fry. "There's also the fiancée to consider. I'm not sure Bambi's smart enough to plan something like this, but she certainly resents the money Mona got. In fact, she strikes me as pretty hostile toward Mona, period, despite the fact that the two of them apparently got together for lunch awhile back. Plus, Bambi was curious about Susie's article. Wanted to know what evidence I had that the newspaper hadn't mentioned."

Michael took out a notebook and began jotting memos to himself between bites.

"Ike Fisher is another possibility, but you know about him already. He sounds like the unstable type and he *did* threaten her." I grabbed the catsup bottle and dumped a bit on the side of my plate. "Are you sure he's really on that cruise?"

"I haven't checked with the ship's captain, but that's where he's supposed to be."

"Of course he could have contracted it out in any case." I started to grab another fry when I saw Michael looking at me. "You want some canned pear and cottage cheese?" I asked.

He laughed. "I'll pass, but thanks all the same."

"You already know about Mona's sister, Alice. I don't know what her motive might be, unless she thought somehow she might inherit. Though, from what I understand she and Mona never got along, so why she'd think that, I don't know. It's odd that she seems to have disappeared just when her sister was killed."

Michael scratched some more in his notebook. "What about this Brandon character?"

I hadn't considered that possibility. Kind of an interesting twist if he'd set it up to look like suicide using a bottle of pills he'd emptied himself. "There was certainly no love lost between him and Mona," I said. "And I don't imagine he's won many good citizenship marks along the way either."

"Well, that's a start. What about men? She involved with anyone?"

I told him about Mendocino and the cufflinks. "But she never said a word to any of us, so I don't know for sure."

Michael asked a few more questions, wrote down the name of the bed and breakfast in Mendocino, then stared pensively into his notebook while doodling little stars across the top of the page.

"What do you think?" I asked.

"It's hard to say. You know the statistics. Spouses and lovers account for an awful lot of homicides." He rubbed his cheek. "The fact that she kept quiet about this guy might mean something."

"Such as?"

"He's someone important maybe, someone with a reputation to protect. Or maybe he was married. The love triangle offers all sorts of room for speculation."

"I don't think she'd get involved with a married man."

Michael's eyes drifted to mine and stayed there. "Sometimes," he said gruffly, "the heart leads us places we wouldn't ordinarily go."

"Meaning?"

"Meaning, in Mona's case, you can't rule anything out." He picked up the check. "Come on, I'll walk you to your car."

Michael wove his fingers through mine as we headed outside. He seemed unusually quiet.

"Are you thinking your heart has misled you?" I asked, with a tentativeness that surprised me.

Michael shook his head. "Sometimes," he said, watching me, "I think it's brought me to a deadend. But never that it's misled me."

21

The gray skies and high winds of the preceding week had passed, and spring was beginning to peek out from under the mantle of winter. It wouldn't last, I knew. It happened that way every year. Just when you were ready to dig out the sunscreen and the lawn chairs, another storm would whip through and convince you that the end of winter was nothing more than a figment of your imagination. All the same, before climbing into the car, I took a moment to savor the sweet scent of jasmine and the feather touch of air warmed by sunlight.

Too bad none of that warmth reached deep inside where I needed it most. Inside, where the images of the past week formed a cold reality of their own.

I'd forgotten about Mona's car phone earlier, but I used it now to call the auto shop. My Datsun, with its four new tires, was ready. There'd been a part of me secretly hoping the tires would be on back-order so I'd be forced to drive Mona's Jag a little longer. Scooting around town in a seventy-thousand-dollar set of wheels changes things in ways that are hard to explain to the uninitiated.

I called Sharon next.

"I got your message," she said. "Don't worry about the meeting, you didn't miss much." Only she didn't say it so much as croak it.

"What's the matter? You sound funny."

"I think I'm coming down with flu. It just sort of hit me all at once and it keeps getting worse."

"Have you taken anything?"

"Vitamin C, Motrin, cough syrup, a couple of decongestants, a flu medicine you mix with hot water, and some Chinese herb concoction my cleaning lady gave me."

"You took all that at once?"

"Not exactly." She turned away to cough. "But pretty much."

Sharon is one of those people who believes that suggested dosage is just a ballpark figure and that drugs are best mixed, something like spices. I've seen her going through her medicine cabinet pulling out a little of this and a little of that, just the way I make chili.

"It might make you feel better to know there's going to be an official investigation of Mona's death." I gave her a brief summary of the latest developments. "The cops will probably want to talk with you at some point."

"They already have." She coughed again. "This morning. Some young guy, looked more like a high school kid than a cop. A long, tall drink of water with a receding chin. He came by just as our meeting was winding down. Could barely conceal his excitement at getting four for the price of one, so to speak."

"Cops figure the more people they talk to, the more likely they are to come up with something."

"He didn't get much useful information from us, I'm afraid. Laurelle didn't really know Mona, of course, but Mary Nell just about talked the poor fellow's ear off. Recounted every conversation she'd had with Mona in the last month. She had plenty of potential suspects too, including that crazy guy who hangs out in front of the auto wash. According to Mary Nell, he got a bee in his bonnet that Mona was his first wife, reincarnated."

"Where did Mary Nell get that?"

"Who knows where she gets any of the stuff she comes up with? Anyway, she was going on and on, while Claire hardly opened her mouth. Seems to me she might have been able to give this cop something useful since she lived so close to Mona. But you know Claire, answered every question in monosyllables. Frowned the whole time, as if she thought murder might be contagious."

I remembered her hasty retreat after our chance meeting in Payless. "Claire suffers from chronic unhappiness," I told her. "I wish I could think of some way to break her out of it."

"Yeah, well, good luck."

A car pulled up behind me and tooted the horn, signalling that he was waiting for my parking spot. I motioned him on. The world of car phones was new enough to me that there was no way I was about to try talking on one and driving at the same time. "I don't suppose you feel up to giving me a ride to the shop so I can pick up my car."

"Sorry, I feel lousy. Why don't you just keep Mona's for another couple of days? I haven't even got around to placing an ad for it yet." Sharon's voice was hoarse and nasal. She sounded miserable.

"Can I do anything for you?" I asked.

She hesitated. "You sure you don't mind?" When I assured her I didn't, she rattled off a list of things she needed from the grocery.

"Just a minute," I said, grabbing a pen from my purse and a scrap of paper from the compartment under the dash. It was a customer receipt from the photo department at Safeway, but it was the only thing I could find. I scribbled Sharon's list on the backside, then promised to pick up Kyle from school. I made a mental note to pick up Mona's photos as well.

"If I'm not better by tomorrow," Sharon said, "you'll have to manage the ticket table at the auction without me. We set up a schedule of shifts at the meeting today, so you should have help. I feel terrible dumping it in your lap like this."

"I can manage," I told her. "Don't worry about anything except getting well."

The next day, Sharon was worse rather than better. I spent the morning transporting raffle items from the school, where most things had been dropped off, to the club, where the auction was to be held. Then I made another trip to the grocery, this time remembering to pick up Mona's photos, stopped by the pharmacy for some heavy duty cough syrup Sharon's doctor had prescribed, and then drove Kyle home from school. Since Sharon was having trouble even making it out of bed, I fixed him a snack as well.

While Kyle ate, I looked through Mona's photos. I'd hoped they might hold some clue to her death. (Wasn't that how it worked in the movies?) Then I'd be able to wow Michael with my cleverness. At the very least I was hoping for a photo from Mendocino, something that would help identify her mysterious lover. But the pictures were family snapshots, mostly of Libby, some of which included Brandon as well. There were several pictures of the interior of Mona's house, presumably the "before" pictures those home decorating magazines suggest you take, one of Sharon and George, which was flattering to neither of them, and a couple of Jodi sitting on Mona's porch swing.

I stuck them back into the envelope and went to check on Sharon. Ever mindful of those pesky airborne germs, I stood at the bedroom doorway while she croaked words of gratitude. I wasn't particularly looking forward to the auction, but I figured my evening was going to be a lot more pleasant than Sharon's.

The Walnut Hills Country Club is private and fairly exclusive, but enough parents belong that there's apparently never any trouble reserving the clubhouse for the school's annual auction. Good thing, since the event would hardly have drawn the crowd it did if we had to hold it in the school cafeteria.

I left the car with the parking attendant and headed inside. I'd arrived early to put things in order, but Mary Nell had beaten me there. She had the reception table already set up, complete with floral arrangement, name tags, raffle bin, even a plate of cocktail nuts she'd appropriated from the buffet.

"It's nice to have something to offer people when they first come in, don't you agree? Make them forget we're after their wallets."

Since people knew that's precisely why they were there, I thought it would take more than a bowl of nuts to make them forget. Of course, there was more. Lots more. Glancing across the room, I saw a long buffet table laid out with enough rolled and puffed and wedged edibles to persuade even the most tightfisted to loosen their purse strings. The bar was sure to help matters along too, despite having to shell out more of your own money to imbibe.

I took a seat next to Mary Nell and started to reach for a nut.

"Maybe you ought to pass for now," she said primly. "We don't want to be running over for refills in the middle of our shift."

"No, I guess not." Though it wasn't like we had to cross the Rubicon to get more nuts.

Couples started arriving almost immediately, some of them decked out to the nines in their fancy evening finery. I figured those were the people whose wallets we were really after, the ones who would bid on the Alaskan cruise and the weekend in Paris. I had my eye on the catered picnic for two and the one hour massage, both of which were enough of an extravagance for me that I'd have never considered them if the money hadn't gone to benefit the school.

Most people had purchased tickets ahead of time so we merely took their stubs for the raffle and directed them to the name tags. I recognized the kindergarten parents and a few others, but Mary Nell seemed to know just about everybody. Whenever there was a lull in arrivals, she'd lean over and do a quick rendition of who's who, a mundane inventory of name, occupation, and number of children.

Among the early arrivals were Susie Sullivan Lambert and her new husband, who she wore on her arm like a jeweled Cartier watch. "I understand my piece about Mona finally got the cops' attention," she said, smugly. "They're investigating her death as a homicide now."

I nodded, without bothering to explain that her story had nothing to do with it. Besides, I was still angry at her for twisting my words and making them public. I wasn't about to say anything more.

Mary Nell had no such compunctions, however. She gave Susie a complete account of her conversation with the police sergeant the previous morning at Sharon's. She hadn't quite finished when Laurelle and Paul arrived, and since Laurelle had been present herself, Mary Nell invited her comments as well. Laurelle, however, had her mind on the living rather than the dead. She ignored Mary Nell, waved to several friends across the room, then turned to hug the couple who'd come in behind her.

The woman, an overly made-up blond with poodle-dog curls, handed Mary Nell their tickets. "Isn't that Mona Sterling's car in the lot?" she asked.

Mary Nell nodded, then introduced me, explaining that I'd borrowed it temporarily. From there she launched into a meandering account of my association with Mona. The woman looked bored and Laurelle examined her nails.

When Mary Nell finished, Laurelle turned her attention, fleetingly, in our direction. "You two managing okay without me?" she asked. This was, I gathered, Laurelle's all out effort at doing her fair share. Without waiting for an answer, she grabbed Paul, who was looking at me rather oddly, and dragged him off.

Susie didn't seem much interested in hearing the details of the police inquiry either. But I figured that was because she was one of those people who doesn't like facts interfering with her thinking.

"Well," Mary Nell huffed, "Laurelle certainly seemed interested enough in Mona's death yesterday."

"Laurelle likes to be in the center of things," I said.

"Isn't that the truth."

After the initial rush of activity, people straggled in more slowly. Mary Nell took the opportunity to straighten the table top, smoothing the linen cover and realigning the name tags and pens. Since not one person had touched the nuts, I grabbed a handful when her head was turned.

"I've been thinking about poor Mona," she said, while I endeavored to unobtrusively chew a cashew. "I've been thinking about her for days, of course, but especially since talking to that policeman yesterday. He got me started wondering and, well . . ." There was a short pause. "I think Mona may have been in some kind of trouble."

"Trouble? What kind?"

"I don't know really. I'm not implying she'd do anything bad herself, of course, but . . . well, she might have, you know, witnessed a crime or overheard some incriminating remark. There was a movie on television a couple of months ago. This woman was married to a sculptor, a real sensitive, artistic type of guy. Well, it turns out that he was using some of his pieces to smuggle drugs. Now, the wife didn't know anything about it at first . . ."

I cut her short. "What else besides this movie makes you think Mona might have been in trouble?"

Mary Nell frowned. "For one thing, nothing else makes sense. It isn't like anyone stands to actually benefit from her death, except Libby I suppose, in the long run. But mostly it's what Raffi said."

Raffi, no last name, was *the* hair stylist among those residents of Walnut Hills who could afford to care about such things.

"I had an appointment this morning," Mary Nell said, "and we got to talking about Mona. Raffi mentioned that she'd dropped by a couple of days before she died, asking about his, uh, friend, Milt."

What Mary Nell meant, of course, was lover rather than friend, but since both Raffi and Milt were male, she couldn't bring herself to say the word. Her main point, however, was lost on me.

"Milt's an attorney," she explained, practically whispering the words under her breath.

I was still lost. "Stan Lundy was Mona's attorney."

She nodded. "But Milt is a *criminal* attorney."

"And you think Mona was inquiring because she needed his services?"

"That's the impression I got."

At first glance it seemed pretty far fetched. Then I thought of the three thousand dollars she'd withdrawn from the bank. And the hold she'd supposedly had over Gary. Maybe Mary Nell was right after all. "Have you told the police?"

"You think I should?"

"It's probably nothing, but yes, I think you should tell them."

Mary Nell's face grew dark. "Oh dear, I don't want to get Raffi in trouble, you know, for breach of a client's confidence."

I sighed. "I don't think the law recognizes hairdresser—client privilege."

She looked at me solemnly, then nodded. "You're probably right," she said, sounding anything but convinced.

At that moment, Claire arrived, chewing at one of her fingernails. "I know I'm late."

"No problem," Mary Nell said. "You want to get a bite to eat or something before you take over here?"

"I don't think so." Claire unbuttoned her coat. "Where's Sharon? She and I are supposed to share this shift."

"Sharon's sick," I told her. "I'll take her place."

Claire went back to gnawing at her fingers.

"Go look around," Mary Nell offered, turning to me, "I'll stay on with Claire."

"I can do it myself. I'm not stupid, you know."

"Of course not," Mary Nell soothed.

"No one was implying you were," I added.

"Nobody ever trusts me. No matter how hard I try."

"We simply thought you might prefer some company," I explained. Then, remembering the photo in my purse, I pulled it out and handed it to Claire. "Here, you might like this picture of Jodi. It's something Mona took, not too long ago from the looks of it."

Mary Nell leaned over to take a peek, but Claire grabbed the photo and stuck it in her handbag without so much as a glance. "I told Jodi not to pester her," Claire muttered, as much to herself as us.

While Mary Nell got Claire oriented, I made a sweep of the buffet, fixed myself a mini ham sandwich, then loaded my plate with an assortment of fancy delicacies, half of which I couldn't identify. Plate in hand, I wandered over to the side of the room where the silent auction items were located, found the listing for my coveted picnic, and discovered that the bids had already surpassed my self-imposed limit. Even in the spirit of supporting education, I wasn't about to fork over seventy dollars for a basket of food. I did bid on the massage, although it was no bargain either, and then on a hardbound atlas of the world. I jotted my name on a few of the smaller items, hoping someone would come along soon and outbid me. I knew that if my name didn't show up in at least a couple of places, I'd hear about it from the powers that be.

When the live auction started, I moved across the room to get a better view. The first few items, a case of wine, dinner for four at the Park Manor, a round of golf with the Club's pro, all went rather quickly. There was a good deal of kidding around among members of the audience, and a few catcalls when the high bid was declared final. After awhile I got tired of watching and headed for the bar. Paul Simms wandered up a moment later, greeting me as though I were an old friend. I'd half expected that he wouldn't remember me, since he hadn't the first time we'd met. But apparently our introduction at Mona's memorial service had stuck.

"Kate Austen," he said, sliding down the bar to join me. "Hey, it's good to see you again."

I wasn't about to offer my hand and say "likewise," so I smiled instead and nodded to the front of the hall, joshing him. "How come you're not out there spending for the good of our schools?"

Paul smiled back. "Laurelle does a fine job of that without my help." It was said pleasantly, but I detected a note of irritation all the same. The bartender appeared and Paul pulled out his billfold. "Let me get this. What'll you have?"

"White wine."

He turned to the bartender. "A glass of the Hidden

Cellars chenin blanc and a double Glenfiddich, straight, no ice."

We again exchanged smiles.

"Say, I wanted to ask you about that piece in the *Walnut Hills Sun*. You really think it's possible Mona Sterling's death wasn't a suicide?"

I nodded. "The article twisted a few things, but it doesn't matter so much anymore. The police have pretty much ruled out suicide. They're investigating it as a homicide now."

"Really."

Our drinks arrived and Paul stared silently into the bottom of his glass. I couldn't see much of his expression because his face was turned, but I was aware that his breathing had picked up.

"What made them change their thinking?" he asked finally.

I didn't know what the police considered public information, and I wasn't taking any chances. "I'm not sure."

"But there was something that made *you* suspicious."

"Just little, intuitive stuff. The only real evidence, if you can call it that, was the scotch." I glanced at Paul's drink and paused for a moment while a thought skittered across my brain. I shook it off. Glenfiddich wasn't your everyday scotch, but it wasn't exactly rare either. "There was a bottle by the sofa," I continued, "along with an empty vile of pills. Sharon Covington claims Mona never drank scotch."

"Interesting." Paul stared straight ahead. He brought his glass to his lips and then set it down again without drinking. "I wonder if they have any leads."

The auctioneer's voice boomed from the other side of

the room. "Going once, going twice, sold to the beautiful lady in blue."

There was a swell of clapping. Laurelle shrieked and waved to Paul.

"Looks like you just bought yourself a weekend at Sea Ranch," I said.

He grimaced. "I'll try to remember the money goes to a good cause."

"At least it wasn't the weekend in Paris," I offered.

"We may get that one yet, in addition." He turned back and gave serious attention to his drink. "You ever been to Sea Ranch?"

"Once, a couple of years ago we visited a friend of my husband's who has a place up there." It wasn't a trip I liked to remember. "My daughter and I were carsick the whole way up and the whole way back."

"Yeah, the road does that to some people. To my mind, Mendocino is a much nicer place. It's easier to get to and more . . . I don't know, more real, I guess. There's a place I like to stay, sort of off the beaten track. A cluster of private cottages nestled among the trees, most with a view of the ocean."

"Sound nice."

"It is. The place is called The Timbercreek Lodge. Expensive, but worth every penny."

Something about my expression must have caught his eye. "You know it?" he asked.

"I've heard of it."

"Not a lot of people have." He offered a conspiratory smile and took another sip of his drink.

My gaze drifted from the glass of scotch to his raised arm, where it froze on the black ebony cufflinks.

Simms. The initial "S."

My heart did a somersault behind my breastbone and my hands began to shake. I took my time setting my glass of wine on the counter, then looked up and asked, "Do you smoke?"

He pulled out a pack of cigarettes. "You want one? You'll have to step outside to light up, I'm afraid. The nonsmoking lobby has penetrated even these sacred walls."

It couldn't be coincidence, there were too many pieces that fit. "You told me you didn't know Mona Sterling," I said, my voice high-pitched and tight.

The color drained from Paul's face. His eyes locked on mine. For a moment neither of us spoke. "I don't know what you're talking about," he said at last.

"No?"

"No." His smile was affable.

But it did nothing to quiet the pounding in my chest. I had a pretty good idea I knew who Mona had been seeing. Knew who had been there at her place Saturday night. Had I also discovered the identity of her killer?

"I'd met her a few times, of course," Paul continued, still smiling. But the smile went only as far as his lips. His eyes were dark and unreadable.

"I . . . I need to get home early," I stammered. "Sitters, you know. So hard to find a good one."

I turned abruptly and left, on legs so wobbly I wasn't sure they'd support me. I needed to call Michael. I made it to the front entrance, realized I had no idea where I was headed, went back inside and found Mary Nell.

"Is there a pay phone around here?" I asked her.

"There's a phone in the clubhouse lobby. You're supposed to log in with your membership number, but I'm sure if you explained you were here with the school they'd let you use it. Or I'll come along and you can use my number. Is it Anna? You look worried.''

Then I remembered the phone in Mona's car. "No, it's nothing like that. If I'm not back by the time they start the raffle, will you cover for me? All you have to do is read off the prize and then pull a ticket from the basket.''

"Don't worry, I'm an old hand at raffles. You sure everything's okay?''

I nodded, looked over my shoulder for Paul, who'd disappeared, then raced to the car. Because of the valet parking, I had to search for it in a crunch of tightly parked vehicles. I found it just as the attendant found me.

"Help you, ma'am?''

I mumbled something about feeling ill, then waited while he moved the BMW that was parked in front, slapped a couple of dollars in his hand and took off down the driveway. My original plan had been to find the car and call Michael, but with the attendant waiting to slip the BMW into my spot, I couldn't simply sit there.

When I got to the bottom of the hill, I turned onto the main road, then pulled off to the shoulder to make the call. I was punching in the number when I felt a hand reach over from the back seat and take the phone from me.

"I'd rather you didn't do that," Paul said.

22

I opened my mouth to scream but managed only a thin, ineffective squeak. A detail that hardly mattered since Paul and I were the only two people within at least a mile. I maneuvered myself to the side of the car, against the door, though that hardly mattered either with Paul breathing down my neck the way he was.

Clutching the phone in his left hand and something small and shiny in the right, he climbed over to the front seat, where he turned to me with a menacing scowl. Although my heart was pounding against my ribs, I forced myself to meet his gaze.

In all honesty, he didn't look any happier about the situation than I felt.

"Sorry if I startled you," he said after a moment.

I ventured a quick peek at the glistening object in his right hand. When I finally determined it was a silver cigarette lighter and not some palm-sized weapon, I allowed myself a deep, full lung's worth of air. "Startled is hardly the word for it," I gulped.

Paul replaced the phone in the cradle, then spent a few moments adjusting his coat sleeves, which had ridden up over his cuffs. "I wanted to talk to you before you did anything rash," he explained.

"Like turn you in?"

"I was hoping I could convince you not to do that." His smile was tinged with an incongruous boyishness, as though he'd been caught by a doting grandmother with his hand in the cookie jar.

"You're kidding."

The smile faded. "No, I'm quite serious."

My throat constricted again. Paul may not have had a weapon, but we weren't exactly on equal footing. He was at least six feet and well muscled. The old adage "go for the groin" didn't do me much good either. Even if I'd been limber enough to twist my knee free of the steering wheel, the damn gear shift was in the way.

"Is that why you decided to ambush me?" I asked.

"Ambush? I was simply waiting for you. How was I supposed to know you'd decide to bypass the valet service?" He readjusted his left sleeve. "How did you find out about me and Mona anyway?"

"You admit it then?"

He cleared his throat. "Let's just say I wasn't being completely truthful before, when I said I didn't know her."

I touched on the key points—brand of scotch, cigarettes, Timbercreek Lodge, cufflinks. "You're one of the few men who still wears shirts without button cuffs."

Paul looked puzzled.

"Mona had ordered a pair of monogrammed cufflinks, with diamonds. Real classy."

Paul ran a hand across his forehead, his eyes half-closed. Even in the dark I could see that his expression was pained.

"What's the matter? You wishing you'd waited until you got your gift before killing her?"

His eyes popped open. "Is that what you think? That I *killed* her?"

"You were there, weren't you?"

He groaned.

"I thought so. It explains why there was no sign of a struggle. What did you do, conk her on the head while you were whispering sweet nothings in her ear?" I pulled back as Paul leaned forward. "Were you getting tired of her, is that why you did it? Or maybe she was becoming too demanding?"

Paul laughed, a hollow sound devoid of all humor. "This is really rich, you know? I've spent the last week drowning in guilt. Soon as I've begun to work my way through that, turns out I'm a prime suspect in her murder."

"Hey, it was you who asked me not to turn you in."

"Yeah, well I wasn't talking about murder, for Christ's sake."

It was clear we were having a bit of a communication problem. "What about the guilt?"

He sighed heavily, rubbed his jaw and then his forehead. "Mona and I were, uh, well, you were right about us seeing each other. It had been going on for a couple of months. That Saturday, we had a fight. A big fight. It was a . . ." Paul paused for a moment, looked away and gave another sigh. "Somehow she found out about Laurelle."

"Found out? You mean she didn't know?"

"Well, she knew. But she, uh, sort of got the impression we were getting a divorce."

It didn't take a genius to figure out where she'd picked up that notion. I wondered if he'd mentioned it in an offhand manner or laid it on thick, rife with emotion.

Paul's eyes flickered in my direction, then away again. He drew in a deep breath. "What a mess. What a total, fucking mess. I can't believe I got myself into something like this."

A moment or two passed while Paul shifted his shoulders and twisted uncomfortably in his seat. He shot me a pleading, helpless look, but I wasn't buying. He sighed and forged ahead anyway.

"She was around the office a lot, meeting with Stan, dropping off papers, that sort of thing. We got to talking and it turns out we're both opera lovers. Laurelle hates anything that doesn't show on a big screen with a good-looking male lead, so when a client gave me a couple of tickets, I asked Mona if she wanted to go." He cleared his throat. "You know how things happen. Mona could carry on a real conversation, which was something of a turn-on in itself. And she had a terrific sense of humor. It's not that Laurelle is stupid, but what with all those babies and everything . . ."

"That's what this was then," I asked sarcastically, "a meeting of the minds?"

"Not entirely. But it wasn't some meaningless affair either."

"Ah, a meaningful affair. Only you couldn't tell Mona the truth about your wife, and I don't imagine you told Laurelle anything at all about Mona."

A car drove past. In the glare of the headlights, I could see that Paul looked a little green around the gills. "That's why I wanted to talk to you," he said, "to see if I couldn't persuade you to keep quiet about this. If Laurelle finds out she'll kill me." Paul's voice faltered. "Sorry, poor choice of words. But it would be the end of everything. She'd run to Stan, and he'd hang me out to dry for sure. I'd be out on my ear with no job, no house, no membership at the club. Nothing."

Paul's suave and sophisticated veneer was melting by the minute, like ice cream on a summer afternoon. Robert Redford transmuted into Danny DeVito right before my eyes.

"Laurelle's his only child, you know," Paul continued. "Stan treats her like a princess."

I suppose it was no wonder then, that she often acted like one.

"I never thought about the repercussions." Paul swallowed a hiccup. "Things got out of hand, and then before I could figure out what to do about it, they got worse."

"Until Mona died, and suddenly they got better again."

"I didn't kill her, for Christ's sake. You can't really believe that."

"But you *were* there?"

He shifted. "For a while."

"And you did fight. The two of you had a drink, talked, she confronted you with the truth about Laurelle, you panicked—"

"But I didn't kill her," he insisted. He closed his eyes and rubbed his temples. "We didn't even have the drink. She launched right into the fight part. I don't know how she figured it out, but she really laid into me, wouldn't even give me a chance to explain. Then when I heard she'd killed herself, I . . ." His voice broke with emotion. "Jesus, you can't imagine what I felt."

His remorse seemed genuine enough, but I thought guilt would probably elicit a similar reaction. My mind replayed the events of that Monday morning. "Did you use the toilet while you were there?"

His eyes shot open. "What kind of question is that?"

"Just answer it."

"I guess I might have. What difference does it make?"

Mona had clearly had a drink with someone that evening. Had there been another person at her house as well? Or was Paul twisting what had happened to suit his own purpose? At the moment, I wasn't sure I wanted to know the answer.

Paul continued to massage his temples. "Christ, I can't believe what's happening here."

"If Mona was alive when you left, there's nothing to worry about."

"I can't prove it though."

"Maybe if you just explain to the police what happened—" I reached my hand toward the ignition.

"Wait a minute."

My hand shot back to my lap.

"She got a phone call while I was there. Someone named Alice. Mona said she couldn't talk right then. There was some exchange about Alice dropping by later. I left about five o'clock. If Alice came over after that, or if Mona returned the call even, it would prove she was still alive after I left."

"Alice? Her sister?"

"I don't know about the sister part, but I heard her say the name a couple of times." Paul gave me another pleading look. "The thing is, I've never done anything like this before. I'd really like to keep it from Laurelle. And Stan. You won't say anything to them, will you?"

"I don't know. I'm going to have to tell the police though."

He groaned. "They'll probably end up telling her. I'll be up shit creek for sure."

I thought being up shit creek was probably preferable to being in prison, but I wasn't so sure Paul saw it that way. I glanced over at him to see if he was readying for some last minute surprise attack. Instead, he was slumped down in his seat, looking glum. He didn't even blink when I turned the ignition.

"You want a ride home?" I asked.

"No," he sighed, "you'd better take me back to the auction. Laurelle will be full of questions about my absence as it is."

Fifteen minutes later I pulled into the same spot by the side of the road and punched the number I'd started earlier.

"Run that by me again," Michael said groggily.

I switched the phone to my other ear. "You weren't asleep, were you?"

"Not totally. Well on my way though. It's been a busy couple of days between this murder business and the arson."

"I thought the reward money had kids talking up a storm."

"Right. Only thing is, I haven't found a one of them who actually knows anything."

"You want me to call back in the morning?"

He humphed. "Lot of good that would do. I'm already awake. Besides, you've got me interested."

I told him about my conversation with Paul, how he'd been at Mona's house the evening she died, and why she was keeping their relationship secret. "He convinced her they had to keep quiet until his divorce was final. I don't know how long he'd have strung her along if she hadn't found out the truth."

"You think Paul killed her?"

"He says he didn't."

Michael drew in a breath. "Damn it, Kate, you can't go around asking people if they're guilty of murder. Sooner or later you're bound to find someone who doesn't take well to that sort of thing."

"The question just keeps popping up."

"Doesn't say much for the company you keep." There was a deliberate pause. "Don't forget this thing with your tires either. You may have already made someone antsy."

I hadn't forgotten. It wasn't the kind of thing you could put out of your mind, even when you tried. Even when you told yourself it was probably the work of some hit-and-miss vandal rather than a killer.

"You listening?" Michael asked.

"I'm not about to do anything reckless," I told him. "But I'm not about to barricade the doors and crawl under my bed either."

"Yeah, well you're a long way from the latter."

"Anyway," I said, steering the conversation back to where we'd started, "the interesting part of all this is that while Paul was at Mona's, she got a call from Alice. He said it sounded like Alice was planning on stopping by that evening."

"Stopping by Mona's?"

"Right."

"That would mean she had to be fairly close by." Michael paused. "You think you could get me a picture of Alice?"

"Sharon probably has one. Why?"

"The cops in Seattle have been asking around, trying to help us out. Turns out Alice is involved with a pretty shady guy. He has a rap sheet long enough to paper a room. When they questioned him about Alice's whereabouts, he got real vague. And he missed work for a couple of days last week, days which just happen to coincide with Mona's death."

"You're thinking Alice and this guy might be responsible for Mona's death?"

"It's a possibility."

"But why?"

"Hell, I don't know. You said they didn't get along. Mona's rich, Alice is poor. Mona has it made, Alice is drifting around feeling life's been unfair. Both she and the guy were dopers. Maybe they just needed money."

"It's as good a theory as any, I guess."

"I'd at least like to talk to her. You never know which contact is going to lead you to the pot of gold." Michael was quiet for a moment. The kind of quiet that comes with thinking. "How well do you know Paul's wife?"

"Laurelle? She has a kid in Anna's class. We were working on the auction together as well. She's not really my type though, and I'm definitely not hers. Why?"

"How does the 'injured wife' scenario strike you?"

"What? Now you think it might have been Laurelle?"

"Just running through the possibilities. In some ways it's a woman's kind of crime. Neat and tidy. Men tend to be messier. They go for knives or guns or brute force."

I tried to picture Laurelle as a killer. She had a nasty enough disposition at times, but what with the high heels, the bracelets and the long, delicate nails, it seemed she'd have some trouble managing the rudiments of the act.

"Goodness," I said, "you're certainly bursting with possibilities."

"Yeah, I guess so." He didn't sound any too excited about it though.

When I got home, Libby was sprawled out on the couch watching television. Anna and Max were sound asleep on the floor.

"I was afraid to move her," Libby said, turning off the set. "I thought she might wake up and not go back to sleep again."

"When she's like that, a jackhammer wouldn't wake her. Did she get some dinner before she crashed?"

"Yeah. And I made sure she got her bath. We were just going to watch a little TV before dessert, and next thing I knew she was zonked out on the floor." Libby stood. "You want me to help get her into bed?"

"Thanks, but I can manage."

"You got a phone call while you were out. Some man named Erikson. I left his number by the phone."

I didn't know anyone named Erikson, or anything close to that. "Did he want me to call him tonight?"

"I'm not sure."

I carried Anna to bed, booted Max out the back door for a quick pit stop, then dialed the number Libby had left. I reached the Pelican Motor Lodge where the switchboard operator rang me through to Mr. Erikson's room. He either wasn't answering or wasn't in. I spent a moment wondering why someone I didn't know would be calling me from a motel I'd never heard of. I checked the phone book and found that the Pelican Motor Lodge did, in fact, exist. Reassuring, though not particularly helpful. Finally, I gave up trying to make sense of it and went to bed.

23

I bundled Anna up and sent her off to school the next morning, even though the wind was fierce and she was clearly feeling under the weather. Not sick really, but achy and listless enough that I'd have let her stay home if I hadn't scheduled another showing with Dr. Caulder. We had an appointment for eleven, and I'd put a lot of effort into finding pieces I thought she would like. So I promised Anna an ice cream for her sore throat if she managed to hang in there until the end of school. Sometimes I worry that I'm a terrible mother, but when I hear about the stuff other mothers pull, I figure Anna won't end up any more warped than the rest of her generation.

Dr. Caulder had allotted me a full thirty minutes of her tightly scheduled time. She'd informed me of this fact in a manner that let me know how truly appreciative I ought to be. Then she took a phone call while I was still setting up and didn't get off until quarter past. My time had been effectively cut in half.

When the call ended, she looked at me with a raised

brow, as though I had been the one holding things up. "Vhat have you brought me today?"

What I'd brought was five very different pieces, any of which would do wonders for the drab and somber beigeness of the place. Each had a different feel, but none of the pictures were in the least threatening or upsetting. Not that I could determine anyway, and I'd given it some serious consideration.

My favorite was a watercolor landscape in greens and blues, with enough rose pink in the blossoms that you could almost smell the fragrance of spring. I showed her that one first.

She dismissed it with a cursory nod. "My patients' lives are not, you know, a bed of roses."

Heck, mine wasn't either. But that didn't stop me from enjoying flowers.

I tried the oil next. A tranquil stretch of sand and sea, richly textured with a wide variant of subdued shades. A string of birds in the upper right hand corner drew your eye into the horizon. Dr. Caulder scrutinized the work from behind her desk, then stood and tried it from a closer angle. I felt my shoulders relax. Success at last.

She turned. "Ees ocean, no?"

I nodded.

She returned to the seat behind her desk. "Vater, especially big vater, it frightens people. Such emptiness and untamed power . . ." She tapped her nails on the polished surface of the desk. "It makes us feel insignificant, no?"

None of the other pieces appealed to her either, not even the black and white abstract I'd thought so unemotional it was almost boring. Dr. Caulder claimed that brought to mind images of female genitalia.

"None of dteese soothe the inner soul," she declared, with a dismissive nod.

She picked up the phone and made another call as I carted the heavy pictures back to my car. I was plum out of ideas about how to proceed and would have told her so except for the fact that she was still on the phone when I returned to the office. I waited a few minutes, then decided to call her later, instead. Maybe she communicated better on the phone than in person.

I opened the door to exit and found myself nose to nose with Laurelle Simms.

She jumped back, startled, then blinked in confusion. "You see Dr. Caulder, too?"

"I was here on business," I explained. "I'm trying to find some art work for her office."

"Ah."

I shifted my handbag self-consciously to my other shoulder. Running into someone you knew in a therapist's office struck me as one of life's more awkward moments, the kind you wish you could rewind and erase. It was right up there with being caught visiting a plastic surgeon or waiting your turn at the sperm bank. But now that her initial surprise had passed, Laurelle didn't seem at all embarrassed.

"Isn't Dr. Caulder just wonderful?" she exclaimed. "So warm and sensitive."

Could we actually be talking about the same person?

"She's really helped me develop a can-do attitude. And she's very direct. I was seeing another therapist for years, all talk and no action. Dr. Caulder's not like that. She focuses on behavior rather than all that deep-seated memory crap. She forces you to confront the things that trouble you, to take control of your life."

An uneasy thought stirred in the corner of my mind. I wondered if Laurelle had suspected anything about Paul and Mona, if taking control of one's life would include killing the woman your husband was sleeping with.

Laurelle smoothed the lavender "Baby on Board" smock over her protruding belly. "She's been such a big help. I don't know what I would have done without her."

The thought slipped from the corner into the center of my mind. It was like an itch I couldn't ignore. "Remember when we were all at Sharon's the day Mona Sterling died? You said you hadn't known her, but then Claire made some comment that indicated you'd been asking about her. Remember?"

Laurelle cocked her head to the left and frowned. Her brows folded into deep furrows. "Gee, I don't."

"It was something about—"

With a quick glance at her watch, she cut me off. "Look at the time. I'd better let Dr. Caulder know I'm here." She was off, leaving me to wonder if Michael had been on target with his injured wife scenario.

I returned the paintings to the appropriate galleries and then went to fetch Anna. The wind had picked up in the past few hours. The gray clouds had grown thicker and lower. There was a damp chill to the air that cut to the bone.

"Are you sure you wouldn't rather have soup?" I asked Anna.

"Ice cream. You promised."

"How are you feeling?"

She scrunched up her face in thought, afraid that this was, somehow, a trick question. Give the wrong answer and she'd never see the ice cream. Finally, she shrugged. A master of equivocation at five.

I reached a hand across and felt her forehead. Maybe a tad bit warm, but not really feverish. "You want a cone or a dish?"

This was a question she could answer decisively. "A dish. The kind with chocolate sauce and whipped cream on top."

I laughed. Anna had her father's talent for turning things to her own advantage. But the anticipation in her expression made me feel a little less guilty about having sent her to school on a day she'd rather have stayed home.

"Okay, ice cream first. Then I need to drop by Sharon's."

We headed for The Creamery in the center of town. It's an old-fashioned lunch spot that serves such cutting-edge cuisine as grilled cheese sandwiches and perked coffee. But they make their own ice cream, which is first rate.

"You sure were sleepy last night," I told her. "You zonked out right there on the living room floor, remember? I had to carry you to bed when I got home."

"Was the motorcycle guy still there?"

"Brandon? He was there last night?"

She nodded. "He let me sit on his motorcycle."

"Not while it was moving, I hope."

Anna gave me one of her "you're hopeless" sighs.

"Did he stay long?"

A shrug. "At first Libby wouldn't talk to him, but he kept banging on the door so she finally let him in. He smelled yucky. Libby thought so too, she told him he needed a cold shower."

Great. I doubted that Brandon drunk was any improvement over Brandon sober. And while I didn't mind Libby having friends drop by, I preferred to be told about it, even after the fact.

"He had a surprise for Libby."

"He did?"

Anna nodded. "He wouldn't tell her what it was. Said she'd find out soon enough and then she'd be sorry she wasn't nicer to him."

"And what did Libby say?"

"She got mad at him." Anna swung her feet up so that her toes touched the dashboard. "Guess what? Jodi got her name on the board today."

I didn't like the smirky overtones of her remark, but I decided to let it pass with a neutral "hmm."

"She punched Nicole so hard she got a bloody nose."

"Why did Jodi do that?"

"Because Nicole called her a bad name. Nicole got her name on the board too and then she got all mad 'cause it was Jodi's fault. Nicole said she didn't do anything but tell the truth."

And this was only kindergarten. No wonder parents were concerned about violence in the schools. "What name did Nicole call her?"

"A battard."

"A battard?"

"You know, someone whose parents aren't married."

"A bastard," I corrected, reluctantly. As long as she had the concept, she might as well get the words right.

"When you and Daddy get divorced then I'll be a bastard too."

I shook my head and launched into an explanation that would have made my mother blush. Then I delivered a lecture on bad language, name calling, and the Golden

Rule. I wound it up by pointing out that Jodi's father had died before she was born so that the word didn't even apply in her case.

By the time I'd finished, we were pulling into the parking lot at The Creamery.

"Do you know what flavor ice cream you want?"

"I want you to read me the choices."

"They're the same as they were last time we came," I grumbled. Reading a list of thirty-odd flavors and supplying a description for at least half of them was not my idea of fun.

I pushed open the heavy door, and for the second time that day found myself face to face with someone I knew. Brandon Weaver gave me a spirited "Hey, how's it going?" then held out the flat of his hand to Anna. She slapped it with the worldly sophistication of a five-year-old. *"All right,"* he said, turning to hold the door for his companion.

The man looked familiar, but it wasn't until they'd strolled off that I recognized him as the blond man I'd seen lurking on the sidelines at Mona's funeral. Who was he? It seemed unlikely that Mona and Brandon would have many mutual friends.

I ushered Anna inside and started to read through the list of flavors, although I was fairly certain she'd end up choosing vanilla, as she always did.

"That's him," she announced as I finished rattling off the first row of flavors.

"I know. Did he teach you that hand slap routine last night?"

"Not Brandon. The other man."

I stopped at peppermint. "What about him?"

"He's the man who gave us candy."

The hairs at the back of my neck stood on edge. "The one on the school yard? You're sure?"

She nodded.

I remembered how she'd described him to the principal. A fairy. It made sense to me now. The man had a kind of spindly build, with a high, polished forehead, fine blond hair and pointy, Vulcan-like ears. His skin was so light it was almost translucent. But what was he doing with Brandon? I ran to the window and looked out. They were both gone.

Something wasn't right here. Swallowing my rising anxiety, I cornered Audrey, one of the waitresses who often served us. "There were two men here, they just left. The younger one was wearing a leather bomber jacket. The older man was thin and blond."

Audrey nodded. "They had coffee."

"Do you know the blond man? Does he come here often?"

"Never seen him before. That boy, Brandon, he comes here quite a bit, but I didn't recognize his friend." Audrey hoisted a tray of milk shakes above her shoulder.

I waited until she'd delivered them to the table of teenagers at the back. "Were they here together?"

"More or less. The blond guy got here first. When Brandon showed up they ordered coffee, talked a bit, though they seemed more annoyed with one another than anything. Didn't even finish their coffee. Not much of a tipper, either one of them."

Anna pulled on my sweater. "Tell me the rest of the choices."

Audrey went off to take an order and I read the rest of the ice cream list in a monotone, skipping every other flavor. My heart was racing, while my mind seemed rooted in quicksand. Was the man at school really some kind of pervert? I couldn't imagine why else he'd hang around the school yard passing out candy. But why would he be at Mona's funeral? And what was his connection to Brandon?

And when I thought of Brandon hoisting Anna onto his motorcycle, his teasing familiarity with her at the door of The Creamery, I felt positively nauseated.

Heavy drops of rain had begun to fall by the time we left. Although I tried to reassure myself with the knowledge that nothing terrible had happened to Anna, I was pretty shaken. I used the car phone to call home. Libby didn't answer. Next I called Brandon and left a message asking him to call me. Then I drove to Sharon's to see about getting a picture of Alice. Sharon had told me that morning she was sure she had one someplace. But the way she'd said "someplace" I had a feeling I'd eventually have to traipse over to Mona's if I wanted one anytime before next Christmas.

Kyle answered the door with a big bowl of popcorn in his arms. As usual, he said nothing. When he left, Anna gave me a sidelong glance and followed.

Sharon called to me from the kitchen. I joined her a moment later.

She was sitting at the table with a frowsy, dark-haired woman who was nervously trying to light a cigarette.

"Kate," Sharon said. "I'd like you to meet Mona's sister, Alice."

24

"**A**lice has been in Los Angeles," Sharon said, her tone deliberately neutral. "She just learned about Mona's death yesterday."

Alice pressed her knuckles against her mouth to stifle a sob. "I still can't believe it's really true. It's just so horrible."

Alice's voice was high and tight, a marked contrast to Mona's full, vibrant cadence, and she was a good deal heavier than Mona, but the family resemblance was strong nonetheless. Both women had deep brown eyes, a wide forehead, and square jaw. On Mona these features had been attractive; they were less so on Alice, whose sallow coloring and limp hair gave her a sort of broken-down appearance.

"I'm sorry about your sister," I said, looking to Sharon for direction. She shrugged and handed me a cup of hot tea.

Alice sniffled again, then inhaled deeply on her cigarette. She was wearing a tight-fitting, pink angora sweater with some kind of sequined pattern across the front. Bits of pink fuzz and fur had drifted from the sweater, clinging, like cat hair, to the black stretch pants below. "Sharon says she was murdered."

"It looks that way." I tried to gauge Alice's reaction. Were the tears a sign of true grief or simply a performance? The two sisters had hardly been close, after all, and I was there at the house for the very purpose of obtaining her photograph as a possible suspect.

"I feel so terrible about it," Alice said.

While nodding sympathy, I again glanced at Sharon, then tried kicking her under the table. Sharon, however, remained oblivious to my frantic, sidelong eye rolling, and merely moved her foot back under the chair when I persisted in kicking it.

"Just terrible," Alice repeated, then dropped her head into her arm and started sobbing for real. "I did this, I just know I did. It's all my fault."

I set my cup down carefully and leaned closer. "What do you mean 'your fault?' "

"Conroy. I'm sure he followed me."

"Conroy?"

Apparently Sharon's mind was not off in space somewhere as I'd feared, because she broke in at that point to explain that Conroy was Alice's ex-significant other. "Seems he has the strength and temperament of a tethered bull," she said. "He was apparently in the habit of taking out his frustrations, of which there were many, on Alice."

"That's why I had to leave Seattle," Alice said, lifting her head. "He wouldn't leave me alone. I didn't dare tell anyone where I was going because I knew he'd come after me." She blinked back a fresh round of tears. "I thought I'd be the one to wind up dead, not Mona."

"You think Conroy killed Mona?"

She nodded bleakly.

"But why?"

"Conroy doesn't need a reason. He's got an awful temper. He gets so angry I sometimes think he's truly crazy. I don't know how he found out I'd been to see her." She wiped her eyes on her sleeve. "I bet Mona wouldn't tell him where I'd gone to, so he killed her."

It seemed to me that Alice had gotten from point A to point B by way of the Twilight Zone. "You really think he'd do something like that?" I asked.

Alice raised her left arm, which was in a cast from above her elbow to her wrist. "I can show you the cigarette burns too."

I winced. Still, Conroy killing Mona didn't make a lot of sense. The man was no Prince Charming, but he sounded like too much of a hot-head to have meticulously planned a murder like Mona's. I told Alice that.

"I don't know," she mumbled, unconvinced. "Conroy's not dumb."

I remembered what Michael had said about Conroy's rap sheet and his missing work around the time Mona died. Was it possible, after all? I was busy sorting it out when Alice started wailing again.

"I feel so guilty," she blubbered, "especially after the way Mona came through for me."

I decided we'd make more headway if we started at the beginning. "Let me get this straight. You left Seattle because you wanted to get away from Conroy, right?"

She nodded.

"And you came to see Mona?"

Alice nodded again. "We hadn't seen each other for years, but when I needed help she didn't hesitate a minute. Got me money and the name of someone in L.A.—" Alice's eyes filled with tears. "It just rips me apart to think of all the awful things I said to her over the years."

Sharon sparked to life. She leaned across the table. "Mona lent you money?"

"You have to understand, I was desperate. I had to get away from Conroy."

"How much money?"

Alice looked down at her hands, embarrassed. "A lot actually."

"Cash?"

"She said it would be better if I didn't leave a paper trail for Conroy to follow."

"How much money?" Sharon asked again. Then, when Alice showed no signs of answering immediately, Sharon rephrased her question. "Three thousand dollars, is that how much Mona lent you?"

Alice looked up, blinked, looked back down at her hands. "She didn't lend it to me actually, it was more like she gave it to me." A pause. "Mona was loaded, you know. Three thousand was nothing to her."

We had the answer to the missing three thousand at any rate. "This all took place on Saturday?" I asked her.

Alice nodded.

"Saturday evening?"

She nodded again. "I went straight from the airport to her place."

Paul would no doubt be relieved to know that he was not the only one at Mona's that night. "The police need to talk to you," I said.

She shot me a wide-eyed look. "Me? Why?"

"Well, you're next-of-kin for one thing. For the other, you were probably the last person to see Mona alive."

Alice's expression grew squinty, then suspicious. She crushed out her cigarette and tossed her head. "That doesn't make me a criminal."

"They just want to talk to you," Sharon soothed. "You may be able to help them. Kate has a friend who's a policeman. Maybe he'll come over right now and you can get it over with."

This time it was Sharon who kicked me under the table. I took the hint and excused myself to go call Michael. I wasn't able to reach him directly, but I left a detailed message with the dispatcher, who promised she'd try to contact him.

Sharon was intently refilling everyone's cup when I returned. Alice was once again looking tearful.

"It was one of the nicest times the two of us ever had," Alice gulped. "For once, Mona wasn't bossy and full of herself. We talked like sisters are supposed to talk, about all kinds of stuff. Got a little tipsy, you know, let our hair down. I used to think she had it so easy, what with being rich and all. But Mona had her problems too."

Kyle and Anna wandered in just then, demanding chocolate milk to wash down the popcorn. I didn't consider the request unreasonable considering that, left to her own devices, Anna would have been calling for soda pop and a handful of cookies (she knows how to manipulate "grown-up time" to the max). Sharon, however, had recently fallen under the spell of some article on childhood nutrition, and was determined to save Kyle from the fat-cell battle she saw as his genetic destiny. He was the only kid in kindergarten, probably the only kid in the whole school, whose lunch box bore such treats as fat-free, salt-free chips and bite size bits of broccoli.

I shot Anna a warning glance and then braced myself for one of Sharon's lectures on the evils of chocolate. But maybe Sharon had decided that fat cells weren't the worst thing that could happen to you, because she not only made each of the kids a large glass of chocolate milk, she placed a flotilla of miniature marshmallows on top.

By the time they'd finished their snack, Michael was ringing the doorbell. Anna gave him a smile and small wave in place of her usual sloppy hug, then sidled up to Sharon and asked if they could each please have one of the cinnamon drops from the bag of leftover Christmas candy in the den.

My daughter, the manipulator. At least I knew that whatever had caused her to feel under the weather, it wasn't the stomach flu.

Sharon shooed Anna away with what sounded like a go-ahead on the candy front, introduced Michael and Alice, and then filled him in on the basics of our conversation. Except for a brief introductory nod, Alice remained silent, her eyes focused on the rim of her cup, her mouth drawn tight.

"I'd just like to ask you a few questions," Michael said softly. "I realize this must be hard on you, since you've just learned of your sister's death and all. But we could really use your help."

Alice lifted her eyes wordlessly.

"You want us to leave?" I asked.

Michael looked toward Alice, who shook her head.

As he took her through some of what we'd covered earlier, Alice seemed to loosen up a bit, though her answers were still fairly lean. Gradually, the tearful edge to her voice gave way to wariness. "I didn't have any reason to want her dead, you know."

"Nobody said you did."

"Nobody had to. I know how you guys think."

"Right now I'm just trying to put together the pieces, figure out as much as I can about what happened Saturday evening. Okay?"

Alice's eyes flickered from Michael's face to the far wall. "If you say so."

"What time did you arrive at your sister's place?" Michael asked, ignoring the unspoken antagonism.

"About six-thirty, I think. It had just gotten dark."

"And what time did you leave?"

"A little before nine."

"What did the two of you do during that period of time?"

She shrugged. "Caught up on things mostly."

"Anything in particular?"

"Not really."

"How about food. Did you have dinner? Coffee?"

"We had a couple of drinks. Mona brought out some cheese and crackers and stuff, but no real dinner."

Michael gave an all-purpose nod, his face expressionless. He slouched back in his chair. "What did you have to drink?"

I recognized the look on Alice's face. It was the same one Anna gets when she suspects a trick question. Alice chewed on a broken fingernail for several moments, then with a sigh, she gave up trying to figure it out. "We each had a couple of drinks, but we weren't bombed or anything. Mona had a martini. I drank scotch. She kept a bottle of pretty good stuff on hand for some guy she was seeing. That's about it, we drank and talked."

"It was friendly?"

"Very." Her tone wasn't.

"What did you talk about?" he asked.

"Stuff."

"Such as?"

Alice looked Michael in the eye. "Men," she said, spitting out the word with distaste.

"Interesting subject."

"Yeah." She lit another cigarette, the blew a plume of smoke across the table.

Michael waited.

"Mona was even more pissed than I was," Alice said. "First off, turns out this jerk she's been seeing is married. Never bothered to tell her that part. In fact, she had it out with him right before I got there, so she was pretty upset. Then she's got that ass of an ex-husband who won't leave her alone. They're divorced, right? But does that stop him from poking his nose into her life, calling to leave nasty messages on her machine? Not by a long shot. There was also some guy on her case because his wife wants to get an education. That really takes the cake, doesn't it? And on top of everything else, she'd had it up to here," Alice drew a hand across her throat, "with Libby's boyfriend. The guy's got sticky fingers but she can never catch him at it."

Alice paused for a quick drag on her cigarette. "Conroy's a first-class ass, but at least he's the only one I've got to deal with."

Michael leaned back, arms folded across his chest. "How did Mona seem when you left that evening, besides being ready to obliterate the entire male species?"

A glint of humor softened Alice's expression. "We weren't, either one of us, ready to get rid of men altogether. Just the ones we had the misfortune of knowing personally."

Michael acknowledged the remark with a faint smile of his own.

"She was in a foul mood," Alice said, "but it wasn't just men. There was something else eating at her too. Wouldn't talk about it, but it must have been heavy. She said it made her realize that even God didn't have it so easy."

"Hmm." Michael chewed on his bottom lip. "Any idea what she meant by that?"

"Nope."

"She expecting any other visitors that night?"

"Not that I know of."

"And when you left, where'd you go?"

"Back to the airport. She offered to let me stay there awhile, but I already had my tickets and I wanted to get as far from Conroy as I could."

"Tell me about him," Michael said, unfolding his arms and leaning forward.

Alice repeated what she'd told us earlier. She was elaborating on Conroy's temper when the peal of the doorbell interrupted. Sharon started to stand, but Alice sent her a beseeching look, so I went to answer it instead.

Claire and Jodi stood on the porch. Claire frowned at me. "I didn't expect to find you here. Is Sharon around? I brought over the wine she won in last night's raffle." She held up a boxed crate of three bottles. "I thought you might have picked it up, but Mary Nell said you left early."

I nodded. "Sharon's in the kitchen." Claire headed down the hallway with Jodi at her heels. Determined to make up for the wrongs poor Jodi suffered at the hands of her classmates, I called her back, then led her to Anna and Kyle, by way of the cinnamon drops. I gave her a whole handful, and stayed around long enough to make sure the other two didn't exclude her. The fact that Jodi was willing to share her bounty enhanced her popularity considerably.

When I got back downstairs, Michael had finished with Alice and was getting ready to leave. I walked with him to his car. The sky was a thick, dull gray, the air heavy with the promise of rain. It was so cold I could see my breath, like little puffs of fog. I wrapped my arms around myself and shivered.

"You cold?" Michael asked.

"Always."

He raised an eyebrow and mocked me with a seductive leer straight out of the silent film era.

"Well, not *always.*"

"Good." The leer gave way to a grin. "You know, if you'd let me move in we could work on that more often."

"Or I could buy some woolen long-johns," I told him, side-stepping a discussion I wasn't yet ready to tackle. "What's your take on Alice? You believe her?"

Michael's grin faded. "Hell, I don't know. Her story makes as much sense as any." Which, from his tone, wasn't saying a whole lot.

"You aren't crossing her off your list then?"

"At this point I'm not ready to write anyone off. There are too many loose ends to tie up first."

"At least it lets Paul off the hook."

"Unless he came back after Alice left." Michael opened the car door and tossed his jacket onto the passenger seat. "We've talked to Mona's ex and that fiancée of his too. They're both defensive as hell. Gary's so polished you know it's a veneer, and Bambi flat out denied ever having lunch with Mona. Now why would she do that?''

He didn't expect an answer, which was a good thing because I didn't have one. "I wanted to tell you something else. I saw Brandon today at the—''

"Yeah, he's still in the running too. The punk's got a real attitude on him.''

"I wasn't talking about Mona's murder. It's about that man who was hanging out on the school yard. When Anna and I stopped for ice cream this afternoon, we saw Brandon talking to someone Anna swears is the same guy. I think I saw him at Mona's memorial service, too.''

Michael's eyes narrowed. "Did you ask Brandon about it?''

"No. They were leaving just as we arrived. Anna didn't even tell me it was the same man until I was halfway through my recitation of ice cream selections.''

He nodded. "I'll try to reach Brandon this afternoon, see if we can't get to the bottom of this.''

I cupped my hands and blew into them for warmth.

"I know you're worried, but there've been no reports recently of anything remotely similar. No attempted abductions, no strangers approaching children. It's probably going to turn out to be nothing.'' Michael leaned across the open door for a farewell kiss.

I brushed him aside. "By the time you get a report,'' I snapped, "it may be too late.''

He sighed. "I'm going to check on it, Kate. And I put out the word when you first told me about this guy. I'm not a magician.''

I knew I was probably making a mountain out of something closer to a speck of dust than a molehill, but I also knew that overreacting was one of the prerogatives of being a mother. Taking out your frustrations on someone you cared about, was not. I touched his shoulder and sought to make amends.

"Why don't you come by this evening," I suggested. "I've got a new recipe for ginger chicken I want to try. You can tell me what you found out over dinner."

"Can't," Michael said flatly.

"Work?"

He hesitated a fraction too long before answering. "I'm having dinner with Barbara."

"Barbara?" As far as I knew, Michael and his ex-wife didn't even trade phone calls. "Whatever for?"

He shrugged. "She asked me."

A current of jealousy shot through me, though I tried to ignore it. "Oh," I said, chirping with forced pleasantness.

"That bother you just a little?"

"No, not at all," I lied.

He grinned. "Yeah, I know the feeling. I'll give you a call tomorrow. And remember, you've landed yourself closer to this murder investigation than is healthy, so be careful."

You too, I said silently. And I wasn't talking about homicide.

Not surprisingly, Anna had no appetite for dinner. I wasn't any too hungry myself, and Libby dropped by only long enough to tell me she was going out for pizza with a friend.

"Brandon?" I asked.

"Are you kidding?" She flung open the refrigerator

door and eyed the contents. "Can I have these leftover noodles?"

"I thought you were going out for dinner."

"I am. But I'm hungry now."

I handed her a plate. "I understand Brandon came by last night while I was out."

"Yeah." She scooped out a mound of noodles, sprinkled cheese on top and stuck them in the microwave. "All his talk about how there's something special between us, then treats me like some piece of used tissue. He paid more attention to Anna than he did to me."

A sliver of fear lodged in my chest as I contemplated just what sort of attention he might have shown her. Suddenly it was all too close.

"I don't want Brandon in my house ever again, do you understand? Whether I'm here or not." I'd intended for us to have a reasonable discussion about expectations and limits, but reason had deserted me. My voice rose with each word and by the end, I was practically yelling.

Libby's face reddened. "We didn't do anything wrong."

"Maybe not, but I won't have him here, and that's final."

Her bottom lip quivered. She dropped her eyes to her hands.

A heavy silence hung between us. I cleared my throat and backtracked. "I just don't think it's a good idea for him to be here," I told her, trying for the sound and sensible tone I'd missed earlier.

She nodded wordlessly and turned back to watch the rotating dish of noodles.

I touched her arm. "I'm sorry. I didn't mean to come on so strong."

"You sounded just like my mother."

"Mothers tend to worry a lot. It's kind of inbred."

Libby was quiet for a moment. "She didn't like him either."

The timer sounded and I handed her a pot-holder. "Last time I looked, you weren't exactly president of Brandon's fan club yourself."

"No, but Brandon does have a sweet side. At least I used to think he did. There were plenty of times he was there for me when no one else was." She retrieved her plate of noodles. "He didn't have such an easy time in the family department himself."

"From what Anna said, I got the impression he'd been drinking last night, or was high on something."

She nodded. "Half of what he said didn't even make sense. He kept talking about some surprise, and how he held the winning ticket in the Missouri lottery."

"Missouri? Does Missouri have a lottery?"

She shrugged. "Even if it does, there's no way Brandon's going to have the winning ticket."

25

I was cranky and irritable all evening. Even Max seemed to know enough to stay out of my way. I tried calling Michael at nine, ten, and then eleven. I told myself it was because I wanted to learn what he'd found out about this blond stranger I'd seen with Brandon, but I knew there was also a part of me brooding about Michael's whereabouts. After all, how long can you linger over dinner?

It was, of course, the after-dinner possibilities that worried me most. They played through my mind with an unwelcome vividness. By the time I left the house the next morning I was in such a funk I didn't even try reaching Michael again, though I couldn't tell if what stopped me was peevishness on my part or simply fear of knowing the truth. Barbara wouldn't be the first woman to recognize that her ex had some awfully attractive qualities after all.

I parked the Jag in Sharon's driveway, then let myself in through the side door. The kitchen table and the area around it were cluttered with paper. Sharon was sifting through a heap of printed forms, her face set in a heavy scowl.

"I've got to get this stuff to the attorney by afternoon," she grumbled, clearing a spot so that I could sit. "I can't even balance my checkbook and here I am trying to come up with a list of Mona's assets and debts. And to make matters worse, George dumped the damn soccer registration materials into the same box. Now I've got birth certificates mixed in with stock certificates, and more pieces of paper than the Federal government."

"I was hoping you might be able to drop me off to pick up my car. I guess my timing's not so good."

She leaned across the table to retrieve a manilla folder. "No, that's okay. I'm going to need a break soon anyway. Why don't you make us some coffee while I finish up with this list of mutual funds, then I'll give you a ride."

I filled the kettle with water. "Where's Alice?"

"She's staying at the Park Manor for a few days."

"Pretty ritzy." The Park Manor is upscale, even for Walnut Hills. A five-star hotel with five-star prices. "I guess she needs to pamper herself a little after Conroy."

Sharon snorted. "It's not like he's the first. Alice has a knack for picking losers, and then refusing to recognize the obvious."

"She did leave him though."

"Yeah, but I won't be a bit surprised if she goes back to him. When she left last night, she was already talking about what a sweetheart he is when he doesn't drink. That's the kind of stuff she does. Used to drive Mona nuts."

When the coffee had finished dripping, I handed Sharon a cup and offered to help pull things together. She nodded toward a stack of papers.

"I think that's all soccer stuff. You might check just to make sure."

There wasn't room on the table, so I held the pile in my lap and flipped through it, checking to see that the picture, birth certificate, and check were all attached to the application.

"Looks like Claire is going to let Jodi play after all," I said.

"I hope so. But you know Claire, she may change her mind again before all's said and done."

"Is that why she only turned in part of the stuff?"

"Oh heck, it must have gotten separated. Everything was all there when I went through it before. Did you know that Claire's real name is Wilhelmina? I saw it on Jodi's birth certificate."

"Good Lord, I can see why she chooses to go by Claire."

"Maybe her formative years were spent as Wilhelmina. It might explain why she is what she is."

"I don't think she's had an easy life, no matter how you slice it." I moved on through the stack of registration materials. "Laurelle's application for Ben is here, but no picture."

"It must have come loose too. Look through the box and see if it's there." Sharon nudged a cardboard box in my direction. "I can't wait to have a word with George. When he decides to help out, he sure helps out big."

I found the picture and clipped it to the application. "Do you think Laurelle suspected that Paul was seeing someone on the side?" I asked.

"Hard to say. I can't imagine her sitting back and letting it go on, if she did." Sharon snapped a rubberband around a thick batch of papers, then gave me a funny look as she listened to her own words. "Why? Are you thinking Laurelle might have killed Mona?"

"What do you think?"

"I asked you first."

"Well," I said slowly, "she had a motive. And yesterday she was talking about how she'd learned to take control of her life."

"The motive part's true only if she knew about the affair. And if she did, I think she'd be inclined to kill Paul as well as Mona. Taking control isn't exactly a skill Laurelle needed to learn."

I nodded. "You're probably right. Paul's certainly worried about what she'll do if she finds out." I set the reorganized soccer stuff in the corner, away from the loose papers Sharon was still sorting. "You want me to do anything with this?" I asked, picking up a package that was in the way.

Sharon gave me a funny look.

"What's the matter?"

"That's Mona," she said slowly.

"Mona?" It took a moment for the words to register, but when they did, I just about dropped the package. "Jesus. You keep her right here in your kitchen?"

"It's only temporary. I talked with Alice about it last night. We decided to have her ashes scattered by air. I think she'd like that."

I set the package down carefully, then dusted my hands against my slacks. I hoped Sharon wasn't counting on my help.

She pushed back her chair. "Come on, let's go get your car."

It was only a box of ashes, but all in all I was happy to get out of there. The notion of keeping Aunt Mildred on your mantelpiece has never had a great deal of appeal to me.

We headed for Sharon's car and I braced myself for the

drive. When she actually stopped at the newly red light instead of tearing through it, I took my first full breath.

"What's the scoop on that man who was hanging around school?" she asked.

"I don't know."

"You mean Michael hasn't talked to Brandon yet?"

"Michael hasn't talked to me."

She arched a brow. "Uh-oh. Do I detect a trace of tension in that comment?"

"He had dinner last night with his ex-wife." I looked out the window, then sighed. "And he wasn't home yet when I called at eleven."

"Not good," Sharon said.

"Hey, you're supposed to reassure me, remind me of the countless innocent explanations."

She grinned impishly. "I was just getting ready to point out that evening hours are ideal for running errands. You know how uncrowded the groceries are at that time. Michael probably decided to get the week's shopping out of the way, and then when the first store was out of, say, toothpaste, he had to go by a couple others to find the right brand."

"You're a big help," I grumbled.

We pulled into the tire center. "You want me to wait?"

"No need, the car's been ready for days."

"Don't worry about Michael," Sharon said. "I've seen the way he looks at you."

Then she peeled off into the flow of traffic, just barely squeezing into the car's length of empty space between two fast-moving delivery trucks. I saw the driver of the second truck extend his arm through the open window to give her the finger. Since Sharon rarely used the rearview mirror for anything but applying lipstick, the guy's efforts were no doubt wasted.

My car *was* ready, I could see it parked at the back of the lot with four brand new tires. But that didn't mean I was going to get out of the shop without a wait. First there was the line at the counter, then the processing of paperwork, which the jowly man at the desk assured me would take only a moment or two. When he pointed me in the direction of the Styrofoam cups and instant coffee, I knew his idea of a moment and mine were not the same.

I settled into one of the plastic chairs and picked up the newspaper from the adjacent table. I'd only glanced at the headlines that morning because I'd wanted to leave in time to walk Anna to her classroom. I warned her she was to go straight to the office if she saw the blond man or Brandon anywhere near school. She'd nodded agreement, but it was the same nod she used whenever I told her to get her feet off the couch or to be sure to brush her teeth with extra care.

The news story which caught my attention didn't do a lot to reassure me. An elementary school janitor in San Jose was being charged with molesting several students. Parents were outraged, school officials stunned. Nobody could understand how the teddy bear of a man who'd befriended students for years could do such a horrible thing. I couldn't understand the behavior either, but I understood all too well how easily something like that could slip by unnoticed.

With an inward shudder, I flipped the page, looking for bland, unemotional news that would allow me to pass the time undisturbed by nagging "what ifs." A fine theory, except that Gary's face was at the top of the business page, under the headline "Sterling Development on the Upswing." It brought to mind a different sort of "what if," but a troubling one all the same.

Although I read the article twice, I didn't understand it completely. There were lots of words like restructuring, flow of funds, refinanced debt, infusion of capital. The gist of the thing was pretty clear though. Sterling Development, which had suffered a string of setbacks in the recent year, was now on solid footing and primed for a bright recovery.

Was the timing of this turnaround coincidence? I couldn't help feeling it was somewhat suspect, coming so soon after Mona's death. When the jowly-faced man at last called my name and handed me the keys to my car, I headed into the valley instead of home. Andy and I had to work out the logistics of Anna's weekend anyway, and it would be interesting to get his take on the Sterling recovery.

Not too many years ago, the southern part of the county was open farmland and pasture, the tallest thing around an occasional oak or Monterey pine. Now the area is fast turning into a sprawl of freeway overpasses, office buildings, strip malls, and regional shopping centers. Sterling Development had done its part to further the flow of progress. The company's newest project was a large shopping mall not ten minutes from several similar and equally large shopping malls. Since they all had pretty much the same stores, I didn't understand the point. But then no one's ever accused me of being a shop-til-you-drop type, so I was probably overlooking something obvious to others.

The company's headquarters were located in an office park a couple of freeway exits beyond the proposed mall.

I parked and climbed to the second floor, where I asked the receptionist for Andy Austen's office.

"Around the corner," she directed, without looking up from her magazine.

The corner wasn't so much a corner as a chest-high partition, and Andy's office wasn't anything but a wood laminate desk and computer terminal. Behind him stretched a wall of real offices, with Philippine mahogany doors and brass name plates.

Before he had a chance to greet me, the intercom on his desk buzzed. "Andy," the voice said, "get me a copy of the geologist's report, the one that came in just a couple of days ago. And then call Fred Barnes and tell him Monday at ten is fine."

"Right."

"Oh, and Andy?"

"Yes, Mr. Rainey?"

"See if you can't dig me up a pencil sharpener that works. This one chews halfway through every pencil."

"Sure thing." Andy flipped off the speaker and jotted a note to himself.

I furrowed my brows. "This is your great career break? The one that's going to propel you into the big time? You're nothing but a secretary."

"Administrative assistant," he bristled. "And when did you get to be such a snob anyway?"

"I didn't mean that the way it sounded."

"No?"

I truly hadn't, though I knew that's the way it had come out. I tried for a different tone. "Andy, you're terrific at sales, marketing, public relations." The sort of career he'd been doing well in until last year when he'd abruptly quit, taken half our savings and gone traipsing around

Europe looking for his lost youth. "You've got a real way with people. You could convince an Eskimo to buy an air conditioner and he'd walk away happy with the deal. Your talents are wasted in a job like this."

He glared at me. "You don't know diddly, Kate. This is a great learning experience. A tremendous opportunity to rub shoulders with some of the big guns in business. Contacts, that's the name of the game." He locked his fingers together and tapped his thumbs impatiently. "Is that why you're here, to keep an eye on me, manage my life?"

This was an old battle, and one I didn't want to get into again. It was one of the reasons we were now going our separate ways. "I'm sorry," I told him. "I just want you to be happy."

Andy's expression softened. "Kate, you're the one who gets upset about these things, not me. And in any case, it's my life now."

"You're right," I said, signaling a truce. "Anyway, that's not why I'm here. I wanted to ask you about the article in today's paper. Sterling Development was apparently having problems, now suddenly everything's rosy. What gives?"

"Whoa." He held up a hand. "You develop a sudden interest in business finance, or what?"

"It strikes me as an interesting coincidence." I lowered my voice in case anyone happened by on the other side of the partition. "Mona dies, and then before you know it, the problems that have plagued the company for the last year or so disappear."

"Yeah, well, businesses have their ups and downs."

They also had their ins and outs. "Did you ever find

out any more about what Mona might have used to put the squeeze on Gary during the divorce?"

Andy shook his head. "I told you before, I work for the guy. I'm not about to go digging up dirt on him."

"You don't care that he may have killed his wife?"

Andy held up his hands as if fending off an attack. "That's a pretty big leap."

"But it fits."

He shook his head. "Not to my mind it doesn't. If Mona had knowledge she could use as leverage against Gary in the divorce, and if he was willing to kill her to keep it quiet, you'd think he'd have done it before signing off on the settlement. Anyway, it's not my job to worry about things like that. It's not yours either, I might add."

One of the polished doors at the far end opened and a voice summoned Andy.

"I'm serious, Kate. I think you should drop it. Gary's a respected businessman and there's no evidence linking him to his wife's death. You start spreading rumors about a guy based on some theory you pull out of thin air, and you're likely to find it comes back to haunt you."

Better that than letting someone get away with murder, I thought. But at the same time, I had to admit that Andy had a point. My misgivings about Gary weren't based on anything but simple knee-jerk reaction. You couldn't hang a man for being a creep.

I turned, retraced my steps around the partition and past the receptionist, who was still engrossed in her magazine. As I reached the double glass doors at the entry, Bambi pushed past me on her way to the ladies' room. She gave me a hard-eyed, hateful look.

"I hope you're happy. All your meddling has finally paid off."

"What are you talking about?"

"Don't go all innocent on me. You know. You've known all along, haven't you? Now he knows too." Her face was mottled with anger. "You snooty society women are all the same."

With that she slammed the door of the rest room and locked it. *Society women?* Me? And what did I know? Whatever it was, it clearly kept me from being on Bambi's list of favorite people.

On the drive home, I mentally ran through the encounter again. It made no more sense in replay than it had live. And though I was able to come up with a long list of things I knew, some of which I'd known almost "all along," none of them were particularly interesting or noteworthy.

Still baffled, I picked up Anna, who was none too pleased to discover that her silver Jag had turned back into a pumpkin. When we got home, I checked the answering machine first thing, even before I set down my purse. Not one single message. I cursed Michael under my breath. He knew I was worried about the man Anna had seen at school. Even if he hadn't been able to find out what was going on, he could have called to let me know he'd tried. Or simply to show that he cared.

Unless, of course, he'd had such a terrific "dinner" with Barbara that I'd completely slipped his mind.

I did a load of laundry, took out the trash, vacuumed the carpet, all of it accompanied by a lot of stomping and slamming. I was mad at Michael, and mad at myself for feeling that way. After all, I was the one who wanted to keep things free and easy.

When he still hadn't called by five o'clock, I called him. I left a message, but I also called back at five-thirty and at six. When I finally did reach him, an hour later, he didn't sound exactly overjoyed to hear from me.

"I got your message," he said. His voice had none of its usual easy roll.

My heart sank. I swallowed. "Were you able to find Brandon?" I asked.

"Yeah."

"Well, what did he say?"

"He didn't. He was dead."

$$\boxed{26}$$

"**D**ead?" I was pretty sure I'd heard him right, but my mind latched onto the word and wouldn't let go.

Michael mumbled something about a train accident. "You might have heard about it on the news," he said.

"Brandon was on the train?"

"Not on it," Michael said, "under it." He cleared his throat. "Sorry, late nights make me punchy."

Particularly if you spend them with an ex-wife, I thought. But I tucked that away for later and focused on Brandon. "What happened?"

"That's what everyone's trying to figure out. The accident occurred in Benicia so it's out of our jurisdiction, but since Brandon lived here, and especially since we wanted to question him on a police matter, there's some overlap." He paused for a moment. "Whole thing doesn't make a lot of sense. They found his motorcycle about half a mile away."

"Did he run out of gas or something?"

"No, tank's full, and the thing runs just fine. Anyway, the spot where he was hit is out in the middle of nowhere. If he was headed any place on foot it would have been a long hike."

"You think he might have been drunk?"

"Maybe. Though it beats me why he'd stumble around for twenty or thirty minutes, then happen to pass out right when he hit the railroad tracks."

The news of Brandon's death had been reverberating in my head, like the clamor of voices too intermingled to decipher. But as the words settled into place, their meaning grew clearer. "What are you saying, that this wasn't an accident?"

"It certainly looks suspicious."

A prickly sensation spread across my shoulders. For a moment my mind was blank, then two thoughts leapt forward at the same time. Neither, I'm ashamed to say, related directly to poor Brandon. My first concern was for Libby. Despite their recent squabbles, Brandon had been a friend, and he was the second person she'd known to die a suspicious death in less than a month. The other thing that struck me was more selfish. We'd lost our only viable lead for tracking down the blond stranger.

"What does it mean?" I asked.

"Wish I knew." Michael sounded tired and disgruntled. "I'm going to need to talk to Libby," he said, after a moment's pause.

"Tonight?"

"It might be a good idea, if she's there. I can be over in less than an hour."

"She's not going to be in any shape to talk to—"

"I'm not in such great shape myself," he snapped, "but I've got a job to do."

Not in great shape. Late night. His ex-wife keeps him awake until the wee hours of the morning and he expects my sympathy?

Then a more benevolent explanation worked its way to the surface. Ever the optimist, I grabbed it. "You were up all night working the case?"

"No. I didn't find out about it until this morning."

"Oh." Not the answer I wanted to hear.

"Got called in at five. After a pretty active night, too."

"Yeah, well life's not always fair." He wasn't getting an ounce of sympathy from me.

"You can say that again. I didn't get to bed until after midnight because the state fire inspector wanted to go over the reports on that arson matter. I had to cut out of dinner early on account of his schedule, then he got tied up on another matter and we got started late. Didn't even get my cup of after dinner coffee to see me through."

"What?" I wasn't sure I had the sequence right. "You left the restaurant early? Without Barbara?"

He grunted. "That was her reaction too. Said it reminded her of all the reasons we were divorced."

I indulged in a moment of selfish satisfaction. I felt bad that Michael had been up late, working so hard, but better that than the alternative.

It was closer to an hour and a half before Michael arrived, which was just as well since it gave Libby a chance to pull herself together. Not that she'd been overcome with grief exactly, though with Libby it was sometimes hard to tell what she was feeling. But she was clearly upset. Shaken as much, I think, by the renewed appearance of death as anything else.

When Michael arrived, I stayed around long enough to make sure Libby was comfortable, then left the two of them alone to talk. I supervised Anna's bath, during which I got the full story about the fight between Ben and Kyle at morning recess, and the stupid substitute yard teacher who punished the whole class because she didn't know who was at fault. By the time I'd read another two chapters in *Ralph S. Mouse* and returned to the kitchen, Libby had gone off to her room. Michael and Max were finishing up the last of the date bars I'd set out.

"He doesn't need dessert," I said, eying the dog.

"No," Michael agreed, "but he likes it."

The fact that Max had polished off a cookie that might otherwise have been mine seemed lost on the both of them. I nudged Max to the side, and sat. "How's Libby doing?"

"About the way you'd expect. Trying hard to hold it all together."

"Was she able to help?"

"Gave me the names of some of Brandon's friends, but that's about it. She had no idea what he might have been doing in Benicia." Michael rubbed his temples. "I gather she and Brandon had a little argument recently."

"More like a major falling out. He wasn't particularly sympathetic when her mother died, and then she found out he was a liar and cheat as well."

"I figured it was something like that," Michael said. "You got any aspirin?"

I handed him a bottle of Motrin. "Personally, I can't imagine what she saw in the guy to begin with. He's . . ." I stopped and looked at Michael. "Wait a minute, you're not suggesting that Libby might be implicated in Brandon's death, are you? I know she comes across a little strong sometimes, but she'd never—"

"Calm down." Michael swallowed the pills without

water. "No, I don't think Libby's involved. But I was hoping she might know something that would point us in the right direction."

"Did she?"

Michael shook his head. "Not really. He apparently told her he was onto something big, but she doesn't have any idea what it was. Could have been just talk, getting even with her for dumping him."

"The Missouri lottery."

"The what?"

"That's what he told her the other evening—that he held the winning ticket. Of course he was also higher than a kite. According to Libby, he wasn't making a whole lot of sense."

"Nothing about this makes a whole lot of sense." Michael closed his eyes and pressed his fingers to his forehead. A grimace deepened the furrows in his brow.

"Let's go into the other room," I told him. "I'll rub your head."

We moved into the living room where I settled on the couch, with Michael on the floor at my feet. I began massaging his scalp and neck.

He moaned softly. "That feels good."

I worked my fingers into the muscles of his shoulders, then up the side of his head. "Brandon wasn't exactly a choir boy," I offered helpfully. "There's probably no shortage of people he'd managed to offend."

Michael made a purring sound which I took for agreement.

"Of course, his tie-in with this guy who was hanging around school is what troubles me most."

He murmured something about "higher." I moved my

fingers to his forehead. After a moment, he murmured again, something about burglary.

"You're working on a burglary too?"

"Not really. It's just interesting that Brandon's print matches one taken from Mona's place after the break-in."

"Well, I imagine he was in and out of that house quite a bit. It could have been there for ages."

Michael made some indecipherable noise deep in his throat.

"What?"

"It could have been," he mumbled, "but from the way it was positioned on the shattered panel of glass, it's unlikely."

I took a moment to consider this. "Are you telling me that it was Brandon who broke into Mona's place?"

"That would be my guess."

What could Brandon have wanted from Mona's? Given the history, he might have been simply shopping for loose cash, pills, that sort of thing. On the other hand, he might have had his eye on something altogether different. But what?

And then another thought hit me. I stopped my kneading. "You think the two homicides are connected?"

"Guys in Benicia aren't convinced it's a homicide."

"But Brandon's death is certainly suspicious."

Michael sighed. "That it is." He nudged his shoulder against my knee, the way Max does when he's feeling shortchanged.

I took the hint and again began working on his head. All the while I'd been listening to Anna's bath-time chatter and reading about the exploits of her favorite mouse, I'd been aware of loose thoughts skittering around in the back of my mind. Slowly, as I worked my fingers through Michael's hair, those same thoughts formed a pattern.

"Suppose Brandon and this elusive blond man were working together in some scheme," I said. "Kidnapping, child pornography, maybe some kind of pedophile ring—"

"We can suppose all you'd like, but you've got to remember that handing out candy to school children, though unwise, is not against the law. You seem ready to indict this guy without evidence of a crime."

"Just hear me out. Mona had something on her mind before she was killed. Something she wanted to talk to me about, remember? And then there was Alice's comment about Mona playing God. What if Mona had begun to suspect what was going on with Brandon and his friend? They could have killed her to keep her quiet. Either one of them could easily have links to the drug world, so the morphine is no problem."

"Except that morphine isn't exactly a street drug."

"Don't get picky. At this stage, we're just supposing."

"Supposing doesn't do any good if you ignore obvious problems of logic."

I dug my thumb into the soft flesh of his shoulder.

"Ouch, not so hard."

"Now this is the way I see it. The scotch is sitting there in plain view where Alice left it, the gin is in the freezer. Brandon wouldn't be likely to know Mona's preference in liquor, so he grabs the Glenfiddich and sets it up to look like an alcohol-and-drug-induced suicide. After the fact, he worries that he left some evidence which would point to him, so he goes back to retrieve it."

"How does that explain Brandon's death?"

I reshuffled my thoughts. "Maybe the evidence actually pointed to the blond stranger. He's worried that Brandon would finger him, so he snuffs out Brandon."

Michael sighed. "You've watched too many bad movies, Kate."

Probably true, but I didn't think it was relevant here.

"And Brandon's boast of impending fortune?" Michael asked.

"Maybe he was trying to blackmail the stranger, and that's what got him killed. There are lots of different twists you could put on this."

Michael sighed again. "So all we have to do in order to wrap up two murders is find this mysterious blond man."

"Right."

"Thanks, Kate. You've been a terrific help."

"Any time."

Michael pushed himself off the floor and onto the couch next to me. "I don't suppose," he said wryly, "that you have any idea how we go about doing that."

"Not yet. But stick around. I'll probably come up with one or two before the night's over."

"If I could stick around," Michael said, leaning over to nibble on my ear, "the last thing in the world I'd want you to be thinking about is finding some other guy."

"What do you mean 'if'? You aren't planning to stay?"

"I can't," he murmured, still nibbling. "We've got a new lead on this arson thing. A witness who got a partial plate." Michael moved from my ear, to my eyes, then down to my mouth.

After we came up for air, I whispered, "I called you last night. When you didn't answer by eleven, I thought you'd decided to spend the night with Barbara."

"That would bother you?"

I pulled away, offended that he'd even consider the

possibility I'd take it lightly. "Of course it would. What do you think?"

He grinned. "What I think, is that maybe this relationship of ours has a future after all."

27

"It's pouring out there," Sharon said, shaking off her umbrella and stamping the water from her boots.

She was dropping Kyle off at my place before school because she had to be in San Francisco for a nine o'clock meeting with George and their accountant. Tax season is one of the few times I recognize the upside of having no money.

"You have time for a quick cup of coffee?" I asked her.

"Just half. If I keep George waiting I'll never hear the end of it." She folded her umbrella and left it on the porch. "Never mind that nine times out of ten it's him who keeps me waiting."

I poured her half a cup of coffee, then added warm milk I'd frothed in the blender, and sprinkled on a dash of cinnamon. A poor man's cappuccino.

"Men are impossible," Sharon grumbled, licking at the foam. "The only people they have to keep track of are themselves, and sometimes they can't do that without help. Last night I chewed George out for messing with my stacks of paper and he swears he didn't touch them. Reminds me of the time I looked high and low for my kitchen scissors, which he professed to never have used. I found them a week later in his tool box in the garage."

"With Andy it was the other way around. He'd misplace things, then accuse me of taking them. I sometimes think the reason he hasn't signed the final divorce papers is because he can't find them."

"Maybe he still has genuine feelings for you."

I shook my head. "I don't think Andy would know a genuine feeling if it jumped out and bit him on the nose."

Sharon caught herself mid-laugh, set down her cup and leaned forward. "That reminds me, I found out something interesting. I talked to Alice again last night. Turns out, Laurelle *did* know about Paul and Mona. Not only that, she was the one who tipped Mona off on the fact he was married!"

"What?"

"Hard to believe, isn't it? Goes against everything we said about her yesterday. Apparently Laurelle suspected Paul was up to something, had him followed, then called Mona that Friday afternoon and confronted her."

The mysterious caller Libby had assumed was Bambi. "No wonder Mona was upset," I said.

Sharon nodded. "Alice said Mona was completely blown away, first to learn there'd been no talk of divorce, and second, to learn that Laurelle was pregnant. She was furious at the way Paul had manipulated her and assumed he could get away with it."

"So that's what Laurelle meant by 'taking control of her life.' "

"Pretty effective, too. I guess she decided if she made a

big scene with Paul, it might really be the end of her marriage. I must say I admire her restraint, but I think Paul's getting off far too lightly."

"I don't think she's about to let him off lightly," I said, remembering Laurelle's spending spree at the auction. Knowing Laurelle, I was sure that wasn't the end of it either.

"Oops, I gotta run," Sharon said with a glance at her watch. "Can't keep George waiting." She stood to go. "Anyway, I think we can forget about Laurelle being our killer."

"I think you're right." Then I told her about Brandon.

"Good Lord," Sharon said, sitting down again.

I poured her a second cup of coffee. By the time we'd walked through all the possibilities linking Brandon's and Mona's deaths, and carefully weighed each of them, Sharon's own demise, at the hands of her husband, was a distinct possibility.

I'd promised to do a special art project with the kindergartners that morning, so after dropping Anna and Kyle off at nine, I returned to school again at ten.

"I really appreciate your doing this," Mrs. Craig said, relieving me of an armload of supplies. "Especially when you just worked in the classroom last week."

"I don't mind. This is the sort of project I love doing." Then, thinking maybe she'd feel I was whining about the other, I added, "Not that I don't always enjoy working with the children."

I'd brought several different kinds of paper as well as brushes and paints, and I set them out around the room. I had one large piece of watercolor paper which I set at the front. I thought I'd use this to demonstrate, calling on individual children to come forward and try their hand as we went along. Since it was a small class, every child would be able to participate in our group effort as well as doing an individual project.

When the bell rang, the class tromped in from recess. Mrs. Craig made a few cautionary remarks, and then, amidst the usual atmosphere of controlled chaos, we passed the hour exploring possibilities of color and abstract design. I urged them away from representational pictures and instead asked them to think about mood and feeling. For the group effort we chose the theme "spring." This was more my choice than theirs, I'll admit, but I needed to treat myself to images of sunshine and fragrant blossoms more than they needed experience in group decision-making.

The kids didn't seem to care what the theme was as long as they got their turn with the big picture in front. When we were finished, what we had was something that looked as if it had been run through the wash with a pair of non-colorfast green overalls (the class was heavily partial to green) and then rolled on repeatedly by the dog (you mix too many colors you end up with brown). Ben had dropped the paintbrush in the center when it was his turn to add sunshine, so we also had drips of yellow, kind of like mustard down the front of your brand-new blouse. Nonetheless the children were thrilled with their vision of spring.

While Mrs. Craig herded them to the cafeteria for a snack, I walked around the room and looked at the individual efforts. The girls tended to paint in clear, sweeping strokes of pink and lavender (and, of course, green) while the boys almost universally filled the entire surface with gray and black. What this said about psychological differences between the sexes was beyond me, but I thought it was pretty clear why men and women had trouble communicating.

"The children had a wonderful time," Mrs. Craig said when she returned. "Maybe we could do something like it again, later in the year. If you'd be willing, that is."

"Sure, if you can handle the mess."

She laughed. "This is nothing. You should see what happens when we do a cooking project." She wet a sponge at the sink and began wiping up splatters and drips. "I understand Libby Sterling is staying with you. How's she doing?"

"In light of all that's happened, surprisingly well. She's basically a sweet kid, though she works hard at disguising the fact."

Mrs. Craig nodded. "Turns out it wasn't Libby that Mona wanted to see me about after all. One of the fourth grade teachers talked to her that day she stopped by. It was apparently something about my kindergartners."

Mrs. Craig laughed again and made a "fancy that" kind of face. Unfortunately, I could fancy it all too well. Wouldn't a teacher be a logical place to start if you suspected a child was being molested? Before I could ask her about it though, the bell rang and she was off to gather her flock.

I made a mental note to call her later, then trudged out to my car with the class picture, which I'd promised to frame, and an armload of supplies. I set them in the back with great care. The last thing my car needed was a multicolor interior.

It had been raining off and on again all morning, but as soon as I started for home the sky opened up. Water pounded the windshield in sheets, sometimes so thick the wipers had trouble keeping pace. Shivering, I turned up the heat. On the radio, the soft swoosh of waves punctuated a poetic delivery of magical names. "Maui, Kauai, the beaches of Waikiki," the voice purred. "Sound too good to be true?" Definitely, I said to myself. "Experience the paradise of Hawaii, now more affordable than ever." Dream on, buster. I reached over and switched stations. Running an ad like that at the height of the rainy season might be good marketing, but it was exasperating as hell to those of us with no means of escape. Still, I allowed myself one fleeting vision of white sand, blue water, and warm sun. The man was right about one thing. It was paradise.

I swung by home long enough to change clothes and wash away the paint from under my nails, then I headed to a small gallery that specialized in animal prints. I was going to make one last stab at finding something which would appeal to Dr. Caulder, and then call it quits.

In a moment of inspiration, I'd remembered the polar bears. I'd stumbled across the piece months ago—an embossed print of two cubs frolicking on ice. White on white, exactly what I'd been thinking about from the start. I was hoping it hadn't been sold in the interim.

It hadn't. As I filled out the forms, I gave silent thanks to my lucky star. I wrapped the picture in heavy paper and then in plastic, placed it in the back of my car, and headed for her office.

When I pulled into the parking garage, Dr. Caulder was just arriving herself.

"Such veather," she exclaimed, shaking her head with disapproval. "I do not like all dtees cold."

At last, there was something we agreed on. Maybe it was a sign. "I've got the picture right here," I told her. "I

think you're really going to like this one. It fits with everything you've been telling me so far. I'll bring it up to your
office right now."

She glanced at her watch impatiently. "I can look at it
here, no need to traipse up and down again." She didn't
add "for nothing," but that's what her tone implied.

While Dr. Caulder tapped her sensible brown walking
shoe against the pavement, I pulled out the picture and
unwrapped it. By now my earlier optimism had all but
vanished.

There was a moment's silence.

"Yes," Dr. Caulder exclaimed suddenly. "Yes, yes, yes.
Oh my, it's perfect."

I took a moment to savor the words, then looked up at
her and smiled. Only Dr. Caulder's eyes were not directed to the polar bear cubs, but rather to the globs of
green and brown from my morning's session with the kindergartners.

"That? It's not, um . . . it's really a . . ."

She stepped closer and peered at me over the tops of
her glasses. "Vhat? It ees too expensive?"

"No, not that. It's just that it . . . belongs to a friend of
mine. I'm not sure it's for sale."

"You'll ask? Please."

I nodded. Kindergartners were an unpredictable lot. I
thought they'd probably go for the money—and fame,
I'd be sure to sell them on that aspect—but I wasn't bank-
ing on it just yet. "Now, about this other piece," I said,
turning slightly to give her a better perspective on the
cubs.

She shook her head. I'm not sure whether she actually
wrinkled her nose (Dr. Caulder didn't strike me as the

nose-wrinkling type), but that was the impression I got. "Dogs?" she said. "Vhy in the vorld vould I vant dogs?"

"They're not—"

But she'd already turned her back and started for the elevator.

The answering machine was blinking away when I got home. I put water on for coffee, then hit play. The first call was from someone named Albert informing me I'd been selected to receive three month's pool maintenance absolutely free. A dynamite deal, if I'd been blessed with a pool. The second message consisted of a mumbled, "Oh shit," which I recognized as shorthand for "I got the wrong number." My third caller was the fastidious-voiced male who advises me almost daily that if I wish to make a call, I should hang up and try again. It makes me wonder what Max does when he's home alone. The final message was from Eve Fisher who apologized for not getting back to me sooner. She'd been out of town, she explained, and had only just returned.

After I made myself a cup of coffee, I returned the call, reluctantly. Why in the world had I ever tried reaching her in the first place? I couldn't imagine what I'd been thinking.

"Hi, you don't know me, but I hear your husband threatened Mona Sterling. Did he also kill her?" It was hardly the way to introduce yourself to a stranger. At least things had progressed to the point that I wouldn't have to work my way through that.

I was hoping Eve would be out. I'd leave a brief message and be done with it. Unfortunately, she was in.

I took a little poetic license with the truth, explaining that I was a friend of Mona's and that I'd called to let Eve know about the memorial service. The timing of the original call was one day off, but I thought it unlikely she was going to figure that out.

"How kind of you," she said. Her voice was thin and high-pitched, like a young girl's. "I just heard the news yesterday when we got back into town from a two-week cruise. What a shock. And I feel so bad about—" I heard a door slam on Eve's end and a male voice in the background. "About everything," she concluded hastily. "And I'm so sorry I missed the service."

"Well, I just wanted to make sure you knew."

There was a brief pause. "You say you were a friend of Ms. Sterling's?"

"Yes. More a friend of a—"

"Could we, uh, maybe get together, for coffee or something? Right now is not a good time for me to talk."

"There's really nothing—"

"Please. I feel so bad that I never explained . . . I mean, I tried to, but then, well, I didn't, and . . . and now I can't. Explain to her that is." Eve took a deep breath. "It would help me if I could explain to somebody," she said at last.

"I don't think that—"

"How about tomorrow?" She lowered her voice. "Just for a short while. We can meet whenever you'd like."

Her tone was so heavy with need I found it difficult to refuse, though I did make another stab at it. But Eve was persistent. We agreed on a place and time, and I hung up, feeling angry with myself for not being more assertive.

Then, in an effort to clean out the clutter of my life, I tried Mr. Erikson once more.

"He's gone," the man at the desk told me. "Checked out a couple of days ago."

I guess he hadn't been any too eager to reach me after all. I crumpled the sheet of paper with his number on it and tossed it into the trash.

"He'll probably be back," the man continued. "Least, he was last time. You want to leave a message?"

And play telephone tag with a traveling salesman? No thanks.

No sooner was I off the phone than it rang again. Claire was calling to see if Anna would be interested in a playdate on Saturday. She actually used that word, "playdate," a term I hadn't heard since pre-nursery school days. It made me realize how little social contact Jodi had with other children.

I don't usually make plans for Anna without consulting her first, but since I'd just agreed to meet Eve Fisher at the very hour Claire suggested, I jumped at the chance to have my babysitting needs taken care of so easily. Besides, this was the first such overture Claire had made, and if I wavered she'd probably freeze up for good.

"That would be wonderful," I told her. "It works out well for me too. I'm meeting one of Mona's students for coffee."

Determined to be sociable, I related the story of Eve Fisher. As usual, Claire responded in monosyllables. I tried a few other topics and didn't get any further. Finally, I gave up.

"See you tomorrow," I said. "And thanks for inviting Anna."

"No problem," she replied, in her usual clipped tone.

My coffee was largely untouched and cold. I dumped it and started to make a new cup. But it was one of those days. The phone rang just as the water started to boil.

"You free?" Michael asked, then continued without

waiting for an answer. "They just picked up some guy in Concord. Tried to lure a seven-year-old girl into his car. She screamed, he took off, and believe it or not, hit a goddamn garbage truck. That's how they got him so quickly. The guy did time a couple of years ago for molesting a neighbor's daughter. His hair's more reddish than blond, but he does have a thin face. I thought you should take a look, just in case he's the one you saw with Brandon."

Despite the cold, my skin was suddenly clammy. "I'm free," I told him.

"Good. I'll swing by in about fifteen minutes."

28

Michael picked me up and we headed for Concord, a town about ten minutes east of Walnut Hills. The rain had turned to drizzle, but the sky was still dark and threatening, the wind given to sudden, explosive gusts. It was the kind of heavy, gray day that chills the spirit and casts sinister shadows on even the most innocuous thoughts. Not that my mind needed any help along those lines.

When we got to the police station, Michael went off to confer with someone named Denny while I sat on the vinyl bench in the reception area and listened to my heart bang against my ribs. What if this man actually was the one I'd seen with Brandon, the one who'd approached Anna and her friends? What did it all mean?

And what if it had been Anna he'd tried to kidnap instead of this girl today. Would Anna have been as lucky? Though I tried not to, I found my mind dwelling, as it had countless times before, on the stark terror of having your child disappear, of never knowing what suffering she'd endured, or was enduring still.

Mercifully, Michael reappeared before I had a chance to work myself into a full-fledged panic. He ushered me through a set of double doors and introduced me to Denny, a burly man with a chipmunk face. I followed them down the hallway to a small, interior room. A dark shade covered half of one wall.

"In a minute we'll open the shade," Michael said. "You'll be able to see into the next room, but nobody there will be able to see out. Take your time, just let us know if any of the guys look familiar. You ready?"

I held my breath, nodded.

Denny pressed a button and the shade rose, revealing another room about the size of our own. Four men stood against the far wall facing us. Every one of them seemed to be looking straight at me. I fought a wave of nausea.

"You sure they can't see out?"

"Positive," Denny said, thumbs hooked over his belt. "You want them to move around a little or turn a different way, you let me know."

I shook my head. It wouldn't be necessary. Not a one of them looked anything at all like the blond man I'd seen at The Creamery. It wasn't even close. But I couldn't take my eyes off the four faces. Three of them, Michael had told me, were cops. But one, I knew, was a convicted child molester, a man who only hours earlier had tried to abduct a young girl close to Anna's age. I tried to figure out which one it was, and couldn't.

"Anyone look familiar?" Michael asked.

"He's not there."

Denny leaned against the wall. "No need to hurry, you know."

"He's not there," I said again. "The man I saw had unusual features, I'd spot him in a minute if I saw him again." Still, I couldn't help staring at the faces in front of me. "Which one tried to kidnap the little girl?" I asked after a moment.

"Second from the left."

I drew in a breath. The man had been at the very bottom of my list. Smooth-faced, with an up-turned mouth, even white teeth, and eyes that crinkled at corners even when he wasn't smiling. He not only looked harmless, he looked downright neighborly. The sort of guy you'd turn to for help if you thought you were in danger. I felt another wave of nausea roll through me, and although I couldn't make myself turn away, I was relieved when Denny once again dropped the shade.

"I thought you didn't hold to the Brandon-stranger-kidnapping scenario," I told Michael when we reached his car.

"I'm not sure I do."

"So why were we taking a look at this guy? Just to appease me?"

"Something wrong with that?"

I shrugged.

"Of course, there's the chance you might be right, too. Even if this guy wasn't your man."

And there was the disheartening chance we might never know for sure, either way. "Anything new on Brandon's death?" I asked.

"Not that I'm aware of. Nothing new on Mona's either. I've had a couple guys interviewing Gary's associates, looking into his finances. Nada." Michael sounded weary and wrung out. He looked it too. The hollows under his eyes were deeper than usual, his expression more drawn.

"Another late night?" I asked, touching his knee in a show of sympathy.

He nodded. "Compounded by the fact that I haven't been sleeping well."

"You?" I laughed. "That's certainly never been a problem I've seen."

It was something of a joke between us the way Michael could sleep through everything from Max's crazed midnight barking to Anna's whimpers. He hadn't even rolled over or opened an eye the time I knocked the lamp off the bedside table on my way to the bathroom.

"No, probably not." He gave me a meaningful, unexpectedly serious look. "But I don't sleep nearly so well when I sleep alone. Not lately."

There was a moment of strained silence while he kept his eyes fixed on mine. I shifted uneasily in my seat. I knew where this was headed. "Guess what?" I said, after a moment, "I talked with Eve Fisher."

"You're changing the subject again."

"She and her husband were on a cruise ship when Mona was killed."

He sighed. "I told you that."

"Yes, but—"

"But," Michael interrupted good-naturedly, "you weren't absolutely sure I was right."

"It just seemed like an odd coincidence is all. I mean Ike threatens Mona, his wife's homework paper is there by the phone, and then Mona's dead."

"That's the trouble with this business, you can't tell what's significant except in retrospect." We stopped at a red light and Michael drummed his fingers on the steering wheel. "I'm right about the other thing too, you know," he added softly.

"What other thing?"

"The thing you never want to talk about."

"Why do we have to push it?"

"Glen's coming back next month. I'm going to have to start looking for a new place soon." Since his divorce, Michael had been subletting a friend's condominium. An easy, interim solution to an issue I hadn't been ready to take on.

I still wasn't. "I know that you're—"

"We could make it official, maybe even buy a new place, one of our very own."

My mouth felt dry. I swallowed and kept my eyes focused straight ahead.

"I want for us to be together, Kate. A couple, everyday and forever."

"Do we have to do this now?"

"What are you afraid of?"

"Living together is so . . ." There was a pressure inside my head, almost a ringing sensation. I didn't even want to think about the official part. "Well, it would change things."

"Yeah, I guess it would." He paused a moment. "But that's kinda the whole point."

"I don't—"

"Is it me? Is that the problem?"

"No, it's me. I'm just . . ." Just scared to death, I thought. Scared of being hurt again, of feeling utterly alone when I'm not. Scared that you'll see my flaws, that you'll grow tired of me or turn against me. Scared, ultimately, that it won't work out. "I'm just . . . not ready," I said finally.

The muscle in his jaw twitched. He regarded me flatly

for a moment, then swung his eyes back to the road. "Sorry I mentioned it."

"I'll think about it, okay?"

"Sure, whatever."

I opened my mouth to say more, then found I couldn't think what to say. We rode the rest of the way in silence.

That evening we were all in foul moods. Anna, who is usually a cheerful and even-tempered child, left the dinner table in a rage after I told her she'd been invited to play with Jodi on Saturday. She stomped into her room and slammed the door like a veritable teen-ager. Libby had been cranky and sullen from the moment she walked in the door, which was a good hour before school let out for the day. "So I cut class," she bristled when I mentioned it. "Big, hairy deal." For myself, disenchantment was like a black cloud, extending to everybody and everything. I was ready to find fault at the drop of a hat.

Which is why, when Libby left the kitchen without offering to help with the clean-up, I lashed out at her for thinking about no one but herself.

"So far, it's unanimous," she said bitterly. "Must be true."

"It wouldn't hurt to dump the attitude either."

She glowered at me, rinsed a couple of plates, then reached for Anna's milk glass and jammed it down hard in the dishwasher. The glass shattered. Libby screamed in pain and yanked back her hand. Bright red blood ran in rivulets across her palm and splashed onto the linoleum. Her face went suddenly white.

I grabbed a towel, wrapped it around her hand, led her to a chair and eased her head down between her legs to keep her from fainting.

"Stay like that," I said. "You'll feel better in a minute or so. In the interim, I'm going to take a look at your hand."

I wet a couple of clean paper towels, then unwrapped the cloth from around her hand and dabbed at the wound. There were two gashes, both long, but neither particularly jagged nor as deep as I'd feared. And there didn't appear to be any splinters of glass lodged in her skin either. I pressed a dry paper towel into her palm.

"It's not as bad as it looked at first," I told her. "I don't think you're going to need stitches, but it will probably hurt for a while."

Libby clutched the towel in her fist.

"Why don't you try sitting up and see how it goes."

She raised her head. Most of the color had returned to her face, but her expression was still marked by distress.

"How's it feel?"

Tiny rivulets of tears snaked down each cheek.

"Does it hurt a lot?"

She shook her head and hiccupped.

I sat beside her and gave her a hug. "I'm sorry about what I said. It wasn't you I was upset with. I guess I just had a bad day."

She wiped her tears with the back of her hand and hiccuped again. "Me too."

"You want to tell me about it?"

A shrug. "Lots of little stuff, like I lost my French book and got a D on my history test."

I murmured something sympathetic.

"And some of the kids at school started saying I was like, you know, a death star. Anybody gets too close to me dies. They'd give me these funny looks and move away whenever I got near."

"Oh, honey, I'm sorry."

"And then at lunch I called my dad. He made a big deal the other day about how I'm his own flesh and blood and how I shouldn't shut him out of my life . . . so I called him to tell him about Brandon." Another hiccup and then she burst into tears. "Do you know what he did? I told him about the train and that Brandon was dead, and he . . . he put me on *hold!* Just like I was some goddamn salesman or something." She covered her face with her good hand and sobbed.

No words of reassurance came to mind that didn't ring totally false.

"I hate him," she said. "I really, truly hate him. He's the one who never thinks about anybody but himself."

"I didn't mean that, Libby, honestly. It was a nasty remark for me to make." I brushed the hair out of her eyes and handed her a tissue.

"You know what he said when he introduced me to Bambi the first time? He said, 'she's someone very special to me and I love her more than I ever believed possible.' "

"That's nice. See, he does care about you."

A fresh torrent of tears made their way down Libby's face. "No, you don't understand. He was talking about Bambi, not me. He's never once told me he loves me. Not ever."

29

I'm always impressed by the curative powers of a good night's sleep. Even a bad night's sleep, which was all I got, seemed to do the trick. Libby's spirits, also, were brighter by morning. Only Anna remained in a funk, and that was largely my fault. I'd made the mistake of reminding her that she was going over to Jodi's a little later.

"She never wants to do anything," Anna whined, looking up from her dinosaur coloring book. "She doesn't even talk, she just sits there looking like a dope."

"Claire told me Jodi's excited about having you over."

Anna looked at me. "Really, Mom," she said, sounding remarkably like Libby. She picked up one of her new fluorescent pink crayons and began outlining the strong body of a Tyrannosaurus Rex. "You know Claire was just saying that because she's supposed to. That's what mothers do."

"I know no such thing. Anyway, it will just be for a couple of hours and I've got some errands to run."

Anna exchanged pink for purple, and gave Tyrannosaurus Rex stripes. "Why can't Libby stay with me?"

"Because," I explained, "Libby has plans of her own." She was going to be spending the day with Sharon, first going over some legal issues, and then shopping. I was hoping Sharon would find time to fit in a hefty dose of supportive counseling as well.

When the appointed hour arrived, Anna wasn't any more enthusiastic than she had been earlier. I walked her to Claire's door and whispered a warning in her ear before nudging her inside. I had to admit there was a part of me that understood her lack of enthusiasm for the arrangement. Jodi, who stood down the hall a good ten feet from the door, eyed Anna silently and solemnly without a flicker of interest. And although she went through all the proper motions, Claire's welcome wasn't a whole lot warmer.

"What time do you want me to come pick her up?" I asked, when the girls had finally disappeared into a back room.

"No hurry," Claire said. "I thought I'd take them to McDonald's for lunch if that's all right with you."

"It's fine." At least Anna wouldn't view the visit as a complete loss.

Claire leaned against the door jam, stuck a hand in her sweater pocket, and scowled at the thick cover of clouds overhead. "This weather's really something, isn't it?"

I nodded. "It's not usually this bad for this long."

She glanced in the direction of Mona's house. "It seems funny, this woman wanting to meet with you. A student of Mona's, out of the blue."

"I have to admit I'm curious."

"She didn't say what it was about?"

"Not really. She's been out of town so Mona's death is

new to her. I think she just wanted someone to talk with about it. I'll let you know when I pick up Anna."

"Yes, do. I'm curious too."

When I got to the cafe, a woman was standing by the entrance, gazing into the parking lot. She cocked her head expectantly as I approached.

"Eve Fisher?" I asked.

She smiled and offered a hand. "And you must be Kate. I really appreciate your meeting me like this."

Eve was not the mousy, timid soul of advanced years I had pictured. Although her hair was mostly gray, it was styled in a fashionable blow-dry feather cut, and her face, though etched with experience, was earnest and attentive. She wore fashionable wool slacks and a sweater, with a yellow and black scarf knotted around her neck. She looked more like she belonged on the pages of *McCalls* than in a news article on women with controlling husbands.

"I felt so bad about dropping Ms. Sterling's class without explaining," Eve said. "Especially after . . . well, after she was so nice to me." We moved inside, found a table by the window and ordered. "I tried to write her a note before we left town, but things were so rushed, and I thought I'd have a chance to explain once we got back. Unfinished business is so . . . ," she drew in a breath, "so untidy."

Our coffee and muffins arrived. Eve stirred a packet of Sweet and Low into her cup, took a sip, and began peeling the wrapper from her muffin. "I shouldn't really be having the muffin. I gained five pounds on our cruise. Eat, eat, and eat. That's about all I did, that and soak up the sun."

It sounded nice, especially the sun part. "Where'd you go?"

"The Caribbean. It's something I've wanted to do for years, but Ike, my husband, always said that . . . well, he was never very enthusiastic. Then one day, out of the blue, he shows up with tickets." She laughed, looked embarrassed and picked up her coffee cup. "Oh, I know why he did it. I'm not stupid. But it was sweet of him nonetheless."

She set the cup down. "That's what Ms. Sterling couldn't understand, and why I feel so bad I never got a chance to explain. Ike never liked my taking classes at the college, but when I started working on my degree, he got really upset. I think he felt threatened, like maybe I was going to pass him up in some way, decide I didn't need him. Or maybe it was just change that scared him. In any case, he kept getting more and more agitated. He even went storming into school one day and yelled at poor Ms. Sterling. I was so embarrassed when I found out."

Eve's cheeks grew pink, as though she were embarrassed now, at the memory. "I couldn't believe he'd actually done something like that. Anyway, Ms. Sterling called me the next day, not angry at all, but worried and very supportive. She went out of her way to offer help, and I know what she must think . . . uh, must have thought when I never came back. That I let myself be bought off for a cruise."

"Didn't you?" It was so close to what I'd thought myself that the words came on their own.

It didn't appear, however, that Eve took affront. "I suppose from Mona's perspective I did, but that's not the way I see it. You've got to understand that I'm fifty-eight years old. I'm not about to change the world or charge off in pursuit of some fancy new career. In the scheme of things, a college degree isn't all that important to me. It was more like a hobby. I know Ike comes on like a raging bull sometimes, but he's actually not such a bad guy, and on balance I'd rather have him happy than angry."

"But if it's something you enjoy—"

"There are other things I enjoy." She paused and offered me a feeble smile. "I wasn't such a hot student anyway, if you want to know the truth. Not that Ms. Sterling was ever anything but encouraging. For instance, I wrote this simply awful paper about a woman who'd lost a child. We read our papers aloud to the class, so I know how much better the others were, but Ms. Sterling acted like she was really interested. You don't find many teachers like her."

I found myself intrigued by the same question I'd had when I'd read the assignment that day at Mona's. "Was it based on your own personal experience?"

A little laugh. "Goodness, no. My children are all healthy and happy, knock on wood. Of course they're grown now. In fact, I was visiting my daughter in St. Louis when the idea for the piece came to me. We were supposed to take a news item and go beyond the facts, write a poem or sketch which dealt with the emotions underlying the event. There was a story in the Sunday paper about missing children that got my attention.

"You hear so much these days about kidnappings and abductions. It's front-page news for a day or a week, but then it's over and the media's on to the next case. I can't help but wonder about the families, how they cope year after year with such a terrible loss. Can you imagine how awful it must be?"

Indeed I could. These past few weeks the thought had never been far from my mind.

"Anyway, this article was based on interviews with families of missing children. It was very moving. I used it as the basis for my assignment, but I turned in the original article as well as my own because I knew my piece didn't begin to do justice to the subject."

I remembered the folded section of the *St. Louis Post-Dispatch* the cops had found that day at Mona's. It must have been the one Eve gave her.

"Most teachers wouldn't have given it a second thought, but Ms. Sterling was genuinely interested. She wanted to know if I was acquainted with any of the families personally and how I'd come across the article in the first place. It's because she was so helpful and encouraging that I feel just awful about dropping her class the way I did, without any explanation. Of course Ike says she probably just wanted to use the information to her own advantage, like maybe she'd interview the McNevitts herself and write her own article, for money."

I choked on the piece of muffin I'd just plopped into my mouth. "McNevitt?"

"That's the name of the family I focused my paper on. Ted and Laurie McNevitt. Their daughter Madelaine was kidnapped at six months. Her twin sister had a doctor's appointment that day, otherwise she might have been the one abducted. Think how that must weigh on the poor child all her life."

I agreed it was pretty terrible, but what tugged at my mind most was the name. Laurie McNevitt, the woman who'd left several messages on Mona's machine, who'd practically pleaded for a return call. About an interview? It didn't make sense.

The waitress came by offering refills on our coffee. We both declined. As we left, Eve said, "You were awfully sweet to agree to meet me. I know it's silly, but this whole mess with Ike and Ms. Sterling made me feel terribly guilty. I feel so much better now that I've unburdened myself."

I assured Eve that I'd enjoyed talking with her, which was the truth. What I didn't tell her, was that our conversation had left me feeling curiously *more* burdened. Maybe it was the timing of our meeting, coming as it had in the wake of my recent anxiety about kidnappers, or maybe it was the memory of despair in Laurie McNevitt's voice. Whatever the reason, Eve's tale clung to me like the shadow of an unpleasant dream. What if it was some kind of omen, a warning from the misty regions beyond? I didn't believe in such things, but I was suddenly seized by a sensation of dread, a sort of free-floating chill that turned my bones to ice.

I found a phone and called Claire to tell her I'd be a bit late. When no one answered, I left a message, then headed for the county library. I was hoping that with a trip to McDonald's under her belt, Anna wouldn't mind spending a little extra time at Jodi's.

The newspaper and periodical room was more crowded than it had been mid-week, so I had to wait for a microfiche machine. And then I had to find a librarian to show me once again how to use the darn thing. Some of us were simply not destined to live in a high-tech era.

I knew the article had appeared on a Sunday, and I figured it had to have been sometime after the first of the year, since Eve wouldn't have been in Mona's class before that. But since I didn't know the exact date, I had to run the spool fast forward from week to week, a process which left me cross-eyed and slightly nauseated. At last, though, I found it.

I skimmed through the page until I found the name McNevitt. The writer talked first about the abduction. Jennifer McNevitt, then six months old, had woken up with a high fever. Her mother made a doctor's appointment, leaving Jennifer's twin sister, Madelaine, with a baby sitter. The sitter had taken the child to a nearby park where she apparently met her boyfriend. What sort of activity the two of them were engaged in wasn't made clear, but when the sitter finally thought to check on the baby, she was gone. There were no witnesses, no leads. Although the sitter had been a suspect initially, she'd been cleared.

The McNevitts had been young, without a lot of resources, but the community had rallied to help, putting up reward money, sending out flyers, fielding calls on possible leads. For the first couple of weeks, the papers had followed every development. The McNevitt name had appeared, in one form or another, almost daily. And then, as Eve had so aptly noted, the story had grown old and faded from attention.

In the interview, Laurie McNevitt talked about the anguish she experienced, the waning hope, as lead after lead went nowhere, as the authorities cut back on their search and the press coverage dried up. For a while, she said, the pain was unbearable, burning inside her like a red-hot iron. It was still there, she explained, but more like an ember that would flare, suddenly and unexpectedly, into four-alarm panic. The hardest thing, she said, was not knowing.

Tears gathered in my eyes as I looked at a picture of the family. Mother, father, Jennifer, and a baby boy who'd been born since the tragedy. A picture-perfect family, except for the black hole at the center of their lives. I flipped onto the next screen for the conclusion of the piece. There at the bottom of the page was a color close-up of Jennifer, the twin on whom the gods had chosen to smile.

I felt my heart rise into my throat as recognition slammed through me.

Jennifer was a carbon copy of Jodi.

30

It doesn't necessarily mean what you think it does, I told myself. Doesn't everybody have a double somewhere in the world? Or maybe Claire and Laurie McNevitt are related, second cousins in a family where nearly all the girls are curly redheads.

I tried to convince myself the similarity was simply coincidence, but deep down I knew it wasn't. The resemblance was too striking for the girls to be anything but twins. Jodi Jorgensen was Madelaine McNevitt, the six-month-old baby who'd disappeared five years ago from a St. Louis suburb. Claire had told me she'd grown up in southern Illinois, left five years ago and never returned. She claimed to be a widow, yet didn't have a single picture of her late husband. Nor did she ever speak of his family. Jodi's birth certificate listed her mother's name as Wilhelmina, which is a long way from Claire. And it listed her birthplace as Boston, which Claire had told me was a short stay. I was willing to bet she'd gone there simply to pick up a birth certificate for the baby she was claiming as her daughter. Besides, Jodi didn't look anything at all like Claire. Not in build, coloring, or features. If truth be told, she didn't look much like a Jorgensen either.

My head felt light, disconnected, as though I were peering the wrong way through a pair of binoculars. My throat had closed up so tight I was having trouble breathing, and my skin felt several sizes too small. I tried rewinding the microfiche but my hands were shaking and I had trouble working the machine. It made a shrill screeching sound, which brought the librarian running.

She scowled, then saw the expression on my face. "You okay?" she asked.

"I'm sorry," I mumbled, pushing back my chair and causing yet another loud racket. "Suddenly I don't feel so well."

As I took off for the door, I struggled with a second harrowing thought. Had Mona seen what I'd seen, come to the same conclusion I had? She'd taken snapshots of Jodi and had tried getting in touch with Laurie McNevitt. She must have known. Had Claire somehow gotten wind of that fact? Was she a murderer on top of everything else?

With a deepening sense of dread, I realized how neatly the pieces fit. Claire didn't drink, so it would make sense that she'd grab whatever liquor bottle she could find without thought as to the contents. She worked at a nursing home too, so she probably had access to morphine. And since she lived on the property, nobody would have thought twice about seeing her there that night.

My mind was a jumble. The thoughts whirled about like dust in a windstorm. I couldn't hold onto any of them. Only one thing was clear. I had to get Anna.

Outside, with the wind and rain lashing at my face, I

scurried toward the car. The pavement was slick, and thick with water. Halfway across the lot I stepped in an ankle-deep puddle and almost lost my balance. Oil and mud splattered my slacks, oozed into my shoes. At the car, I fumbled in my purse for the key, and then had trouble fitting it into the ignition. Finally, the car started and I pulled into the street, making a left turn across two lanes of traffic. Pushing the accelerator to the floor, I made it through the stop light just as the yellow flicked to red, then zig-zagged lanes impatiently, passing every car in my path. By comparison, Sharon would have qualified as driver-of-the-year.

Stay calm, I repeated to myself, mantra-style. Stay calm. You're going to park in Claire's driveway, knock on her door, plead an appointment if she asks you in, but linger long enough to chat about the girls' morning and thank her for inviting Anna for a visit. Smiling and cheerful, that's the image you want. No point raising her suspicions or letting on that anything has changed.

It took seemingly forever to weave my way through the traffic and onto the freeway. Conditions there were no better. Cars slowed and moved at a snail's pace as three lanes narrowed to two. Cal Trans in its endless endeavor to improve our roadways. I forced myself to take the slow, deep breaths I'd learned in Lamaze class, then thought of Anna again and felt tears prick at my eyes.

I was still working on my breathing when I pulled into Claire's. Her car was gone. I rang the bell anyway, then knocked. How could they not be back from lunch?

I checked my watch. It had been over an hour since I'd called and left a message. Even if they'd gotten a late start, they'd have to be back soon. I returned to the car to wait, wishing I'd thought to call Michael before rushing over to Claire's. But I didn't want to leave now, not when they would be returning any minute.

Inside, the car was damp and stuffy. And finger-numbing cold. Rain drummed against the roof, and the windows began to fog over. I shivered, turned on the engine for heat, and tried to ignore the sense of unease that rose, like molasses, in my throat. I didn't want to think the unthinkable. Didn't want to give in to panic. I turned on the radio, listened to a song about heartache, a commercial about headache. I checked my watch again. Maybe they'd taken in a movie or stopped to do some shopping.

Then, in a white flash of terror, I remembered that I'd told Claire about Eve Fisher. Told her about the paper of Eve's I'd found by Mona's phone. And I remembered too, Claire's pointed interest in our meeting. Lord, please, no. Don't let Claire recognize Eve's name, don't let the paper be what alerted her to Mona's suspicions.

I raced to Claire's door again and started pounding, as if by sheer will I could make Anna appear. Next door, an older woman I recognized as one of Mona's neighbors pulled up and began unloading groceries. She waved to me.

"You haven't seen Claire, have you?"

"They left, all three of them, right after you dropped your little girl off. Figured they were late for a party or something the way they took out of here."

Lord, please. Please. I tore back to the car and made it to McDonald's in record time. One o'clock on a rainy Saturday. The place was jammed. Shrieking kids and screaming babies, and parents yelling to be heard over the din.

I jostled my way to the counter, ignoring the scowls directed my way. "I'm looking for a friend," I said, "a little taller than me, large boned, short brown hair. She had two little girls with her." I realized I'd just described half the people there that afternoon.

The man in front of me gave me an angry look and angled his body so that I had to speak over his shoulder. "One of them had red curls," I said, then stopped short. Not any more, I reminded myself. Claire had cut Jodi's hair short, probably dyed it as well since it appeared darker and less red, thus radically changing her appearance. Now I knew why. I reached into my purse and pulled out Anna's picture. "This is one of the girls," I said, leaning past the man who was making every effort to nudge me aside.

The woman behind the counter couldn't have been more than a girl herself. She had a flat, bovine face marked with acne. She glanced at the picture, shook her head indifferently, then turned back to her customer. I started to work my way down the counter when I realized the futility of it. No one was going to remember who'd been here, and what difference did it make anyway? Disheartened, I called Claire's once more in the hope they might have returned, then drove home.

My house felt empty and cold, like a crypt. A sudden, suffocating helplessness rolled over me. I took a deep breath, then another. Stop it, the voice of reason admonished. Get a hold of yourself.

I called Michael and left a message, using the word "urgent" so many times I lost count. Then I shed my wet shoes and socks, and put a kettle of water on for tea. Max had greeted me with more than his usual enthusiasm and was bounding from one side of the kitchen to the other, but when I opened the door for him to go out, he refused.

"The rain won't hurt you," I grumbled, but I wasn't in any mood to force the issue. Sooner or later he'd decide the need was greater than his disdain for inclement weather.

When the water was hot, I poured a cupful, dropped in a tea bag and sat down at the table. I felt useless sitting there, doing nothing, but I wanted to stay by the phone for Michael's call.

Anna's coloring book was lying open on the table where she'd left it that morning. The mighty and ferocious Tyrannosaurus Rex rendered harmless by Anna's strokes of purple and pink. A lump rose in my throat. She hadn't wanted to go to Jodi's, and I'd forced her. Reprimanded her when she'd complained that Claire was creepy. I bit my lip, fought the tears, tried to reassure myself with the memory of all those times I'd been sure something terrible had happened, and it hadn't.

I sipped my tea, which, despite the deep golden color, tasted like stale tap water. Max sidled up next to me and whimpered. Scratching the fur behind his ears, I tried to comfort myself as well. My imagination had gone into overdrive was all. This wouldn't be the first time. They may have been stuck in traffic, or decided to take in a movie. Besides, it wasn't like Claire was a stranger. The police would have no trouble getting her picture, her license and social security numbers, her bank account. She couldn't simply vanish into thin air.

And hadn't I made some rather sizable deductive leaps anyway? Even if Jodi was the missing Madelaine McNevitt, that didn't necessarily prove Claire was the kidnapper. Nor did it mean that Claire was a killer. There were Brandon and Oscar to consider as well. Brandon and Oscar, two less than exemplary characters whose association with each other seemed suspect at best.

Finally, Max settled at my feet. I took another sip of tea, rocked back in my chair, and looked at the phone. Why didn't Michael call?

Outside, the sky had darkened. I watched the trees bend in the wind, listened to the branches scrape against the house. I heard a rustling sound, turned, saw nothing. I managed a smile at my own spookiness. I rubbed a bare foot against Max's fur and turned back to watch the heavy drops of rain pound against the patio. In the glass, I caught a reflection of something behind me. I turned again, and saw Claire standing in the hall doorway, my heavy kitchen cleaver in her outstretched hand.

31

Claire stepped towards me slowly, without speaking. Her eyes were dark and intense, her expression flat. The hand that held the cleaver was as steady as her gaze.

"Where's Anna?" I asked, in a near whisper.

A thin smile, cold as ice, played on her lips.

"Is she all right?"

"She's going to be fine, Kate. Just fine."

Claire's voice was like a fingernail against chalkboard, it sent a shiver down my spine. "Where is she? You didn't hurt her, did you?"

Another steely smile. "That's not really what you should be worrying about right now."

I swallowed. My throat felt as though it were stuffed with cotton. "How did you get in, anyway?"

"The key under the brick out back. You told me about it yourself not too long ago. But that's not really what you should be worrying about either."

Max pushed himself out from under the table and started prancing around the room with excitement, his tail wagging so hard his whole rear end shook. Terrific. A dog who would fiddle while Rome burned, or in this case, while his devoted mistress was chopped to pieces.

"Did you and that Eve woman have a nice chat?" Claire asked, ignoring the canine festivities taking place at her feet. "Did she bend your ear with her pathetic, woeful tale about the baby who was kidnapped from the park?" Claire took a step closer. The metal blade glistened in the light.

I was still sitting at the table, afraid that any sudden move on my part would trigger the same in Claire. But I had to do *something*. "Put that thing down," I said, looking at the cleaver, "and let's talk." I tried for the even, unruffled tone of a television heroine, but I missed it by a mile.

Claire shook her head. "Talking never does any good. Never did, never will. People only hear what they want to hear."

"We can work something out, I'm sure of it."

She shook her head again.

"If you try anything, I'll fight back and we'll both be hurt. What's the good in that?"

Claire held up her other hand. She was grasping what looked like a rectangular plastic box.

"Recognize this?"

I shook my head.

"It's a stun gun. A most useful device." A snicker rose from her throat. "Kind of like my American Express card—I never leave home without it. A tad uncomfortable, I've been told. But I don't imagine it's as bad as this." She raised the arm holding the cleaver.

An involuntary shudder worked its way down my spine.

I felt a deep, nauseous fear in the pit of my stomach. "Why are you doing this?"

"Come on, Kate. Let's not play games." She gazed at her reflection in the shiny metal blade. "It's not like I enjoy this, you know."

She was thinking, perhaps, that I did?

Claire sighed, lifted her eyes from the blade. "I was actually quite fond of Mona. But when I spotted that newspaper article on her desk, and then saw the way she looked at me . . ." Claire shrugged. "I had to do something."

"So you killed her." No game playing there.

"I thought it would be such an easy solution, but nothing in my life is ever easy." Claire sighed again. "Who else would wind up with a baby who happened to be a twin? Without that, I'd have been home free."

Probably true. I swallowed and tried to concentrate. Keep them talking, I was sure I'd read that somewhere. "You didn't know she was a twin at the time?"

"How could I? The baby was alone in the buggy, tucked under a yellow blanket. I didn't even know if it was a boy or a girl. Not that it mattered either way."

"Why did you do it?"

"You wouldn't understand. Things have always gone right for you."

"That's not true."

"True enough. Nothing's ever worked out for me. I was always the kid who ate lunch alone, the last one chosen for a team, the partner no one wanted. I was thirty-one years old and I'd been on two dates in my entire life, both of them arranged by one of my aunt's co-workers."

Claire's voice grew more agitated. Deep red splotches colored her face. "It was pretty obvious I was never going to find a husband. And I've got some medical problem, the doctors said I probably wouldn't be able to have children. Then, at the park that day, it was like a sign from God. This woman pushed the carriage down the path and parked it under a tree, not five feet from me. I was so envious I could feel it, kind of like acid eating away at my insides. The woman was young and pretty, all the things I wasn't, and she had a baby, which I never would.''

"You could have—"

Claire's eyes narrowed and she cut me off angrily. "Do you know what that woman did? She left her baby, that precious little child, all alone. Didn't even check on it before walking off into the bushes with some stud. Oh, I watched them for a while, kissing and pawing at each other until I couldn't stand it another minute. It was so unfair.''

Claire was waving both arms about as she talked. I inched back, out of the ever-expanding path of danger. "But that wasn't the mother," I said, "it was just the baby sitter.''

"You think I was going to take the child back when I learned that? Laurie McNevitt was no saint herself, either. She should never have trusted a woman like that with her baby. Never. Besides, she still had the other child, she didn't need two.''

Claire's words were rendered all the more horrible by the reasonableness of her tone.

Just then the phone rang. "Don't answer it," Claire ordered.

I held my breath, waiting for my chance to lunge for the phone. But Claire positioned herself so that I couldn't. After four rings the machine clicked on. Michael's message was brief. "Call me when you get in.''

Claire looked agitated. A shadow passed over her face. "I never wanted to hurt anyone. Not you, not Mona, not even Brandon. But you do what you have to do."

"Brandon?"

"See what I mean, how things never work out for me? I thought getting rid of Mona would be the end of all this. But Brandon found out, too. He had that newspaper article and . . . ," she swallowed, ". . . and the death certificate for Jodi Jorgensen. He'd overheard Mona talking to someone about it on the phone, but since she hadn't mentioned any names, he didn't know who she was talking about. After Mona died though, he saw his big chance. He went through her things searching for more information."

Claire's expression grew tight, her features sharp and scrunched together. "I looked everywhere for that damn newspaper Saturday night, and I couldn't find it. Brandon, though, he found it right away."

Her breathing was becoming shallow and quick. She paced two steps to her left, then to her right. Her eyes were fiery and intense, but they never left my face.

"He wanted money," she said indignantly. "I don't have money, not the kind he wanted."

"So you killed him too?"

"I had to. I told you that." Her voice was pitched high and plated with a frantic uneasiness. "I get no pleasure from this, you know. It's not what I wanted to have happen." With a sudden jerk of her wrist, she glanced at her watch. "Get your shoes on. I want to get this over with."

The stagnant, brassy taste of fear filled my mouth, rose into my nose and down my throat. I looked around for a weapon, anything to defend myself. A coloring book and a cup of lukewarm tea. It wasn't much. "Where are we going?"

"For a drive. You're going to have an automobile accident, Kate. I'm sorry you can't go peacefully into the night the way Mona did, but it should be over fairly quickly."

My eyes were focused on Claire's hands. I probably had more of a chance against the cleaver than the stun gun, but I couldn't figure out how I was going to get either one.

Claire tossed me my shoes. "Lace them up," she said, "then tie them together. No tricks, I'm going to check."

My mind still frantically searching for a plan, I did as she said. The shoes were cold and clammy on my feet, and they squished when I stood.

"Take your purse," Claire said, extracting the car keys and then tossing it to me. "We want this to look authentic."

She stayed far enough away that it was impossible to swing the purse at her. And with my feet hobbled, I couldn't move more than a few inches at a time anyway.

She held the door. "After you."

Outside, we made our way toward my car, Claire at my elbow, her stun gun readied. My eyes searched desperately for some neighbor or gardener or encyclopedia salesman making his rounds. I would even have welcomed a messenger of the Lord. But the day was dark and blustery, the kind that kept sensible people indoors.

Claire opened the door on the passenger side and shoved me in. I felt the panic surge through me. This was it. Once I was in the car with her, she'd zap me with the stun gun and it would be all over. Quickly, and without thinking, I reached for the doors and locked them. Then I started fumbling with the knots in my laces.

But I wasn't fast enough. Claire was around the car in an instant. She inserted the key, opened the door and raised the arm with the stun gun. Holding my purse out in front like a shield, I leaned on the horn. And held my breath. Claire yanked the purse from my grip and tossed it into the back.

"That was stupid," she said, scowling.

The only thing stupid about it was that it hadn't worked.

Just then a jogger rounded the corner. I prayed that he wasn't tuned in to his Walkman, then hit the horn again. I also started screaming—loud, raw screams that I'd never in a million years imagined myself capable of.

The man looked up, perplexed. I kept screaming, and started waving my arms as well.

Claire stood by the door, frozen in a moment of uncertainty.

From behind us, the heavy bass of a car stereo pulsated with a deafening beat. The jogger said something, but I couldn't make out his words. Finally, he started toward us. Claire pivoted, and dashed the other direction, into the street.

There was a screech of brakes, a heavy, sickening thud, and then silence, broken only by the steady, throbbing beat of a rap tune.

32

For a moment everything was still, like a freeze-frame photo. My ears rang with the nerve-shattering screech of tires and the horrifying, almost silent thump, of metal against flesh. Then, seconds later, Michael's car and two blue-and-whites pulled onto the street.

"It's Claire," I sputtered, pointing to the limp figure lying by the side of the road. My voice shook as terribly and uncontrollably as my body. "She was . . . she was going to kill me. Just like she killed Mona and Brandon."

The jogger had run over to check on the injured woman. Two of the patrolmen joined him, while the third endeavored to talk to the young male driver who seemed unable to stand still or say anything beyond, "Shit, man. She came out of nowhere."

Michael touched my shoulder. "Are you hurt?"

I shook my head, gasped for air, found that I'd forgotten how to breathe. "But she has Anna. Oh God, Michael, what if something's happened to Anna?"

The next few hours passed in a blur. The paramedics loaded Claire into the ambulance and took off amidst sirens and flashing red lights. The young man was escorted into a patrol car and driven away. A second uniformed officer talked to the jogger and the assemblage of neighbors which had materialized out of nowhere. There were tow trucks, fire trucks, television trucks, even one of those deli-on-wheels trucks. A regular beehive of activity, which was amazing considering that only a short time earlier, when I'd been desperately searching for some sign of life, the street had been utterly deserted.

Michael immediately put out a bulletin on Anna and Jodi, then called in a forensic specialist to go over Claire's car inch by inch. "See if we can pick up any clues as to where they might have gone," he said.

I nodded stiffly. I didn't need him to tell me they were also looking for signs of torn flesh or blood.

I'd given him the story in bits and pieces, but he had me go over it once more. This time he took notes, asked questions, nodded periodically, then looked at the other officer he'd introduced as Peter.

"Everything matches," Peter said. "Too bad we didn't put it all together a couple of hours earlier."

When Peter left to make a call, I rested my head against Michael's shoulder. He wrapped his arms around me and kissed the top of my head. I was too frightened to cry, but I couldn't stop trembling.

"It's going to be okay, Kate. We'll find the girls and we'll find them unharmed. There would be no reason for Claire to hurt them."

But she's crazy, I thought bleakly. There was no telling what she might do.

Peter called Michael from the kitchen. "We've got the map laid out and the distances marked. You want to come take a look?"

"Why don't you go lie down," Michael suggested,

touching my cheek. "I'll come check on you in a little bit."

There was no way I was going to sleep, or even rest. But sitting like a stone statue in my living room wasn't doing anything for me either. I headed for the bathroom, peeled off my clothes, which were stiff with mud and sweat, and stepped into the shower. I was no less frantic when I got out, but at least I was clean.

I was in the hallway headed for the kitchen when the phone rang. I stopped and held my breath.

"Speaking," I heard Michael say. There was a pause. "I see."

His tone was grave. My body turned to ice. The conversation played out in my imagination. They'd found two girls, strangled or stabbed or God knew what, but not alive. They'd want someone to make a positive identification.

"Right. I'll bring her over."

The silence that followed was deafening. I forced myself to the doorway. Michael turned, saw me, and gave me the thumbs up sign. His grin was as wide and bright as a summer's day.

"They picked up both girls about ten minutes ago," he said. "They're scared, but otherwise fine."

That's when I started crying, and I cried all the way to the station. I was still mopping up tears when I pushed past the police sergeant to get to Anna. I hugged her tight and blubbered in her ear.

"You shouldn't have been worried," she said airily. "I knew exactly where we were the whole time."

As it turned out, Anna had, in fact, handled herself admirably. Claire had left them at the movie theater in the mall, saying that she had shopping to do. She'd told them to wait for her on the bench outside the ice cream shop if she was late, then softened the deal with the promise of cones. Anna hadn't enjoyed or understood the movie, which was some avant-garde Japanese film, and she'd grown tired after thirty minutes sitting on the appointed bench. Peeved though she was, she'd nonetheless tried to be a good sport. But finally, the injustice of the day had gotten to her and she'd done exactly what she'd been taught to do when she needed help—find a policeman or security guard. It was hardly her fault that she'd mistaken the telephone repairman for a cop; he was, after all, in uniform, and it had all worked out in the long run anyway.

Or worked out for some of us.

As Anna filled me in on what had happened, I watched a woman police officer talking to Jodi at the far side of the room. Anna's adventure had a happy ending, but no matter how you sliced it, Jodi's didn't. It seemed terribly unfair that the big loser in all this was an innocent child. A child who would once again be forcibly snatched from a woman she knew as mother. My only consolation was the hope that with time, Jodi would blossom in the love of her real family. That she would learn to laugh and romp and revel in the joy of being a child. And that she would ultimately lead a much fuller, happier life with her parents than with Claire.

Just then the side door opened and a man appeared. The blond, elflike man I'd seen with Brandon. I turned to Michael. "That's him," I whispered.

Michael laughed. "I know." The man approached. "Kate, I'd like you to meet Oscar Erikson, private investigator working for the McNevitts."

"Guess my instincts aren't so good," I told Michael the next morning. "I was ready to send Mr. Erikson away for life, yet I trusted a kidnapper and killer with my own child."

"Mmm." Michael nibbled a piece of croissant. He'd brought over a whole bag of them, still warm from the bakery, plus several baskets of fresh, ripe strawberries. Libby and Anna had devoured their share quickly and were now in the front room engrossed in a game of checkers, leaving the two of us to a leisurely and unexpectedly civilized Sunday brunch.

I rested my chin on my hands. "I still don't understand why Brandon and Mr. Erikson were together the other day."

"As far as I can make out, Brandon's sole interest in this matter was what was in it for him. He had his eye on the big bucks, and he was willing to play both sides to see which was most lucrative. He was hoping he could convince the McNevitts, through Erikson, to up the reward."

The Missouri lottery. And Jodi was his winning ticket. That the McNevitts actually lived on the Illinois side of St. Louis seemed to have escaped him. "That's pretty disgusting," I said, "using a child's misfortune for your own gain."

"We both know Brandon wasn't any boy scout. It might have worked, too. You can imagine how desperate the McNevitts were, especially after Mona's phone call raised their hopes."

"She actually talked to them?"

Michael shook his head. "She contacted the police there, wanting information about the case. She didn't let on that she knew anything, but word got back to McNevitts. They hired Erikson and asked him to follow up on it."

"Why not the FBI?"

He broke off an end of a croissant and tossed it to Max. "Well, for one thing, what they had wasn't exactly a solid lead. Besides, they blamed the feds for botching the case in the beginning and they weren't willing to take a chance on having it blown again. By the time Erikson arrived though, Mona was already dead, supposedly a suicide."

"And the poor McNevitts were back to square one." Worse, really, because they'd thought they might be getting somewhere.

"Erikson thought it was strange, that's why he called our office and asked if we'd found anything suspicious about the death. He nosed around for a couple of days, tried to talk to Libby, at school of all places—"

"He tried to talk to me, too," I added, remembering the phone call he'd placed from the Pelican Lodge.

"He didn't handle any of it very well, in my opinion,

but he was concerned about keeping a low profile. He was afraid if word got out, whoever had the child would simply move on." Michael reached for a second croissant. "When the family got a call from Brandon asking about the reward, they told Erikson to get in touch with the guy. But Brandon wouldn't tell him a thing, except that the price wasn't right."

"But you knew it was Claire. Somehow you figured it out before I told you."

He nodded. "I'd only just put it together late yesterday. Brandon's father was going through his belongings and came up with a death certificate for a month-old baby named Jodi Jorgensen. He thought it was odd and figured it might shed some light on his son's death. I think he was worried that Brandon might have been the baby's father."

I did a quick calculation. "He'd have been only fourteen at the time."

Michael shrugged. "The father must have had some reason for thinking the way he did. The name didn't mean anything to him, but it went off like a neon light for me."

"You actually remembered Claire's last name?" I thought I'd only mentioned her once or twice in passing, and I wasn't sure I'd ever mentioned Jodi.

"Not from anything you'd said. If you recall, I told you that we had a break in the arson case. What we had was a partial plate which led us to Claire Jorgensen. We questioned her Friday and got nowhere. It seemed pretty farfetched anyway. What motive could a suburban housewife possibly have for setting a school fire? But when Erikson came forward with this stuff about the kidnapping, it made more sense."

Not to me, it didn't. I shook my head in confusion.

"The school had a copy of Jodi's birth certificate," Michael explained. "Claire wanted it destroyed."

The light bulb went off. She'd taken the birth certificate from Sharon's soccer files as well. Poor George, Sharon had blamed him unfairly.

"I went back to see Claire again yesterday afternoon," Michael continued. "She wasn't there, but I got to talking to a neighbor who told me you'd been there too. That you'd been half hysterical, in fact."

I felt a chill just remembering it. The terror, the anxiety, the panic. I didn't want to think about what I'd be feeling today if Anna hadn't been found. What Laurie McNevitt must have felt everyday for the past five years. "You've no idea how terrible it was."

His eyes were soft, as was his voice. "I can only begin to imagine, and even that's pretty awful."

I felt tears prick at my eyes, as they had periodically since yesterday afternoon. I couldn't help thinking about what might have happened, what in fact had happened to one little girl five years ago. I got up to reheat the coffee and wipe my eyes on the sly. Michael pulled a section of newspaper from the heap at the far end of the table.

"If Eve Fisher hadn't been in Mona's class," I said, after a bit, "if she hadn't been visiting her daughter the week the assignment was given . . ."

"If Jennifer McNevitt hadn't taken sick one night five years ago. That's the way life works, Kate. You think about it too much, you go crazy."

I poured us both a second cup of coffee, then stared off into the drippy, gray morning while Michael read the paper.

Suddenly he rocked forward in his chair with a wild, loopy laugh. "Hey, they found your slasher."

"My slasher?"

"Your tires, remember? The guy was caught red-handed by two little old ladies out walking their poodles. Seems he has a thing against you 'knee-jerk liberals.' "

The other day I'd been called a snooty society woman and today I was a knee-jerk liberal. At least I wasn't in a rut. But I wasn't exactly following Michael's point either.

"It's that bumper-sticker," he said, caught up in the humor of it all. *"It will be a great day when the schools have all the money they need and the air force has to hold a bake sale to buy bombers.* This guy's on a campaign to teach 'your type' a lesson."

A man with a cause. However misguided, it was a step above being stalked by a killer. I gave an inward sigh of relief. "If only he'd made that clearer to begin with—"

"See what I mean about not knowing what's germane to a case until it's over?"

I nodded.

But Michael didn't want an answer. He leaned across the table, suddenly serious. "I've been so worried that someone was out to get you. Even after we knew about Claire, I wasn't sure it was over. You managed to stir up a lot of people over Mona's death, you know. Any one of them could have had a reason for wanting you silenced." He reached for my hand and began tracing a pattern on my palm. "If something were to happen to you—"

I recognized the tone—we were approaching heavy discussion time. I removed my hand from his and tried steering the conversation back to the simpler subject of murder. "There were a lot of things that seemed germane and weren't," I observed. "Things that made me think it was Gary who'd killed Mona. Or maybe Bambi. He had such an obvious motive and she's, well, she's just weird."

Michael raised an eyebrow. "You going to change the subject every time we get personal?"

"I believe it was you who changed the subject first."

He pursed his lips, then started to say something, but I cut him off.

"Not only did Gary have the financial motive, I'm sure Mona had something on him, too. Why else would he have agreed to a settlement he was so clearly unhappy with?"

"Gary may well be guilty of some offense, but chances are we'll never know what it is. Not unless the IRS gets interested anyway. Bambi, now that's a different story." Michael leaned back in his chair and popped a strawberry into his mouth. "Seems manicurist wasn't Miss Bambi's first chosen career. Until last year she worked as a dancer, so to speak, at a back-alley strip joint."

"You're kidding?"

He shook his head. "Apparently this was a part of her past Bambi wasn't eager to share with her future husband. During the divorce, Mona hired someone to dig into Bambi's background, then used the information as leverage. Mona would keep her lips sealed if Bambi could persuade Gary to accept the settlement offer."

"My, my." I don't know why exactly, but I found myself more favorably disposed towards Bambi the ex-stripper than Bambi the fluffy-headed fiancée. Maybe the woman had some character after all. "Life sure is full of surprises," I mused. "You think you know a person, but you never do, really."

"Speaking of which . . ." Michael reached into his

pocket, pulled out an envelope and slid it across the table to me.

"What's this?"

"Tickets."

"To what?"

"Not what, where." He had an odd look on his face, solemn and unsure, yet tinged with boyish impatience. "They're tickets to Maui," he said softly. "For spring break."

I'm sure my own face, in response, looked every bit as odd.

"You've been complaining of the cold and all, and I thought . . ." He paused for a breath. "And I thought that if we went away together, spent an entire week with each other, it might convince you . . ." Here he stopped altogether and looked at me. The silence rang in my ears. ". . . Well, it would be a chance to see if you could stand having me around, you know, on a regular basis."

I felt a ping in my chest, a kind of breathlessness deep inside me. "It's a . . . a nice idea," I stammered, "but I can't leave Anna for that long."

Michael nodded, then gave me a slow, impish smile. "There's a ticket there for her, too."

"Oh." I brushed the crumbs from my plate into a little pile and worked at getting air into my lungs. "Well, there's Libby to consider as well. I mean, she's been through a lot and I'd hate to just shuttle her off somewhere."

Michael pulled out another envelope. The smile grew to a grin. "I figured you'd say that so I got an extra ticket."

"Oh."

"Oh?" His eyes were a soft, liquid gray. As warm and

inviting as his smile. All at once the breathlessness in my chest gave way to a tidal wave of feelings. Most of them, I have to admit, were pretty nice. I opened my mouth to speak.

Michael shook his head. "Sorry, they don't allow dogs without a six-month quarantine."

"That's not what I was going to say."

"No?"

"What I was going to say was, it sounds lovely. The very best idea I could imagine."

I returned Michael's grin with one of my own.

ABOUT THE AUTHOR

Jonnie Jacobs lives with her husband and two sons in northern California. She loves hearing from readers. You can write to her c/o Kensington Publishing Corporation. Jonnie can also be reached via e-mail at jonnie@jonniejacobs.com, or you can visit her Web site at http://www.NMOMysteries.com.

It started with my father's death and nearly ended with my own, though both these events were somewhat peripheral to the murders that rocked the town of Silver Creek early last summer.

It was my father's funeral that brought me home in the first place. When I left Silver Creek twelve years ago to attend college, I vowed I'd put as much distance between the town and myself as possible. And while I ultimately ended up less than four hours away in driving time, my life in San Francisco was light years away in other respects. I was a senior associate in one of the city's small, but notable, law firms; I owned my own architecturally significant (albeit heavily mortgaged) house in the Berkeley hills; and I was in the early stages of what I hoped might become a fairly serious relationship with the firm's star litigator, Ken Levitt. If you had asked me, I'd have said that I'd finally brushed the last of Silver Creek's dust from my shoes. Which goes to show just how wrong a person can be.

My father and I had one of those relationships which improve with distance. Although I was diligent about calling on alternate Sundays, my visits home were infrequent and usually quite brief, sometimes lasting only an hour or so as I drove through town on my way to some more glamorous destination. I would have liked my stay that June to have been as abbreviated. To drop in for the funeral, the way Sabrina did, and then out again less than forty-eight hours later, leaving the loose ends of an emptied out life for others to deal with. But Sabrina had children, a husband, and several thoroughbred horses, all of whom needed her at home, while I had not so much as a single house plant that required my attention.

"You're so much better at these things anyway," Sabrina told me as she slid into the airport limo that Friday morning. It was no use arguing, but I knew the only thing I was better at was getting suckered into taking on responsibility she didn't want. It had been like that as long as I could remember. Of course, Sabrina had at least shown up, which is more than could be said for our brother, John, who pleaded an inflexible schedule and sent an ostentatious arrangement of lilies instead.

The patterns of our childhood, it seemed, hadn't changed much. As the oldest, and only boy, John had more or less assumed a posture of aloofness, deigning to mix in family matters only on those occasions when it suited him. And my parents, knowingly or not, had encouraged his behavior by treating John as someone whose affection was to be wooed. Sabrina, on the other hand, had cast herself in the leading role at every opportunity. Two years my senior, she was very much like our mother—bubbly, fun-loving, and conveniently helpless when it came to anything tedious. Growing up, the three of us had been like the points of a triangle, each pulling in a different direction. I couldn't say we'd worked out our differences really, but over time we'd come to accept them.

Which isn't to say I wouldn't have liked a little help in winding up my father's affairs.

Still, I was managing just fine until the day after the burial when I found myself alone with my father's springer spaniel, Loretta, and a houseful of memories I never knew existed. I hadn't counted on that. I'd figured I could sweep through the house fairly quickly, tossing most of what was there into the big Goodwill boxes I'd brought with me, and the remainder of the stuff into the trash. But I'd been at it since seven that morning, and I wasn't even half through with the kitchen. I simply couldn't decide what belonged in which pile. I'd even started a third pile, things I might want to hold onto. And while it wasn't yet large, its very presence confused me more than I cared to admit.

By late afternoon I'd had it. I picked up the phone and tried calling Ken, whose own world fell so easily into neat little piles it sometimes scared me. As usual, he was in conference and couldn't be disturbed. This could mean anything from a heavy negotiating session to a late lunch, and his secretary, a stern old-school type who didn't approve of women attorneys, wasn't about to clarify the issue for me. "I'll tell him you called," she sniffed, then added with emphasis, *"again.* I'm sure you realize what a terribly busy man Mr. Levitt is." I did, although I was still a trifle peeved that he hadn't come with me to the funeral.

"It's not like I knew your father," he'd explained before I left.

"You've met him," I countered, "and besides, you know *me.*"

"I'm sorry, Kali, but the timing's terrible. I'm swamped with work. And the partner's retreat is that weekend."

Reluctantly, I'd conceded the logic of his argument, but that didn't stop me from feeling put out. And the fact that he'd been tied up in meetings the last two times I'd called hadn't helped matters.

I went back to packing, but didn't make it past the lumpily woven pot holder I'd made my mother one Christmas years ago. It was stuck in the back of a drawer filled with her homemade aprons and hand-embroidered dish towels. Like a sudden nighttime fever, the past swept over me and filled me with longing. There I was, Ms. Cool-Headed Efficiency, propped against my father's greasy old stove, blinking hard at the worn linoleum floor in an effort to contain the rush of tears.

Which all goes to explain why, when Jannine Marrero called and invited me to a barbecue that evening, I accepted without a moment's hesitation.

"I hope you don't think it's rude, inviting you at the last minute like this, and so soon after your father's passing. Eddie says it's downright insulting, but I figured you might be ready for a little diversion by now."

Jannine's voice has a kind of twang to it which I've always found comforting. We were best friends all through high school but somehow, without meaning to, we'd drifted apart after graduation. Although we exchanged Christmas cards and occasional phone calls, I hadn't seen her in five or six years.

"I'm not insulted at all," I told her truthfully, "and I'd love to come."

"There won't be many people you know, mostly other

teachers from the school and stuff, but now that I know you'll be there, I'll see if I can't get some of old gang to drop by, too." She paused to take a breath. "Gosh, Kali, it's going to be good to see you again."

I didn't know about that. I thought there was a good chance we would run out of things to say to one another very quickly, but I was pretty sure I couldn't stand my own company for the whole night either.

Jannine greeted me at the door with an expansive hug. "Shoot, Kali, you don't look a day older than you did when you left home. Or a pound heavier. Must be that big city drinking water or something. Maybe I ought to try a jug or two myself."

We looked each other over, discreetly at first, then much more candidly. Jannine, who had always been a little plump, was now a good thirty pounds overweight. Her overly permed hair hung at odd angles, forming a shapeless mass around her face. But she had always been one of those people blessed with true inner beauty, and that had not diminished. When she smiled, her whole face lit up with an honest, down-to-earth pleasure that caught you up in it, willing or not.

"It's good to see you, too," I told her, surprised to discover I truly meant it.

She squeezed me again, then clasped my hand as though I were an errant child and dragged me into the back yard. "Eddie, come look who's here."

From across the yard, Eddie turned and gave me one of his prize smiles. It hit me in the stomach just the way it had in high school. He had been handsome then, the stuff girl's dreams are made of, and if anything, he'd grown better looking over the years. Curly black hair, dark eyes and straight white teeth. Even the slightly thicker middle looked good on him. "Hey, kiddo, long time no see."

I gave a self-conscious laugh. "Well, here I am."

"She looks terrific, doesn't she, Eddie?"

He slapped Jannine playfully on the fanny. "Damn sight better than you, sweetheart, that's for sure."

"Jannine looks wonderful," I protested, but she'd already given him a solid jab in the ribs with her elbow. This was apparently an old argument.

"I'd like to see what you'd look like after four babies and two miscarriages."

Eddie raised his arms to fend off an imaginary blow. "Jesus, don't go pulling that woman stuff on me again." He reached into the ice chest and dug out a beer. "Want a drink?"

"Sure." I took the can, then looked at Jannine.

"Nah, Jannine doesn't want any," Eddie said, with a laugh. He draped an arm loosely around his wife's shoulder. "It addles her brain. Doesn't it, sweetheart?"

Jannine laughed too, though not quite so heartily. "My brain's always addled."

"How's life in the big city?" Eddie asked, turning his attention back my way. "You rich and famous yet?"

"A long way from both."

I'd gone into law initially with the intention of righting wrongs, of tipping the scales of justice in the direction of fairness and decency, but I'd discovered that people with sizable student loans couldn't afford such lofty principles. Although my five years at Goldman & Latham hadn't done much for the general good of humanity, it had made a fair dent in the size of my indebtedness. Still,

I wasn't rich and I wasn't famous. Sometimes I wondered if I was even happy.

Eddie took a long slug of beer. "I'm working on my M.B.A. now," he said. "Did Jannine tell you?"

"She hasn't had a chance to tell me much of anything yet."

"I've got plans. Someday I'm going to be a hotshot myself, just like you."

"Eddie Marrero," I said, in a tone which was only half-playful, "you've always been a hotshot. It was you they had in mind when they coined the phrase."

Eddie grinned, cocking his chin and shoulders like Jose Canseco stepping up to bat.

"Hey, Marrero," a voice called from the porch.

Eddie turned and waved. He tossed a pretzel into the air and caught it in his mouth. "Catch you later, Kali, I got to go check the grill."

Jannine shook her head. "To listen to him, you'd think he was headed for the big time." She grabbed a beer and popped the tab. "Come on into the house for a minute while I finish up with the salads. A high school girl was supposed to come over and help, but she had to cancel at the last minute so I'm kind of behind schedule."

We moved into the kitchen, where Jannine began pulling plastic baggies of vegetables from the refrigerator. A minute later a lank, freckle-faced girl slid past Jannine and reached for a Diet Coke from the refrigerator.

"Erin, honey," Jannine said, draping an arm around her daughter, "this my friend Kali, the one I've been telling you about."

Erin offered me a weak smile.

"She was just a toddler the last time you saw her," Jannine said, beaming. "Now she's eleven. Eleven, going on sixteen.'' Erin gave her mother one of those icy glares girls her age are so good at, but Jannine let it slide right past. "You want some chips, too? You can take a bowl up to your room if you'd like.''

"Mom!'' Erin made it a two syllable word.

"Skinny as a rail,'' Jannine said, as Erin scooted past us on her way out the door, "and she thinks she's overweight. Won't eat anything but rabbit food. If only I had that kind of willpower.'' Jannine blew an affectionate kiss, which Erin, surprisingly, returned. Then she wiped her hands on her apron and dug out a big plastic salad bowl. "I was sorry to hear about your father,'' she said, turning to face me. Her voice was soft, weighted with things left unspoken.

I shrugged. The father I missed was not the reclusive shell of a man who had died of a stroke four days earlier, but the gentle, even-tempered man who had slowly withered away following my mother's suicide my freshman year in high school. I didn't need to explain, though; Jannine understood as well as anyone. She had lived through those years with me almost by the hour. Her family had, in fact, become my own.

"We sent a donation to the hospital in his name,'' she said. "Since there was no funeral, we didn't know what else to do.''

By my father's own request we'd had a simple, private burial. Whatever sense of loss accompanied his death was also borne privately. It was a marked contrast to my mother's funeral years earlier and the emotional fallout that followed. I hadn't realized until she was gone how strong a force she'd been in our lives, and how much my father had relied on her energy and strength.

Of the three children, I bore the brunt of it. John was

away at college by then, in a world where even living parents rarely made an appearance. And Sabrina had her boyfriends, an ever-changing parade of star quarterbacks and prom trotters who were more than willing to offer comfort. The only person I knew to look to for comfort was my father, and he couldn't provide it. I've never truly forgiven him that, nor my mother for being the cause of it.

"We didn't see each other all that often," I said. "It's like he's been gone for years."

"Still, death is so final." She began tearing lettuce into a bowl. "So what are you going to do?" she asked, after a moment.

"Do?"

"With the house and everything."

"Sell the house, if anyone will buy it. There isn't much else."

She grabbed a handful of chips and munched as she worked. "I wouldn't worry about the house, I bet it sells quickly. It's big, even if it does need work."

The whole time I was growing up I'd thought our house small and tight. I'd been surprised to discover that it was, in fact, quite spacious. Considerably larger than my own house in Berkeley.

"Silver Creek has changed," Jannine said. "It's not the sleepy little town it was. Heck, we've even got a new movie theater going in on the east side of town, and I guess you know about the K-Mart over where the bowling alley used to be." She paused to scoop up two year old Lily, who had appeared out of nowhere clutching a fistful of crackers in one hand and a mashed strawberry in the other. "This one here," she said, nuzzling Lily's head, "she wasn't even in the hatchery last time I saw you. I can't believe how time flies. So, catch me up on the last, what's it been, five years?"

While I finished my beer, I filled her in on my stint with the D.A.'s office and my subsequent transformation to corporate veteran. It didn't take long. As I'd discovered on previous occasions, the life of a lawyer rarely lends itself to the heady anecdotes people seem to expect.

"How about men?"

"They come, they go. What's new with you?"

Jannine shifted Lily to the other hip. "You know, same old stuff. Right now we're gearing up for a summer of football practice." Eddie, one-time high school hero, was now the high school coach. "Football's big in this town," she said with a sardonic laugh, "that's one thing that hasn't changed."

"Neither has Eddie," I told her.

"Yeah, still the star, cocky as ever."

Before I had a chance to respond, a woman with dark, close-cropped hair sidled up next to me.

"Kali O'Brien. I'm sure glad Jannine warned me you'd be here, or I'd swear I was seeing a ghost."

It took me a moment, but I finally figured out the woman was Nancy Walker who, at seventeen, had had stringy blonde hair and a reputation for cutting more classes than the rest of us combined.

"I thought you were in the East," I said.

"I was, but my husband traded me in for a newer model so I came back here. I teach at the high school. English no less. Dumbest kid in school and now I teach there." She laughed good-naturedly.

"You weren't dumb," Jannine said.

"No, probably not, but I didn't know that then."

"Hey, Jannine!" Eddie's voice rose above the din of